A WYATT BOOK for

ST. MARTIN'S PRESS

The
Changeling Garden

WINIFRED ELZE

A WYATT BOOK for
ST. MARTIN'S PRESS
New York

Design by Sara Stemen

Library of Congress Cataloging-in-Publication Data

Elze, Winifred.
The changeling garden / Winifred Elze.
p.   cm.
"A Wyatt book for St. Martin's Press."
ISBN 0-312-13449-5
I. Title.
PS3555.L97C48   1995
813'.54—dc20   95-23539
CIP

First Edition: November 1995

10 9 8 7 6 5 4 3 2 1

The Changeling Garden

Chapter 1

David burst out of his parents' station wagon before it had stopped.

"David!" Annie called after him, but she knew he was too excited to hear. He was already around the corner of the new house and on his way to the back garden, his feet crunching on the gravel, his dandelion hair flying.

"He runs fast for a five-year-old," Mark said. He looked through the windshield at the old Victorian with its slate roof and its wide, welcoming porch, then turned to Annie. "Do you still like it?" he asked.

Annie laughed. "Of course I still like it. I'm not going to change my mind before I've even moved in."

"Just thought I'd check before I had those guys unload the truck," he said, pointing to the moving van parked in front of them. The movers stood around on the lawn and drank coffee. Thin curls of their cigarette smoke rose toward the perfect blue sky. "Just wanted to be sure you're still happy with it." He leaned over and kissed her. His cheek was scratchy with a one-day-old beard, and he smelled lightly of shampoo.

Annie kissed him back, then jingled the house keys in his ear.

"Right," Mark said. "Their time is our money."

Mark took the keys and went to talk to the movers. Annie walked toward the house. The front porch was laced over with a gnarled tangle of wisteria vines, not yet leafed out, and a thorny mass of old roses separated the house from the lawn. The ground beneath the bushes was bright with star-of-Bethlehem, their blossoms turned toward the May sunshine.

Annie followed the path David had taken between the main house and the garage, formerly a carriage house. The arborvitae beside the carriage house crowded the path and grew up to the building's second story. They must be almost as old as the building. She glimpsed part of a dusty window above the foliage, and remembered there were servants' quarters up there.

Annie found David in the back garden, bent over, talking to a daffodil. He paused, listening intently, oblivious to her presence.

"That's called a daffodil," Annie said.

David looked at her, taking the name in. "It's glad we're here," he said.

A bee hummed by Annie's ear but, ignoring her, went straight to the daffodils. The bee's thick little body went to work in the trumpets: in and out she went, making the flowers bob with her weight and getting herself dusty with pollen. When the baskets in her legs were full, she flew off, still humming.

"The bee's glad we're here, too," David said. He reached his arms out to the bare garden, where last year's frost-browned stalks lay on the earth, radiating out from the new buds that had just cracked the surface. "They're all glad!"

Annie could sense the pent-up energy ready to burst forth,

leaves unfurling in visible growth. She was suddenly, acutely aware of all the white-tendriled roots tangling through the ground, growing pale cell by pale cell, drinking in the rains and getting ready. She felt she too had roots, she sensed it all so clearly, then abruptly pulled herself back into the sunlit world, where only the budded tips of columbine and delphinium hinted at what was going on beneath the surface.

She breathed deeply, steadying herself in reality. Must be lack of sleep from staying up so late packing, she thought; I have to get a grip on myself. She laughed at that because, yes, she certainly did have to get a grip on herself if she was going to go sliding off into plants like this. It was too weird to be real.

David smiled and tugged at her hand. "Want to play, Mommy?"

"Annie, the movers want to know where to put things," Mark said helplessly from the back porch, as though it had never occurred to him the movers would ask for this information.

"I'll be right in."

"Come on, Mommy," David said.

"David, I have to help Daddy with the moving men." He was hanging on to her arm, weighing her down.

"David, I have to borrow Mommy for a while," Mark said. "Can you lend her to me?"

Suddenly David was standing on his own feet, but still near her. He looked from his mother to his father, and back again. "For a little while," he said, and ran off toward the old apple tree that grew in one corner of the irregularly shaped garden.

"You can play anywhere inside the fence," Annie called after him. She and Mark went into the cool dimness of the house. There were boxes everywhere, and furniture—heavy furniture—in the wrong places.

"The couch goes in here," she said, pointing to the larger of the two front rooms. "Aren't you going to have them lay the rug first?"

"It's still in the truck behind a bunch of other stuff. Where do you want the sideboard?"

Finally it was all in. Mark paid the men, they closed up their truck, and rumbled down the street. Annie sat down on a full packing carton. Everywhere she looked, there were full packing cartons, all waiting to become empty packing cartons.

"Maybe I'll develop a headache and go lie down in a cool, darkened bedroom, with a handkerchief dipped in cologne, while you take care of these few little things down here," she said to Mark when he came in.

"You can lie down in the bedroom, if you like, but there's no bed set up yet. It's awfully quiet in here. Where's David?"

They looked at each other, suddenly realizing how long David had been left alone, unwatched. They hurried out the back door and into the garden.

"David!" she called.

There was no answer.

"I hope he didn't wander off," Mark said. "Did you tell him to stay inside the fence?"

"There he is!" Annie said. She pointed. David was high in the apple tree. His bright head could be seen among the blossoms, up where the branches become thin. She didn't know what could be keeping him from falling, and she was afraid.

"My God," Mark said quietly. He put his hand on Annie's shoulder. "Keep him calm. I'll look for a ladder." He disappeared into the garage.

"David," Annie said, refusing to let fear edge into her voice: She didn't want to frighten him any more than he must already be frightened. She walked slowly toward the tree.

David saw her and waved. "Hi, Mommy!"

He didn't sound afraid. At least he wasn't frozen up there, then; he was just too little to understand what a dangerous spot he was in. Did they even have a ladder that would reach that high?

"David, honey, can you come down?"

"It's nice up here, Mommy. I can see our roof!"

"David, I think you should come down now. It's time for lunch."

"It's okay, Mommy, the tree won't let me fall. It promised."

"That's nice, David, but I still would like you to come down now. Can you do it, or do you want Daddy to get a ladder?"

"It's nice up here."

"Aren't you hungry? Wouldn't you like some lunch?"

"What are we having?"

"Whatever you like. Daddy has to go to the store."

"Can I go, too?"

"Yes, David. But you have to come down first."

He began the descent, and she couldn't understand how those twigs could hold even his slight weight—they didn't look strong enough to keep a cat up. He went from branch to branch unhurriedly, just as if he were climbing down from a chair. The most ordinary thing in the world.

"I can't find the extension ladder," Mark said quietly from close behind her.

"He's climbing down. Don't say anything to distract him," Annie warned.

David dropped softly to the ground, unhurt. Annie and Mark simultaneously took deep breaths, then looked at each other and laughed ruefully, realizing they'd both been holding their breath while they watched David make his descent.

"We've got to make him understand he could kill himself doing that," Mark said.

David hugged his mother, then, turning to his father, he held out his arms. Mark swung David up to ride on his shoulders.

"That's as high up as I want you to go," Mark said.

David giggled, enjoying the ride and holding on to Mark's hair with both fists.

"Really, David," Annie said. "It's dangerous, climbing so high in a tree."

"I told you the tree promised not to drop me."

"David, it's nice to imagine things, but trees can't promise anything."

"They can too. They can do anything they want, except walk around. I bet they could do that too, only they forgotted how."

"David, promise me you won't climb that tree again."

"What's for lunch? Can I have tuna of the sea?"

"David."

"What?"

"Promise."

"It would hurt the tree's feelings."

Annie looked to Mark for help with this.

"David," said Mark, bringing the boy down from his shoulders and holding him before him. "If you climb that tree again I will personally give you a spanking you'll always remember. Is that clear?"

"Yes," David said.

"Good. Now let's go buy lunch."

The boy ran ahead. Mark winked at Annie, then followed David into the house.

Annie felt uneasy: David hadn't promised. She looked back at the apple tree. It was an old tree, its bark lined with the fissures of many years' growth, but you had to look carefully to notice its age, because today it was in full bloom, its flowers a glory against the cloudless sky. Maybe David would lose interest in it when the flowers had faded.

A vision of a swing presented itself inside her head, but it wasn't her thought. Who had put it there?

The scent of apple blossom flowed over her, sweet and thick. She could almost see it, like dust motes in a sunbeam, enveloping her in a haze of fragrance. She began to lose a sense of where her body was, her fingertips fading in the distance, her feet long ago become part of the earth. Slowness overtook her, and a patience that had forever at its disposal. The sunlight was in her hair; her hair became the sunlight. She was welcomed to a world of constant, slow growth, imperceptible but unlimited change, where loss did not exist because all things were used, were in transition, were part of the constant recycling of nature.

Annie felt herself slipping away and was terrified. The fear brought her out of it and she was standing in the meadow, shaking, but in her own body and only her own body. What kind of place was this?

She looked at the apple tree. It welcomed her. She swallowed, found the swallowing hard, took a step backward.

A swing. The tree wanted a swing for David. David would love a swing, and the tree brought her attention to the perfect branch for one. They'd just have to make sure they put a cut tire over the branch, to protect it from the rope, and David could play on the swing and forget about climbing. Was it a bargain? the tree asked.

Annie swallowed again. "All right," she said.

The tree was pleased. It offered . . . She wasn't sure what it offered. Confused visions, feelings, possibilities overwhelmed her mind, things frighteningly alien to her.

Terrified, she turned and ran toward the house.

Chapter 2

By the time Mark and David got back with lunch, Annie had convinced herself that what had happened in the garden was her imagination—trees don't talk to people. Her heart rate had slowed to normal, and she decided she just didn't want to think about it.

They lunched on take-out sandwiches and soft drinks from the nearby convenience store. Then Mark and David went upstairs to set up the beds while Annie tried to make some sense of the kitchen. She found it cluttered with packing cartons, but clean. On the counter by the sink there was a parcel wrapped in brown paper and addressed to her from Ada Avent in a spidery hand.

"Do you know where there's a hammer?" Mark asked, coming into the kitchen.

"Mark, look. The lady who owned the house before left us a package."

Mark looked over her shoulder and put his arms around her. "Not us: you. It's addressed to you. Open it."

"It feels like a book."

"Maybe it's a cookbook. I hope it's got the recipe for that cake she served us."

Annie undid the wrapping and found a brown velvet book that closed with a metal clasp. She opened it. "It's an old photo album," she said. "Look, this first picture must have been taken just after the house was built." There was no wisteria in the picture, and the porch had fluted columns. The oriel window on the second story was stained glass, and the slate roof looked shiny and new, its edges unchipped. She turned to random pages. "It's full of pictures of the house and garden. What a nice thing to leave behind. Wasn't that sweet of her?"

"Yes. But do you think you could put it away for now, and help me find a hammer? And could you please help me with my assistant? I can't get a bed together while he keeps jumping on the mattress."

They put the beds together and found the immediate necessities of bedding, clothing, and crockery. They laid the living room rug and shifted the large pieces of furniture into place. By then, the boxes were turning to dim shapes around them, and the light from the windows had dwindled.

"I'm sorry I have to leave so soon," Mark said, "but at least I want to get the big stuff squared away for you before I go."

David came in, carrying his teddy bear. His face was flushed, and his hair clung damply to his forehead. "I'm hungry," he said, and flopped onto a footstool. He'd been rushing in and out all afternoon, helping, then running out to play, which was actually more helpful, and Annie thought he looked exhausted.

"Daddy's going to get a pizza," Annie said.

"Pepperoni?" David said, smiling. But then the smile faded and he looked at his mother suspiciously. "Aren't you going to cook in this house?"

"Yes, dear, but I'm too tired tonight." She looked at the field-stone fireplace that dominated the sitting room. "Why don't we eat in here tonight? I'll make a fire while you get the pizza."

"There's no wood," Mark said.

"There has to be some in the garden: twigs, fallen branches. There always is," Annie said. A feeling of anxiety rose in her at the thought of going into the garden again, but she put this aside as nonsense, something to be faced down. "David, do you want to help me make a fire, or do you want to help your dad get the pizza?"

David thought this over, and Annie realized she'd unwittingly given him a problem in diplomacy. "I better go with Dad," he said, "and make sure he doesn't get mushrooms on the pizza."

Annie approached the apple tree warily. It stood outlined against the dusk, its white flowers tinged with the same lavender as the sky. Just a tree. A quiet, somnolent tree, drowsy with contentment after a sunny afternoon. Nothing to be afraid of.

She soon found an armful of fallen apple branches and some dead mock orange canes for kindling. The last light of the day pointed long shadows toward the house, and sent her own burdened shadow there before her. She dropped her armload of wood onto the porch and went back for another before the dark came.

The apple tree murmured sleepily and its fragrance grew sweeter, more soothing.

Annie stiffened. Trees don't get sleepy, or reassure you that they're not dangerous.

The tree chuckled indulgently at her mistake. All around her, shrubs and trees reached out, asking politely to be pruned. The iris complained of crowding and asked to be divided.

"I know," Annie told them. "You need a lot of work. I'll get to it."

They thanked her, putting forth their best manners, except

for the iris, which was a little whiny. I'd be whiny, too, if my feet hurt, Annie thought. The scent of apple blossoms curled through the garden like a lullaby, with a current of narcissus making a plaintive note within it. Anne could tell they were all taking care not to frighten her again.

"All right," Annie said. "I'll come out the first nice day and do some yardwork." She looked around then, hoping none of the neighbors had heard her talking to the plants. Did David and Mark hear them too?

The plants greeted her promise warmly. They seemed friendly enough, but Annie didn't trust them: She could tell they were holding something back, even though they denied it. She retreated warily toward the house, keeping watch in case they tried anything. None moved. She hoped they couldn't. She turned suddenly and ran for the kitchen. The wood she'd gotten already would have to do. Having achieved the safety of the back porch, she looked back, breathing heavily. The garden looked ordinary enough on the surface.

She had a fire crackling by the time Mark carried in the pizza. He set it on the hearth, and poured wine for the two of them, root beer for David.

"I'm glad you changed your mind," Mark said. "This is a great house."

"Me?" said Annie, giving David a slice of pizza on a paper plate. "Changed my mind about what?" The fire made dancing shadows of everything in the room. David perched on one end of the hearth and ate quietly.

"About not wanting to buy a house until I was settled in a job that didn't require so much traveling."

"You'll always travel. The company's always going to send its engineers out to set up new equipment," Annie said. "When did I say I didn't want to buy a house because of that?"

"Just every time I brought up the subject."

"I don't remember that." Annie lifted her glass. The fire made the red wine glow from within. She sipped it and set it down. What could Mark be talking about? "I always wanted this house."

"From the time you saw it, yes," Mark said. "Before that you never wanted to settle down."

"Because we hadn't found this house yet," Annie said. It was perfectly plain to her, but Mark was wearing the indulgent look he put on whenever she said something he considered nonsensical but cute.

"I like the fire, Mommy," David said. "It grows."

"The senior engineers don't travel so much," Mark said.

Annie watched the fire sprout in hot red tendrils from the fissured wood. A branch collapsed, breaking apart into embers that reseeded the flames.

"It's a funny blossoming, that consumes itself and produces only ashes for fruit," she heard someone say.

"What?" said Mark.

Annie looked at him. "I didn't say anything. What did you hear?"

Mark looked puzzled, but shook his head. "Something about this being an ideal time to sell. Maybe the house is haunted. Anyway, haunted or not, it's true that this place is a great investment."

"Investment?"

"It's a good-sized piece of land, for where it's located. I thought we'd have to haggle over the price more, but I think Mrs. Avent liked you."

"How, investment?"

Mark tilted his head to one side and looked down, a dead giveaway to Annie that he was sidling up to an idea he knew she wouldn't like. "We could sell and make a profit tomorrow. Charlie Legere from the bank has already approached me: They want to build a branch office."

"I want to stay here, Daddy," David said.

"We will, kiddo," Mark said. "We're not moving. But that back lot is huge, and they're offering more for half the land back there than we paid for the whole property."

"Sell the garden?" Annie said.

"And pay off the mortgage. Why not? Not all of it, but there's a couple of acres back there. It's going to be hard to keep up. Do we really need it all?"

Do we? Annie wondered. The apple tree, the meadow, the back garden—everything that had frightened her. Why not sell? It would all be gone, bulldozed away.

A scream filled the inside of her head; long and despairing, it vibrated through all her feelings of compassion. She stood, the wineglass slipped from her fingers. She dimly knew it shattered on the hearth, that Mark was picking up the shards and cleaning up the mess, that he was saying something. All she could hear was that wail, like an unborn child who suddenly knows his time will never come.

The wail faded to a whimper. She saw Mark staring at her, David huddled and silent at the far end of the hearth. She was shaking. "We can't sell the garden," she said to Mark.

"Why not?"

"Didn't you hear that scream?" Annie said. "We can't do it. I won't let you kill it."

"Easy, easy," Mark said. He tried to put his arms around her, but she fought him off.

"How can you want to sell it when it screams like that?"

"Nothing is screaming," Mark said. "But we don't have to talk about selling, not now." He captured her finally and held her close. "You're just overwrought. Calm down. Everything will be fine."

She leaned against him. He was warm and solid and reassuring. When she felt more in control, she pulled back and looked up into his face. "We can't sell."

"I'm only thinking of our financial security."

"Didn't you hear it?"

"I heard nothing."

She pulled away from him and looked at David. "Did you hear it?"

David nodded solemnly. "Yes," he said. "It was sad."

"Don't get David believing this," Mark said. "He'll have nightmares." Mark frowned, reached for another slice of pizza. She knew he was trying to get the situation back to normal. "We don't have to think about it now," he said.

"No!" said David.

"I can't have more pizza?" said Mark, but the attempt at a joke fell flat. Annie noticed he put the slice down on his plate without eating any of it.

"You can't sell my garden. My mommy won't let you."

Mark laughed. "I guess I'm outvoted. It's nothing for you to worry about, David. It's nothing for anybody to worry about."

David faded quickly after dinner, and Annie tucked him into bed while Mark locked up downstairs. They made a halfhearted attempt to unpack clothes, until Mark came across the small television and plugged it in in their bedroom.

"Oh good," Annie said. "I'm too tired to think." She lay on her familiar bed with its unfamiliar orientation and sank her head onto her pillow.

Sometime in the black night Annie was awakened by crying. The television was off and she had been covered with a blanket. Mark slept beside her. David was crying. She woke from heavy sleep, layer on layer above her, standing too soon so that everything blotted out and she was dizzy. She walked unsteadily toward

David, banged her leg on a chair that wouldn't have been there in her old room, remembered where she was, and woke sufficiently to find her son. He was sitting in his bed, screaming and staring at something straight before him.

"What is it, honey?" she asked, sitting beside him. He clung to her, still crying and screaming. "It's just a bad dream. Is it about the garden?"

He sobbed out something unintelligible, and pointed. She turned and felt the same fear he did. A spectral shape was in the room, menacing, of sinister and unknown purpose. Then she saw with relief that it was the window, uncurtained, which reflected their own shapes to them by the dim light of his nightlight.

"It's just the window, honey. Reflections, like a mirror. See?" She went over to it. He grew more calm as understanding came. "It scared me, too," she said. "It does look like a ghost, but it's nothing. Tomorrow we'll put up curtains on this window." She hung his robe over it. "This will do for now, all right? You go back to sleep."

It was worth a try. She was tired and wanted to go back to bed, but she could see he was still too frightened for it to work.

"I can't sleep, Mama. I'm hungry."

"All right. Let's go have some warm milk with honey in it."

They went down to the kitchen. She kept pace with him on the stairs, his small, plump hand enclosed within hers.

"I'm cold, Mama," he said as he sat on the kitchen stool watching her heat the milk. She remembered she'd left his robe draped across the window. Mark's sweater hung on the back of a kitchen chair.

"Here, put Daddy's sweater around you." He wore it proudly, the sleeves dangling below his ankles. She added honey to the milk, and poured two cups.

"Do you want anything with that? There are donuts left from lunch."

He bit into a donut, dropping flecks of powdered sugar onto the sweater.

Mark came in. "What's going on here? A party, and I wasn't asked?" He gave Annie an I-told-you-so look.

"I didn't think it was a party you'd want to be invited to," Annie said, "but there's more milk and honey if you want some."

"I think I will." He poured himself a cup and sat down with them. "Any of those donuts left?"

She pushed the box toward him, then leaned her head on one hand, elbow on the table, and yawned. "I don't know why you two are so lively," she said. "I'm exhausted."

"What was all the screaming about?" Mark asked. "There was all that noise, and then you didn't come back to bed. I thought something had happened."

"There was a ghost in my room," said David.

"It wasn't a ghost," said Annie. "And you know it. Don't go trying to scare your father. It was the reflection in the window. It was scary, though. I have to put up a curtain for him tomorrow. Can we go back to bed now?"

"Wait," David said. He slipped off the stool and went purposefully to the door, but it was locked and only rattled when he tried to open it. "I have to go out."

"Honey, tomorrow. It's dark out."

"I don't care about the dark in the garden. That dark's all right. I have to go out."

Mark opened the door.

"No," Annie protested.

"We don't want him to be afraid of the dark," Mark said.

They stood in the doorway, watching David. He walked through moonlight to the bottom of the steps, then stopped. He bent down, a small figure in the shadows, talking to something or someone by the porch. Unfamiliar shapes bulked around him, some solid, some made of the dark itself. But David seemed unconcerned. He came up the porch steps and back into the kitchen.

"Who were you talking to?" Annie asked.

"The rosebush."

"Did you go out to tell it good night?" asked Mark.

"Don't be silly, Dad. I asked it to grow big thorns all the way up to my window, so nothing can get in."

"Is it going to?"

"Yes."

"It would be a practical solution," Mark said to Annie. "Ready to go to bed, Tiger?"

David nodded and Mark swung him to his shoulders.

"I'll lock up," Annie said.

She watched them go upstairs, then slipped out the back door and stood, listening. The night was still. She went down the porch stairs to the spot where David had crouched talking, and waited quietly. At first she was in the garden, in the dark, and that was all. But after a while she could hear the small, cellular movements of photosynthesis, much as she could hear her own heart beating. Then came the rustle of growth: The rose was trying to please David. She wondered how soon the difference would be visible, how great David's influence over the plant would be. Annie walked slowly up the stairs, considering whether all this was due to David's influence over the plants, or his influence over her imagination. She glanced back at the garden, then went into the lighted kitchen and closed the door behind her.

Chapter 3

Annie mixed orange juice, but neither the bright color of the juice nor the cheerful smell of brewing coffee, nor the sunny morning outside her kitchen window, did anything to lift her low spirits.

"I'm sorry to be leaving you with such a mess," Mark said, removing a coloring book from a chair and sitting down. "So David's up?" he asked, dropping the book onto the table.

"No. I packed that around the coffeemaker so it wouldn't break." Annie thought about all the cartons lying in wait throughout the house. "Don't feel left out. There'll probably still be a mess when you get back," she said, handing him a glass of juice.

David came in, sleepy and tousled, and looked at his dad. The knowledge of what Mark's shirt and tie meant registered on his face. "Why do you have to go, Daddy?" he asked.

"I have to set up the machinery so companies can make paper so little boys can have coloring books to draw in," Mark said, pointing to the book.

"I can draw on the sidewalk." David emptied the contents of his pocket onto the table: two pennies, some seedpods, a piece of chalk. "See?" he said, holding up the chalk.

"I also have to make money so we can pay for our house and our food. You're a bright little boy. You can understand that."

"I have money. You can have my pennies." David slid the pennies toward his father.

Mark sighed. "That's not enough. But thank you anyway, that's very nice of you to offer me your pennies. You keep them for your piggy bank."

"There's English muffins and strawberry jam for breakfast," Annie said, but David didn't smile. He managed to put away two muffins, though, so she wasn't too worried about him.

After breakfast, Annie stood by with David, still in his pajamas, while Mark loaded his suitcases into the car. "I'll call," he said, and kissed them both.

David cried when his father drove away, and Annie picked him up. "Daddy will be back," she said. "Tell you what, we'll do some exploring together later. Would you like that?"

David nodded and gulped down a sob. His father had rounded the corner and was out of sight. "In the garden?" he asked.

Annie hesitated. "I suppose we should see what's out there," she said. "It'll probably look very different now that morning's here and we're rested." She set him down on the porch steps. "You go get dressed while I clean up the kitchen, okay?"

He went inside, and Annie noticed the newspaper on the porch. It had a note on it from the paperboy, saying this was a complimentary copy and would they like a subscription. She carried it into the kitchen, poured herself a second cup of coffee, and unfolded the paper.

The front page carried an Associated Press story about arms talks, and a bigger headline about a local murder. Even in a nice little town like this, she thought, skimming the article about how the young woman's body had been found but there were no suspects yet.

She hadn't finished the newspaper when David came in. "Let's go, Mommy," he said, and opened the kitchen door.

She looked at the unwashed breakfast dishes, then at the child waiting impatiently, one hand on the doorknob. He'd dressed in a sweatshirt and jeans. She checked his feet to see that his sneakers were fastened. They were. Thank goodness for Velcro, but she supposed whole generations would grow up not knowing how to tie shoelaces. The house was a mess, but it wouldn't get any messier while she was outside, not so long as David was with her.

"Okay," she said.

She followed him into the kitchen garden and onto the brick path that led on the right to the front of the house, straight ahead to the other gardens. Everything seemed cheery in the sunlight. There were chives about four inches tall, and parsley ready to cut, and in one corner, a sundial stood surrounded by thyme that was turning newly green. It seemed a benign place, and she felt silly to have been frightened. She was big enough not to be afraid of her own imaginings. All the same, she was careful to avoid any consideration of Mark's wish to sell part of the land.

They went through the gate, and a weighted chain closed it behind them. Annie would have liked to check the perennial garden and the rose garden, both of which were to their left, or the orchard and greenhouse on the right, but David ran straight ahead to the meadow, drawn irresistibly to the open space.

The meadow was a big triangular area, bounded on its base by the gardens and orchard, on the left by a hedgerow along a neighbor's property, on the right by the stone wall that separated it from the quarry garden. Where the hedgerow and wall met, there was a huge pine, its lower branches drooping to the ground. David ran straight toward it and disappeared into the branches.

"Look, Mommy, a secret hiding place!" David said when Annie followed him under the tree.

"So there is," Annie said. There was far more room than she had expected, room enough for her to stand up. This was because the base of the tree was actually about four feet lower than the level of the meadow. A circular retaining wall held the dirt back and formed a round, stone-walled room with the tree at its center. The living branches were its roof, and a thick mulch of needles softened the floor. The air was drowsy with the scent of pine.

"This is my room," David said, and Annie knew the first place she'd look for him anytime he turned up missing.

David ran around his room once, then found toe-holds in the fieldstone and climbed out. Annie boosted herself up and followed him.

"What's this?" David asked, pointing to a seed pod, split open and dried, its seeds long since flown.

"Milkweed," Annie said. The meadow was a tangle of milkweed, of brown grasses with stiff, caterpillarlike seed pods, of wild asters whose blasted flowers were still recognizable by their shape, even though the purple color had gone with December's hard freeze. Wild strawberry leaves were unfurling close to the ground. She wondered what else waited dormant, ready to burst into life.

"Why?" David asked.

Annie looked at him.

"It doesn't look like milk," he said.

"The sap does. I'll show you later, when the new plants are growing. If you break open a stem, it looks like it's full of milk."

Behind David there was a band of crocus. Annie followed it with her eyes along the meadow, all around them in a bright circle broken only where they had come up from the house. A fairy ring, like the ones her grandmother had planted, but far larger. Odd that crocuses were blooming in May. If this were a shady spot where ice lingered she could understand it, but out here in full sunlight? Still, the flowers welcomed her, and she smiled.

Annie looked quickly at the apple tree in the corner of the meadow by the perennial garden. The apple tree didn't give anything away, but she was sure it knew everything that had happened here, and why. So did the pine. They were just playing dumb so as not to alarm her. No, she didn't want to believe that, it went against common sense. But she found she did believe it anyway.

"The plants are quiet today," David said wistfully.

"Good. Plants are supposed to be quiet."

"I like it better when they talk."

"They're not supposed to talk. They're supposed to just sit there and grow and make fruit, and that's all."

David laughed. "No they're not. Look at the little house, Mommy," he said.

"That's a bird feeder. We'll get some seed next time we go shopping."

She looked around for birds then, and saw a flock of sparrows watching her from the hedgerow. A trill of birdsong floated out of the apple tree, but Annie couldn't see the singer among the blossoms.

"We'll plant some sunflowers out here this summer," she said, and the birds twittered their approval. "And we ought to clear away these fallen branches, and prune the shrubs. I promised the garden I'd take care of it. Do you know where your wagon is?"

David nodded.

"Would you like to help me haul some wood back to the

house? Or maybe there's a wheelbarrow in the greenhouse. Let's go look."

She took his hand and they walked toward the orchard and greenhouse.

"Where's the greenhouse, Mommy?" David asked.

"Right over there. Straight ahead." She pointed to where glass glittered in the sunlight, and felt a tug on her other arm as David stopped short.

"Boy oh boy," said David, shaking his head in disapproval. "That's not green, Mommy. That's glass." He let go of her hand and ran into the orchard. Since the trees were all dwarf varieties, Annie didn't worry about his climbing them, and continued on to the greenhouse.

It was in good shape. A couple of broken panes could be repaired easily. The plants were all dead of neglect and ready for the compost heap, but it wasn't too late to get a head start on some annuals. There were some tools under one of the tables, but no wheelbarrow. Little red wagon it was, then.

She went outside and was walking toward David when something hummed past her ear. A bee or a small bird, she thought at first, but she looked in the direction it was moving and saw an arrow slam into the bark of a fruit tree. It had been traveling in a direct line between her and David. A startled blackbird flew squawking from the tree. She whirled around, and saw movement in the hedge that separated their property from the road.

"Wow," said David.

Annie was furious. She ran toward the hedge, ready to confront whatever fool had shot an arrow that could have injured her son. Or herself: She could still feel the ghost of its movement past her ear.

She pushed through the hedge to the sidewalk and looked

around. No one was in sight. There was light traffic on the road, but no pedestrians. That just proved the little beast could run fast, probably around the corner or into one of the houses across the street. She noticed she was shaking. With no idea which way he had gone, there was no way she could chase him, so she turned and went back through the hedge.

She found David looking up at the arrow. "The tree caught it for me," he said. "Thank you, tree."

Annie pulled the arrow out. It was a nasty-looking thing, with a metal point that looked like it meant business. It had stuck firmly into the wood. She tried to remember: Had there been a blur of movement, had the branch interposed, just before the arrow struck? It had happened so fast.

"Can I have it, Mommy?" David asked.

"No. It's too sharp. I'm going to save it and show it to Daddy. You can show it to him, if you like."

"We have good trees," David said.

Annie looked at the orchard, just bursting into a white-flowered riot. A vision closed around her of trees dancing in celebration, abandoning themselves to the brief frenzy of spring and happiness that David was unhurt. She took a deep breath to free herself, but her lungs filled with perfume and it wasn't until she noticed a pain in her hand that she could pull her mind back.

"You cut yourself on the arrow, Mommy," David said.

"I wish we had thicker hedges," said Annie.

"Want me to ask it to grow thicker, Mommy?"

"No. I mean, you're not able to do that. They'll grow thicker on their own, just naturally. It's normal for hedges to do that. Let's go back to the house now. We have a lot of unpacking to do."

He took her hand carefully. "I'll put a Band-Aid on it," he said in his most grown-up tone.

Annie looked back over her shoulder as they went, and thanked the tree, just in case all this was real and it *had* saved David.

Annie worked out her anger at the archer by throwing herself into the housework, but she couldn't escape a feeling of apprehension. She and David ate lunch on the back porch, and she found herself checking the sight lines to different parts of the property, wondering if she and David were vulnerable to attack.

In the afternoon, David asked to ride his tricycle on the rose garden paths. With some misgiving, she said yes. They couldn't let themselves be held hostage in their own house because of fear, and the kid who'd fired the arrow had probably been as frightened by what he'd done as she had been.

The house became shadowy in the afternoon, the curtains spiderwebs against the eastern sky. She could hear silence reaching all the way to the attic, and from the other side of the window glass, the faint and occasional chime of David's tricycle bell.

Annie had checked on David from the sitting room window and was passing through the hall when she noticed a man's shape outlined on the front door's frosted glass. His arms were raised, as though he were trying to see inside. She grabbed the broom, set it within reach, and suddenly opened the door.

The boy who was standing outside fell back, startled. He looked about thirteen, smaller than his shadow, and had a round face sprinkled with freckles. His hair was reddish brown and unruly, as though he didn't think much about it.

"Yes?" Annie said, wondering if he'd come to confess about the arrow.

"Um, I'm the paperboy for the *Gazette*," he said. "I left a paper this morning, and I was wondering if you'd like a subscription."

"Oh," she said, and noticed the canvas bag with the word

GAZETTE stenciled on it that was slung over his shoulder. "Yes. Yes, I suppose we would. Sorry if I startled you."

He wrote something with a stubby pencil in a notebook that looked like it had seen better days, then looked up at her. "Your name?"

"Annie Carter. Do you happen to know anyone in the neighborhood who has a bow and arrows?"

"No. What's the point? There's nowhere to shoot arrows around here. I'm Jeremy Wesson," he said, giving her a card with his name printed on it in a childish hand, and a series of dates machine-printed around the edge. "That's to mark when you've paid," he said.

"Somebody shot an arrow into my backyard this afternoon."

Jeremy frowned. "My mom'd ground me forever if I did something like that. We got pets around here."

"He nearly hit my little boy."

Jeremy looked worried at that, and turned his head and whistled. A little black terrier came running up to him, wagging its tail. "Good boy," he said. He looked up at Annie. "I'll tell my mom and dad about that. It's probably illegal or something."

He moved off then, the terrier jumping around him and tugging on his delivery bag. Annie watched him go, and laughed at herself. Poor kid probably thought she was crazy. Well, at least she didn't have to worry that the paperboy was the mystery archer—not as fond as he was of his little dog.

Chapter 4

"Vroom!" said David, making motorcycle noises. "Vroom! Vroom!" He rode in circles around the kitchen table on a plastic motorcycle that rattled and thundered.

"You're making more noise than the weather," Annie said. She wondered whether the rain would ever stop. Three days of it, and of David and his motorcycle. It had kept them both out of the garden, and she'd spent the time sorting out the house and rationalizing her reactions to the garden, so much so that she felt ready for the sunshine to come back. She was confident David's game of pretend had suggested all the things which, in her overtired state, had seemed real. He probably had never been as high in the apple tree as she remembered him being.

"I'm thunder!" David shouted. He pulled up beside her and smiled happily, then revved up the toy with a crank set into it and added his own imitation to the noise it made. Then he was off, rattling across the bare wood floors. A second of quiet came when he went into the dining room: He's crossing the rug, she thought.

Then he came back into the kitchen and the noise crescendoed toward her. It was like living in a roller rink.

"Vroom!" he shouted as he came up close to her. The pedal grazed her ankle and the sudden pain made her lose what patience the constant noise had left her.

"David!" she shouted, grabbing the motorcycle. The sudden stop threw him off balance. He fell and began to cry.

"All right," she said, struggling for control. "No more motorcycle." She went into the hall where the boxes of clothes were stacked and emptied three of them before she found his boots and raincoat.

"Here," she said. "You can go outside and play."

He looked up at her, his face tear-stained and resentful.

"David, I'm sorry, but Mommy's had enough noise for a while. And see what you did to my ankle?" She showed him the scrape and the blood that was congealing along part of it.

"You hurt me," he said.

"I'm sorry," she said. "But you hurt me, too. Come on, there's an empty milk carton in the kitchen. I'll make you a boat while you put your boots on."

"All right," he said. He slowly, painstakingly, pulled his boots on and put on the yellow mackintosh. She helped him with the zipper, then he accepted the boat and went outside.

Annie closed the door behind him and leaned her forehead against the cool glass. She had a headache. Maybe a cup of tea, in peace, will help, she thought as she put the kettle on.

The rain had softened to a gentle drizzle thicker than a mist. And it was warm out. He should be fine.

She couldn't see him from the kitchen window, so she went into the library, whose deep bay window gave the best view of the perennial garden.

There he was, splashing through a puddle that had formed itself into a miniature lake between the flower beds. Daffodils, bedraggled, were wetly yellow above one edge. David's boat had sailed into them, and he went over and pushed it aside. He gently lifted the blossoms out of the puddle and tried to tip the water out of the trumpets and to blow the petals dry, but they were too wet. He let them go and stood a moment in drooping imitation. The water, faintly rippling, reflected both the yellow flowers and the yellow-coated child. Annie had a momentary illusion that they were the same, differing only in size, but she brushed it aside.

Then David began splashing in the puddle. The boat was forgotten and the flowers forgotten, while he busied himself sending shimmering masses of water back toward the sky. He'll be soaked when he comes in, she thought; a raincoat only keeps rain off when it falls from above, the way it's supposed to, not when it falls from underneath.

The kettle whistled. She made a pot of tea, and while it brewed she struck a match and lit the kindling in the kitchen fireplace. It was convenient having the wood set up, although the primary reason for doing it had been to discourage David from using the fireplace as a passage from the kitchen to the library. It had been clever of the builder to make one fire service two rooms by setting the mantels back to back in the one chimney, but he couldn't have been thinking about little boys when he did it.

The photo album from Mrs. Avent was on the mantel. Annie took it to the kitchen table and paged through it while she sipped her tea.

The pages were of bristol board glued together and covered with glazed paper. There were openings cut to display the photographs, which were slipped in through slots cut in the paper. The paper was blue-gray, and had a border of flowers that framed the photo, different flowers on each page, but always white with green leaves. Each page was protected by a sheet of tissue paper bound into the book. She'd seen books like this in antique shops. It was a generous present as well as a thoughtful one.

The book contained photographs of the house and gardens, taken at intervals from the house's construction and the planting of the seedling apple and pine. The first photo was sepia-toned, and had the date *1869* written in white on the lower corner. So if anyone tried to tell her the house had a secret room because it had been a station on the Underground Railroad, they'd be wrong.

She liked the fluted columns in the first picture, and wondered when they'd been replaced. They wouldn't show under the wisteria, anyway. That came in the fifth picture. One photo was taken from across the street, and showed magnificent elm trees on either side of the carriage house. The trees were there for two photos, then were gone. Through the years, the curtain styles changed, the paint was sometimes dark, sometimes light; someone had added shutters, then they were gone. The bay window puffed out, and stayed.

Each house photo had accompanying pictures of the garden, which always expanded a little. The kitchen garden and the meadow were first, then the orchard. After that, the perennial garden, the greenhouse, the rose garden, the tennis court with its hedges. Always in the background, the pine tree, and growing up to its left like a younger sibling, the apple tree.

The last picture caught her by surprise. It was like going though a stranger's photo album and suddenly finding your own face looking out at you; her first thought on seeing the last picture was that it was home.

Of course it was. This was the version of the house that she'd bought; she lived here. It was home. But there was something more to it. She tried to push the feeling away, and looked to see if the photo were dated. It was: in Ada Avent's wavering hand, the year 1965. Annie had been born in 1965. Maybe she'd noticed the date subliminally, and that had given her this odd recognition.

The back third of the book contained empty pages. Maybe that was why Mrs. Avent had given it to her: to fill and pass on. Or was there something she was supposed to notice? The book seemed to mean something more, something just outside her understanding, like the garden.

No, that was silly. The book was just a photo album and the garden was a pleasant bit of land with plants growing on it. Neither of them meant anything more than that. If she thought she'd heard a scream, it wasn't because . . . She couldn't sell because she'd promised Mrs. Avent she wouldn't. Of course, that was it: The scream had just been her subconscious reminding her of her promise. And they couldn't sell the garden. She felt much more comfortable now that she had a sensible reason for the impossibility of selling. It was so much easier now that she had something plausible to say, something Mark could understand.

David came in, tracking water across the floor.

"I'm cold," he said.

"I'll make you some cocoa. Take those wet boots off, and anything else that's wet."

"Everything's wet," he said proudly. "I'm wet all over."

"Then take everything off."

She got him into dry clothes, and he was warming himself by the fire while she made the cocoa, but when she turned around with it, he was gone.

"David!" she called.

"I'm here."

She found him in the library, kneeling on the cushioned seat in the bay window.

"I thought you wanted cocoa."

"I do. But look at my boat." He pointed. She gave him the cocoa and sat beside him.

The rain was heavy again, borne in on strong winds. The air

was thick with it, and a mist rose from the ground. David's milk-carton boat spun around, driven by conflicting winds.

"Wow," he said.

"That's quite a storm," Annie said.

David snuggled against her, sipped his cocoa. "It's mine," he said.

"What is?"

"The rain. It makes me grow. It makes me strong."

"Rain doesn't make little boys grow. Naps make little boys grow."

"Rain makes me strong."

"Yes, honey, you're very strong. And you need a nap."

But they sat watching the topmost twigs of the apple tree whip their froth of blossoms against the silver sky.

"Rain makes the trees strong," Annie said.

"That's what I told you," David said. "I just told you and told you."

Annie felt a chill that had nothing to do with the gray sky or the wind blowing ripples across the puddles. She watched a drop of rain hit the windowpane and stick, firm as a comfortable fact, then another, and another, until the tension between them grew so great they joined, first two, then three, then more, and they ran down in a rivulet: comfortable, clinging facts washing themselves away. If her facts weren't strong enough to hold on to, and David spoke the simple truth, then what was the garden doing to him?

Protectingly, she hugged him tight. "You're a little boy," she said. "You remember that."

Fair weather returned the next day.

"Let's go shopping, David," Annie said. "You can pick out the cookies."

David ran ahead of her, rattling his wagon along the old slate sidewalk. The tree branches above them held the faintest haze of green from thousands of newly opening leaf buds, and the spring sun, newly hatched, shone warmly through the tracery of branches.

"We're the noisiest things out," Annie said. "Remind me to oil your wheels."

"I don't have wheels," David said, stopping momentarily to jerk the wagon over a tilted slate.

"Your wagon wheels."

"Oh." He frowned at the pavement, which had been made irregular by the growth of tree roots. "It's a lumpy walk," he said.

"It's like a roller coaster," Annie said. "Do you want me to pull you?"

"Okay." He climbed into the wagon and rode in state to the grocery store, his weight helping to muffle the sound.

After their stop, two brown paper bags of food and a sack of birdseed took David's place in the wagon. He walked beside it, helping push it over hard places and eating chocolate chip cookies from one of the bags. Annie stopped outside the hardware store.

"I need cup hooks," she said.

"Cup hooks?" he asked incredulously.

"Those little metal things you screw into a shelf and then hang the cups on."

"Oh," he said, sounding disappointed. He'd evidently had a more fanciful idea of the purpose of something called cup hooks. "I'll wait here."

"All right, but don't go away. You can sit on the back of the wagon." She wasn't concerned: she could see both David and the wagon from the store.

Annie stepped into the darkness inside. A bell tinkled. It was an old store—the floors were of wood and the boards ran all along the narrow length of it, making parallel lines that converged in the rear. Two men came from behind a curtain that concealed the back room. One was the proprietor. He came and stood behind the counter, which had bins of nails all along its front. The other stayed a little behind, waiting to resume the interrupted visit or perhaps planning to use the interruption to take his leave.

"Can I do something for you?" the man behind the counter asked.

"I'd like some cup hooks, please. About two dozen."

"What size?"

"I didn't know they came in sizes."

"Quarter inch, half inch, three-quarters."

"For teacups. Half inch, I guess."

He moved to one of hundreds of wooden drawers that were built into the wall behind him. He seemed as old as the store. She felt he resented her, or disapproved, but maybe that was just his manner.

The other man was in the shadows, watching. He leaned against a glass display case as though it had been put there expressly for that purpose. He was a large man, thick, with heavy thighs and arms and fingers, and reminded her of some of Picasso's massively formed people, all muscle and no nerves.

He was waiting. Dark little eyes glittered in his face, the only lively thing about him. He had an apple in one hand, and slowly he brought his other hand up to meet it. Watching her, he grasped the apple with both hands and twisted. The apple split in two with a cracking sound.

"You moved into old lady Avent's house, ain't you?" he said.

"Yes," Annie said, not smiling. She didn't like the way he was looking at her. She was conscious of her breasts, the curve of her body. She regretted having come in, but couldn't leave until the store owner completed his slow search for the cup hooks.

"I used to live there." Annie didn't believe him, and it must have showed in her face, because he went on. "It's true. That's my

apartment over the garage. When I was a kid. My father did ..."
He paused, and gave a smile that was more of a leer. "Odd jobs
for her."

The store owner set a little paper bag of cup hooks in front
of her, and she paid him.

"I do odd jobs, too," the man said. "If you need anything."

"My husband takes care of our home repairs," she said. She
accepted her change and left, the bell tinkling again behind her.

"I'm tired, Mommy," David said. "Can you pull me?"

"All right." She wanted to be off. She tugged on the wagon
with its heavier load, uncomplaining, and went in the wrong direction, wanting to go home by a different route. She stopped several
times to make sure she wasn't followed.

I'm getting paranoid, she thought. Besides, this is silly: He
knows where I live.

The tranquillity of the day was gone. Its surface, so shiningly
beautiful, was crazed like a badly fired piece of ceramic and threatened to crumble and flake away, exposing something frightening
underneath. She breathed carefully, to not disturb, not expose the
hidden shape.

Back in their kitchen, she made David a sandwich, all the
while listening to the noises of the house with a newly educated ear.
She tried to distinguish each one: that's the pump, that's the refrigerator coming on, that's only the wind in the blind. It's not someone coming in. Mice scurried overhead, and a bird flapped its wings
at the window.

"Eat your sandwich, David."

She made one for herself, but couldn't eat it. Instead, she
stepped outside into the sunshine. Munching, David followed her.

"Your rosebush is growing," she said. It did seem noticeably
taller; the rain might account for that.

"Yes," he said. "It's nice and fat." He bent over and patted it.

"Careful of the thorns," she said.

"I know." He said it with such satisfaction that she knew he was remembering the night he had talked to it. He must think he made the thorns grow bigger, she thought.

She looked at the bush more carefully. The thorns did seem bigger than those of the other bushes. It was a vigorous plant, too: it had shot up toward the house and seemed to be hugging the trellised wall by the porch. It was growing rapidly up toward David's window.

"It must be the variety," she said to convince herself, but David heard her.

"It's the same kind as the others," he said.

She looked at the thorns. They were large thorns, and sharp. As large as lion's claws. Soon they would be hidden by leaves and by blossoms. Annie asked the question she didn't want to ask. "Did you make the thorns grow bigger, David?"

"Yes," he said proudly.

She took him by the shoulders and looked into his eyes. They were the same blue eyes he'd always had: clear, truthful, no hint of change. "People can't make plants grow different just by wishing," she said.

"They can if the plants want to."

"Plants can't want anything. They're just plants."

He looked hurt, as though she'd just lied to him. "Yes they can."

"No, David. You're just imagining this."

"I'm not! My rosebush does anything I want."

"You know all about the plant, then?"

"Yes."

He was angry now. "All right," she said, reaching for the name tag and reading it: Pink Perfection. "What color flowers does the rosebush have, David?" she asked, overcome by an urge to test him. Silly, she told herself, but still she couldn't resist doing it.

"Red," he said with conviction.

"No, honey. The name tag says pink."

"Red!" he shouted, and a vision of the future suddenly engulfed her mind, the plant showing her what it would become. It blazed against the side of the house, red roses covering it. She could see them so clearly, but they weren't there, not yet.

David was crying. "Red," he said again. "Red."

She hugged him to her. "Don't cry, David. If it's imaginary, I guess we're imagining it together."

She thought again of the man in the hardware store. She thought of him, and of the roses, and the roses seemed to be warning her about him. They knew him and didn't like him. David grew quieter, and over his shoulder she could see the thorny bush, offering protection.

She wondered if Mrs. Avent remembered the man. She'd been meaning to write a thank-you note; she'd ask about him at the same time.

She smiled at David and wiped his tears away. He smiled back.

Chapter 5

Annie was pruning the hedgerow, and David was supervising, when Mark came home. David saw him first, because Annie had just noticed a big piece of metalwork stuck in the middle of the shrubbery, and was wondering what it was and how it had gotten there. Some kind of frame for training the plants?

"Daddy!" David yelled, running across the meadow toward his father, who was just emerging from the kitchen garden. Mark wore a dress shirt with the sleeves rolled up, jarringly white against the brown and green that surrounded him. He threw David into the air, caught him, then walked toward Annie carrying the boy.

Annie met him halfway across the meadow. "Hi," she said, leaning across David to kiss Mark. "You must have made good time. I didn't expect you till late tonight."

"The good news is I'm home early. The bad news is, I have to leave again day after tomorrow."

"No!" said David, squirming down.

"You can't even stay for the weekend?" Annie said.

"Afraid not." He put his hand out toward David. "I'm sorry, Tiger. I'll make it up to you."

David stayed out of reach. "You never stay home!"

"I'm not home as much as I'd like," Mark said. He walked toward David.

"No!" David shouted.

A blackberry cane snaked out of the nearby clump and tripped Mark. He fell, scraping his face on a milkweed stalk on the way down.

Annie was amazed David could make a plant move so quickly. "David! That's no way to behave," she blurted out, not even considering that it might have been an accident or David might have had nothing to do with it.

David looked at her defiantly and she knew her instinct had been right.

"You hurt Daddy," she said.

Mark sat on the ground, brushing grass and mud from his hands. He seemed surprised, and there was a smear of blood on his cheek. When David saw the blood, his expression changed to remorse and he began to cry.

"Hey, it's not your fault, Tiger," Mark said, getting up. "These shoes are just too slippery for out here. I'm fine, see?"

Mark's taking all this well for a man who's just had a tiring drive home, Annie thought. On his best behavior because he feels guilty about leaving again so soon?

David hugged his father and calmed down.

Mark looked at Annie. "Have you had lunch? I'm starving."

"I'll fix something," she said. He put his arm around her and they walked toward the house. "Didn't you see that blackberry snap out at you?" she asked.

Mark laughed. "No, I guess I must have missed that one."

Annie realized she no longer believed she was mistaken about these things, but she understood how Mark could miss it: She'd denied enough incidents herself. Now she just wished she knew what it all meant. Could something be real to her and David, but not to anyone else? "There's a letter for you from the bank."

"I saw it. Is that all the mail that's come?"

"That's it. The junk-mail people haven't found out where we live yet. What did the bank want?"

"There are an awful lot of boxes in there still. Have you unpacked anything?"

"Of course I did; it rained for three days."

"I splashed in the puddles," David said. "Mommy made me a boat."

"That sounds exciting. I wish Mommy would make me a boat, about twenty feet long, with sails."

David laughed and ran ahead, arms up, pretending he had sails.

"Mark, I still want to know what the bank wants."

"They're making offers."

Annie stopped suddenly and Mark tripped forward. The garden became alert; she could sense it, like a cobra rising up, opening its hood. "Mark, we're not selling."

"Don't get upset," he said. "That's why I didn't want to tell you. I knew you'd get upset. Offers aren't acceptances."

"But that's why you're being so patient and polite: You're still thinking about it."

"One of us has to be practical."

Annie was suddenly aware of all the branches above and around them, all the tangled roots they'd have to pass before they could reach the house. David could make them move; could they do it on their own? She was sorry she'd brought this up outdoors. "We can't sell, Mark. I promised Mrs. Avent."

"Don't get mad at me. I've been going against all common sense and saying no, just to please you. They keep raising the offer. Read the letters when they come if you don't trust me."

"I trust you, it's just . . ." She could tell the garden was angry, not with her, but with him.

"It's just that you don't want to sell. I know." He put his hand under her chin. "So we won't unless you change your mind. Now can we forget it so I can enjoy my few days home?" The plants backed down then, coiling up into a less threatening posture, but still alert.

"Sure," she said, and they walked to the house, Annie keeping watch for unruly plants along the way.

Mark went upstairs to change while Annie made lunch.

"David, come here a minute," she said, before he could escape from the kitchen. She crouched down to talk to him at eye level. "David, you know what you did to Daddy in the garden? I don't want you to do that again."

He looked at the floor.

"You could have really hurt Daddy. You can't just get mad and hurt people like that. People won't like you. The garden won't like you."

David's chin quivered. "I'm sorry," he said.

Annie hugged him. "It's all right this time. No real harm was done. Just don't do it anymore, okay?"

He nodded.

"Good," she said. "We'll say no more about it. Now go wash your hands and face and we'll have lunch."

Annie checked the refrigerator and decided egg salad was the best thing to make. She took the scissors out to the kitchen garden, and was snipping chives when it hit her that she had just told her five-year-old not to cause the plants in the garden to hurt people. She closed her eyes. The smell of cut chives encircled her. It was absurd to think David had some kind of telepathy going with the plants.

She opened her eyes again and moved to the parsley, cutting sprigs of curly leaves. The parsley smell cleared her mind: Absurd or not, that was what was happening. At least she hoped so, or David would be telling all this to a psychiatrist someday.

After lunch, David was keen to get back outside.

"See all the firewood, Daddy!" he said, climbing onto the stack of branches they had piled on the back porch.

"Wow!" said Mark. "Did you do all that?"

David nodded, and Mark caught him as he jumped from the pile.

"I suppose you've explored everything without me," Mark said.

"Not quite," Annie said. "We saved the quarry garden for when you were home."

"Quarry garden? You mean that old pit on the other side of the wall?"

"Let's go, Dad," said David.

They went across the meadow, and as Mark walked by the blackberries, Annie thought she saw the canes quiver.

"Down, boy," she said.

"What?" asked Mark.

"Nothing," said Annie. She could feel the blackberry's disappointment.

The hinges on the gate into the quarry were rusted, and Mark strained to open it. "I see why you left this one till I came home," he grunted.

The hinge gave way, and they went into the garden.

"Wow," said David. "What made this?"

Opposite them was a sheer granite cliff. At its top, a wall separated their property from the street and gave them privacy; at its bottom, a pool of water lay still and dark, reflecting the sky. On their side, the ground fell in terraced steps to the water. Additional steps had been cut where necessary to facilitate access to the pool, and the terraces were planted with rhododendron and juniper and low blueberries. Creeping alpine plants sprouted from pockets of soil, and softened the stones.

"People digging for rock made it," said Mark.

David ran ahead on the path to the water.

"Be careful, David," Annie called. "You could fall."

They caught up with David at the bottom of the path. A wide ledge sloped gently into the water, and David leaned, peering in. "I can see myself," he said.

The water was clear but of uncertain depth, dark where the ledge ended. When Annie turned to look behind her, she saw that the terraced slope formed an amphitheater and she and Mark and David stood on its stage. Or its holy place: There was a table-flat stone that would make a good altar.

Mark looked up at the top of the wall. "It's quite a drop. Anybody who fell over that wall would break his neck and sue us for everything we've got."

"I don't see how he could do both," Annie said. "It's a beautiful spot."

"Can we swim here?" David asked.

"Not by yourself," said Annie.

"I wonder if it dries up in the summer," Mark said. "It looks to me like it's spring-fed. There's the overflow for snow meltoff and rain." He pointed across the pond, where small openings in the cliff were letting excess water drain away.

"This is my beach," David said, lying spread-eagled in the sun.

The pose jolted Annie into thinking of an altar again, and she looked up quickly to catch a glimpse of worshippers. There was nothing.

"Whatever else I do while I'm home," Mark said, "I'm going to put new hinges and a lock on that gate up there. Keep a certain party from coming down here alone. Is there anything else you want me to take care of?"

"If you could climb up and clean out the gutters. The rain was backing up onto the roof, and I'm afraid it'll leak under the slates." She looked around the quarry. "It's different down here, isn't it? Unusual."

"Might make a pretty good swimming hole in August. Save us having to drive to the lake," Mark said. He looked at the top of the wall again. "I think the bus stop's up there."

She couldn't see any sign of a bus stop. Just a long, jagged-edged wall, with the sun at its edge, shining down in a dazzle of rays.

"The wall's more than six feet tall at the bus stop. That should be all right," Mark said.

Annie looked at the pool, not at all sure she wanted to swim in it. "It looks cold," she said.

Mark laughed. "I'm sure it is, now. But by midsummer, the sun will warm it up, shallow as it is and rock-bottomed."

Annie looked at it again, and wondered why he thought it was shallow. She couldn't see the bottom of it. The water was black and cold and reflecting. She couldn't tell whether it had a bottom.

Chapter 6

 After Mark left on his next trip, Annie decided she'd better get back to fulfilling her promise of pruning. For one thing, she wanted to stay on the garden's good side; for another, she needed to figure out exactly what was going on. She said to David, "It's too nice out to stay inside unpacking. Let's get back to pruning the hedgerow."

She'd gotten as far as the metal thing before, and still wondered what it was. It was impossible to tell through all the branches; no matter how hard she tried to push them aside, she couldn't even reach it. Maybe if she clipped some of them away.

"What do you think that thing is?" she asked David, who was leaning his whole body-weight against the hedge.

"A gate."

"A gate? What's the point of having a gate inside a hedge? It can't open. It's probably some kind of old topiary frame."

"It used to open."

"To what?"

"Next door. Use the clippers and see."

"What if you're wrong?" said Annie. "We'll have a big hole in the hedge for nothing."

"It's a gate," said David. "The hedge told me."

"How did the hedge tell you? Does it use words, or how?"

"It showed me a picture of how it used to be. Do you want it to show you?"

"No! I don't. You mean a picture like the rosebush showed us, don't you?"

"Yes."

"You shouldn't let them show you too many of those pictures, David."

"Why not?"

Annie felt she had to speak carefully, surrounded as they were by the hedge. "Because they're plants, and you're not. You're a little boy."

"I know that," David said, his patience wearing thin.

Annie felt the hedge getting sulky. "That goes for you, too," she said to it. "You remember it, too."

David shook his head. "It won't show you anything anymore today, Mom. Are you going to cut through?"

"I suppose I shouldn't do this," Annie said, "But it's the only way to find out."

She cut out several years' growth before reaching an old cast-iron archway and gate, rusted, but not past saving.

"You were right, David."

Annie cut away the last of the branches, and was surprised to find that although the gate was in the center of the hedge, the opening to it on the other side had already been cleared away.

"Open it," said David.

"Honey, that's somebody else's garden over there."

David climbed onto the gate and peered over the top.

Through the arch, they could see a formal arrangement of flower beds and brick paths. Narcissus and tulips bloomed. A gazebo stood on the left, its interior hidden by latticework. A pair of flowering trees marked the edges of the garden and framed a view of lawn leading up to a white clapboard house.

A yellow ball bounced out of the gazebo and rolled along the path. A red-haired baby of about two years toddled after it, retrieved it with much careful bending and attention to the placement of her hands, then trotted back inside the building. Again, the ball came out in a low, slow arc, and again the child followed, giggling. She was a pretty little thing, very fair, her hair a curly haze around her head. This time she tripped and fell, crying, into the path.

A woman wearing blue jeans and a sweater emerged quickly from the gazebo and picked up the child. She, too, had red hair. The sobbing child clung to her. The woman kissed the palm of each chubby hand and the baby quieted.

The woman saw Annie and David at the gate. She smiled and walked toward them. She must be the child's mother, Annie thought; the resemblance was undeniable, and her age was right for a mother. She had an angular face, thin, striking because it was atypical. Was it pretty? It was a face that made you rethink what you meant by "pretty."

"Hello," the woman said. "You must be our new neighbor. I'm Mariah Fenton."

"I'm Annie Carter, and this is my son David." She held up her pruning shears. "We just discovered the gate."

"I told you it was here," David said.

Mariah gazed at him thoughtfully. "Erica," she said to the baby, "I want you to meet David." Erica hid her face shyly in her mother's hair. "If a prince had just cut his way through a thick old hedge to meet me, I'd at least look at him," said Mariah.

"I didn't," said David.

"You notice he doesn't deny being a prince," Annie said. "I see you keep your side of the gate clipped."

"Yes. I like the look of the gate. It used to be clipped all the way through, but the grounds got to be too much for Ada to keep up."

"Is she fragile, or can I play with her?" David asked, pointing at Erica.

"Both," said Mariah.

"Mom says babies are fragile."

"I was talking about your cousin," Annie said. "He was a newborn. This baby can walk and play with a ball."

"Let me see," David said. He climbed down from the gate and shook it, trying to open it.

Annie stuck the pruning shears in her pocket and helped him. After the initial resistance of built-up rust, the gate opened smoothly. "You know, a wire brush and some Rustoleum and this gate should be fine. It's lucky you kept up your side."

"Hi, baby," David said. Erica hid her face, then peeped out. "Hi, baby," David said again.

"She's a little shy," Mariah said. "But I'm sure she'll be happy to play with you when she gets to know you better."

"How's she going to get to know me if she won't play with me?" David asked.

"Tell you what, why don't you and your mom come up to the house, and you can play with Erica while your mom and I have a cup of tea." Mariah looked at Annie. "There aren't many little children in the neighborhood."

"Okay," said David.

"For a little while," said Annie. "I have a ton of unpacking to do, and I've been avoiding it."

"So avoid it a little longer," Mariah said, leading the way to her house.

"That's a handsome gate," said Annie, looking back and noticing the ivy pattern that gave way in the arch to something that could have been a purely decorative motif, but which looked like writing in an alphabet she didn't know. "But why do you suppose it's there?"

"My grandmother owned the house I live in, and her sister owned yours. They had the fence with the gate put in so they wouldn't have to walk all the way around the block to visit. The fence is still in there, you just can't see it because the hedges have overgrown it."

"Why bother with a fence at all?"

"Keep the kids and dogs sorted out, I guess. I don't think they always got along all that well, either."

Annie still wondered about the fence. "Is this garden like ours?" she asked David quietly when Mariah went ahead to open the door.

He shook his head. "No. It's sleeping."

Mariah's kitchen was large, with exposed ceiling beams and a fireplace that had been built for cooking as well as heating. There was a fire burning, and Mariah added a log to it.

"Keeps the chill off," she said. "Erica, why don't you show David your playroom?"

Erica nodded, and led David down the hall.

"This house is older than ours, isn't it?" Annie said.

"Yes. It was one of the first houses built in the area. Our family used to own a big farm, but they sold it off gradually." Mariah put the kettle on. "Yours is more civilized, though. Aunt Bess was a lady. Also she was building in a more refined time."

"I think this is wonderful," said Annie, looking at the herbs hung to dry from the ceiling, and the leaded-glass casement window that gave onto the garden.

"Have a seat," Mariah said, putting two cups down on the

trestle table by the window. She pinched a sprig of leaves from one of the bunches of leaves and put it into a teapot, then spooned in tea leaves.

"Do you use all these herbs?" Annie asked.

"Yes," said Mariah.

"She's got the reputation of being a witch."

They turned at the sound of a man's voice, and Mariah introduced her husband John.

"I have not got the reputation of being a witch," Mariah said. "And you ought to be at work."

"Just passing through. Don't let her give you any herbal medicines," he said to Annie. "You come to see me if you have any problems."

"John's a doctor, when he's working," said Mariah. "He likes to introduce me as an herbalist. He thinks it's funny, but I always make a point of telling people it's supposed to be funny, because someday somebody's going to take him seriously."

"Mrs. Harris already did."

"That should be a lesson to you. Are you going to be home for dinner?"

"I don't know. I'll call. Nice to meet you, Annie. I like that name. Solid. Normal. Be good to have somebody normal in this neighborhood for a change." He left.

"John is colorful," said Mariah, pouring tea. "I do my best to stop him, but I haven't been very successful."

"You don't really give out herbal remedies, do you?"

"Of course not. Mrs. Harris did say once that my peppermint tea did more for her digestion than all John's medicines, and John has been running with it ever since."

Annie sipped her tea. "He's going to be disappointed about my name," she said.

"Why?"

"Annie's just a nickname. Is this peppermint tea?"

"No. What's your real name?"

"I don't tell people that. It's too horrible. I feel like I'm floating. What herb did you put in this?"

"Catnip," said Mariah, and refilled their cups.

"I'm starting to understand what cats see in it," said Annie.

"So what's your name?" Mariah asked.

Annie giggled. "Philantha Godiva."

Mariah giggled too. "Why?"

"My mother. My parents. It's a long story."

"Tell me."

"John wouldn't approve. It involves a witch doctor."

Mariah laughed. "He's not here."

"Oh. Right. Well, the Godiva part means 'gift of God.' My mother had trouble carrying a baby to full term. I was her only pregnancy that didn't end in a miscarriage, so she says I was special and a gift from God. My mother's a language scholar and very big on giving things appropriate names. You wouldn't believe some of the names our cats had. Actually I've always suspected she named me after the chocolates."

Erica came running in, followed by David. "Cookies!" Erica said.

"Of course," said Mariah. "And milk." She put their snack on the children's table and they sat down to eat it.

"More tea?" Mariah asked Annie.

"I don't think so," Annie said.

"Relaxing, isn't it?" said Mariah. "But I guess you're not used to it."

"Fast!" said Erica, and she and David were off down the hall, cookies in hand but milk left behind.

"Well, they're having a good time," Mariah said. "So where does the witch doctor come in?"

"Oh, my dad's an anthropologist, and he was in South America when my mother wrote to say she was pregnant. He couldn't come home, and he was worried, and he swears he made some kind of deal with some native priest or witch doctor, and that's why I was born all right. He's got proof, too." Annie pulled the loose neckline of her sweater to one side. "See that birthmark on my shoulder? He says it's the mark of some Mayan god. Says it's the god's face."

"It does look like a face. It could pass for Mayan," said Mariah.

"Obviously he saw the birthmark and made up the story to go with it, but he swears it's all true. Sure, Dad. I'm really going to believe that one. And his answer to that is, part of the spell or curse or whatever, is that I won't believe any of it until the proper time comes."

"Your dad sounds clever."

"He is, but he's got a warped sense of humor and my mom's overeducated. It got strange sometimes."

"So what's Philantha mean?"

"Oh, that. Philantha's Greek. It means flower lover. That one they got right. Self-fulfilling prophecy: My mom used to drag me to her horticultural society meetings every Saturday of my preschool life. In kindergarten I rebelled. She claims she was preparing me for my future; I think she just didn't want to hire a baby-sitter."

"It's a wonder you didn't grow up to hate plants."

"I suppose it is, in a way." Annie sipped her tea. "I'm finding the garden around my house . . . interesting. Have you noticed anything unusual about it?"

Mariah gave her an unguarded look of surprise, then paused before answering. "No," she said. "It's unusually large."

Annie didn't believe her. Mariah wouldn't have had to think so long before giving a truthful answer to such a simple question.

"So where are your parents now? I'd like to meet them," Mariah said.

"They retired to the south of France." Annie's gaze drifted to the hanging herbs. "Do you know what they're all for?" she asked.

"I know what they're supposed to be for. I haven't tried everything. My grandmother taught me, and she left me her notebook."

"Ada left me a photo album," Annie said. She watched the sunlight shimmer in her half-drunk tea, then looked back at the herbs. "Would you teach me?" she asked. "I'd like to know more about what plants can do."

Mariah smiled. "Sure," she said. "Ada told me we were going to be friends."

Chapter 7

 An owl's cry wakened Annie. She sat up quickly, feeling she'd just been warned, trying to remember where she was. She recognized her bedroom and the new lace curtains, but not the shadow beyond the curtains, and not the scraping sound at her window. She listened. The scraping continued, as though someone were trying to get in.

She turned on the lamp beside her bed. Immediately the shadow disappeared in a crash, followed by scurrying and then by a second crash, metallic and lingering.

Annie hurried downstairs, putting on her robe as she went. She flicked on the kitchen light and went out the back door. The full moon was bright on the garden paths, and she went around the corner of the house to the area under her bedroom window.

Whatever it had been, it was gone. Her trashcan was overturned, and a ladder lay sprawled across the path. It was her ladder. Where had Mark left it? He'd cleaned the gutters, but had he put the ladder away or left it against the house? Nice going, Mark: just invite the burglars in.

She looked up at the house. The branches of a maple had fully leafed out. Had the leaves brushed against her window? Was it their shadow she'd seen?

She checked the flower beds beneath the window. The marks of the ladder were there, and something heavy seemed to have fallen or blundered through the plants. She looked around her, trying to see into the shadows, but anything that might be in them was hidden.

Annie suddenly felt vulnerable, standing in the moonlight while whatever had disturbed her sleep might be hiding in the dark, watching her. She returned to the back garden.

Light from the kitchen streamed across the porch and made a bright patch on the brick path. She felt comforted, until she realized she'd left the door open and out of sight, and that if there were a burglar he could have walked right in. She went slowly up the porch steps, her heart beating faster when the third one creaked. In the doorway, she looked around the kitchen, saw it was empty, and quickly stepped inside and locked the door.

As quietly as she could, she got a carving knife from the cabinet drawer and made the rounds of the house, turning on a light in every room to drive out anything that might need dark. She checked all the closets, and the lock on every door and window, checked the attic and, hardest of all, the cellar. When she was certain no one but she and David were in the house, and that there was an unbroken barrier of wood and glass between herself and the outside, she began turning the lights off again, finishing in the kitchen. By then she realized she wouldn't fall asleep again. She made cocoa and took it into the darkened library to sit with it on the window seat and look out.

The garden was without color in the night. Shiny, moonlit leaves alternated with felt-black shadows. She set the cocoa mug down and leaned her cheek against the cool windowglass. She could see the sky and knew there were clouds because the full moon rimmed their edges with light, and because the patches within the outline were barren of stars. One triangular shaft of darkness, rising almost to the heart of the moon, she knew was not a cloud but the mass of the old pine tree at the back of her meadow. She felt drawn to it as if it were home.

Without warning, she found herself perched near the top of the pine tree, her wings folded against her body, her owl's eyes looking toward the house. Moonlight flowed silver across the slate roof, and she swiveled her head to catch sight of the moon riding free beyond a rift in the clouds. She stretched her wings and left her perch.

She flew below the clouds on feathered wings that stroked the night. She looked down and saw distinctly everything below. There was a field mouse in the meadow, and she hungered for it, but instead she watched the man's figure, alone on the street, making its way from her part of town into the poorer section. She followed it until it disappeared into the warren of shops and apartments downtown.

She wheeled over the downtown area, saw a rat on a building roof and stooped to catch it. It squealed when she flew off with it, back to the meadow, where she tore it apart and feasted on the warm meat. Her night vision revealed the world that belonged to the opossum, the skunk, and the cat. She flew for a while for the joy of it. A bat, out hunting, changed course to avoid her. When the eastern sky began to lighten, she circled back home and flew to the top of the pine tree, to her hidden perch among its highest branches, to sleep the day through.

Annie awakened on the window seat at dawn. She looked at

her hands, expecting to see them stained with blood and fur, then rubbed her face and was surprised to find not a beak, but soft flesh. She shivered. That had been the oddest dream.

She pulled her robe tight around herself and went out onto the front porch. The wisteria vines with their new leaves made a screen of privacy all around, but through the opening the stairs made she could see the lawn, dew-covered, stretching toward the street. In the early light, each grassblade held its own rainbow. The neighborhood was quiet, except for birdsong.

With a soft thud, the newspaper landed on the porch. She stepped forward to get it and the paperboy, seeing her, circled his bicycle in front of her house.

"Looks like some dog got into your trash," he said.

She waved to him. "I heard it last night," she said.

He continued down the street, and she watched the flight of a newspaper onto the porch of each of the next three houses, until he disappeared from her view.

She unfolded her paper to glance at the front page. The headline said there'd been no murder last night. She laughed; since when did somebody not being murdered merit a headline? But as she skimmed the piece, she understood there'd been three murders discovered now, and by the murderer's timetable, another had been due between nine and eleven last night. She lowered the paper and gazed thoughtfully across the perfect morning. She wondered, along with the writer of the article, why—but Annie's wonder was tinged with fear. Was there a connection between the intruder frightened away from her window and last night's lack of a murder? Surely a murderer would be more persistent than that.

She pushed a stray lock of hair back from her face and was surprised to find something caught in her hair. Probably twigs from the roses near the house, she thought, but when she brought her hand away there were pine needles, sticky with resin, clinging to her fingers. She let the newspaper slip to the porch floor unheeded, to blow in the light morning breeze. The only pine tree on the property was the one at the back of the meadow. Was there an owl perched near its top, and did it remember being someone else last night?

Chapter 8

David and Annie sat at Mariah's kitchen table, watching Mariah harvest seeds. She'd tied the flower heads inside paper bags, and hung the plants to dry, and now she shook the bags to loosen any seeds that might still cling to the plants. The seeds rattled against the paper.

"I should have done this months ago," she said, taking herb stalks from a bag and stripping the leaves into a bowl. "You look tired," she said to Annie.

"I didn't sleep well last night," Annie said.

"What's that?" David asked, peering into the bowl.

"Basil," said Mariah. She crumpled a leaf under his nose. "Smell."

He breathed in the scent as though trying to memorize it. "What's it for?"

"Cooking. I use it on beef and pasta. Historically it's supposed to draw poisons to it."

"That's good to know," said Annie.

David pulled the bag of seeds to him. "There are rocks in here," he said.

"Those aren't rocks," Annie said. "They're seeds. You put them in the ground, and new plants grow from them."

David looked at her skeptically. "Aw, come on, Mom."

"It's true. Mariah, help me out here."

"Seeds are those black things in apples," David said.

"Those are apple seeds," said Mariah. "These are basil seeds. Every plant has its own kind of seed, that grows into that kind of plant."

"Oh," said David. "Can I plant some?"

"Sure," said Mariah.

"I'll show you where to find seeds," Annie said, taking a stalk from a bag not yet opened. "See, this used to be the flower. Then it turned brown, and the seeds grew, and when it's all dry, the seeds are ripe and you can plant them."

"All plants have them?"

"All plants with flowers."

"Oh. How come you never told me before?"

"You never asked before." She looked at Mariah. "He's lived all his life in an apartment until we bought the house. It can be amazing, what you don't realize they don't know."

Mariah poured the basil seeds into a labeled jar. "That cupboard at the end of the room has lots of jars with different kinds of seeds in it, if you'd like to look at them. Just be careful with the jars."

"Okay," David said, and went to investigate.

Mariah shook some more seeds loose. "So how come you're not sleeping? You're not nervous, being alone, are you?"

"I wasn't until last night. Then some clown climbed a ladder and tried to get in my bedroom window."

"Burglars are carrying ladders around with them now?"

"No, it was Mark's ladder. He forgot to put it away."

"It doesn't sound too serious, then," Mariah said. "Probably just some kid or some nosy neighbor taking advantage of the opportunity. If it were anybody who meant business, he wouldn't count on having your own ladder handy to climb up, would he?"

"That's what the police said," Annie told her. "I called them this morning. There's not much they can do. Drive by a little more often, is all. They told me to make sure my doors and windows are locked, and to leave the porch lights on all night."

"It's good you called them," Mariah said. "Make them a little more aware."

"Sure. If anybody kills me, they know'll it was an intruder. They'll have a lead."

"If he comes back, call us. I mean, call the police, too, but we can get there faster. Just the sight of somebody coming at him with a flashlight's probably enough to get rid of the guy."

"Thanks. It bothered me a lot, but I feel better just getting out and talking to another adult," Annie said. And she did, too. Maybe isolation was part of her problem. But she wouldn't talk about the business with the owl, she decided. No sense convincing Mariah she was crazy, and on such short acquaintance, too. "I wish you had some herbs I could hang over the doorway. Garlic only works on vampires, doesn't it? Not burglars."

"Not burglars. Bittersweet's supposed to work on burglars."

"You're kidding."

"No. They used to call it felonwort. If you could rub the berries on him, it would get rid of him faster, but hanging some over the doorway's supposed to be effective. I've got some, if you'd like to try it."

"Sure. Can't hurt. Have you used it?"

"For Christmas decorations," Mariah said. "Nobody's burglarized our house at Christmastime." She took down a box and got out some white twigs with red berries attached. "I spray them to keep the berries on, but that shouldn't matter. Here's a branch for the front door and one for the back. Just don't tell John."

"Oh, I don't think I'll tell anybody," Annie said.

David brought a jar of seeds over to the table. "These are rocks," he said.

"Those are beets," said Mariah. "But if any seed looks like a rock, it's a beet seed."

"Beets taste like rocks," David said.

Annie held the jar up to her eye level. "I think they look remarkably like kitty litter."

"Is that baby of yours ever going to wake up?" David asked.

"Not for another hour, I hope. She'll be grumpy all afternoon if she doesn't nap long enough," Mariah said.

"Come on, David," said Annie. "We have some decorations to put up. Maybe Mariah will bring Erica over later."

"Okay." David leaned forward and patted the bittersweet. "Nice plant," he said.

Mariah saw them out the door. "I'll bring Erica over this afternoon," she said, but David was busy looking at the ground.

"Are these things seeds?" he asked.

"The acorns? Yes. They grow into oak trees like that one," Mariah said.

David looked where she pointed. "Wow," he said. "Can I have some?"

"You can have them all," said Mariah.

"Thanks a lot," Annie said. "There must be thousands of those things."

"He'll get tired of it," Mariah said.

David busily filled his pockets.

After lunch, Annie settled David down for a nap and collected her mail from the entrance hall. Three bills and a letter from Mrs.

Avent. She tossed the bills onto the hall table and carried the letter into the kitchen, where she sat down to have another cup of tea and read her letter in peace.

Ada was pleased she appreciated the book, and was happy the garden had gone to someone who could understand the garden's soul. She'd had several groundskeepers living over the garage through the years, and some of them had had sons. There was one father and son who might fit Annie's description. The son had been a chunky boy, something of a bully, and was always shooting a slingshot, an arrow or a BB gun at something. Ada had fired the father partly because of the boy's behavior, but mostly because she'd caught him stealing. They'd both had the same name, Harley Baer and Harley Baer, Jr.

Annie supposed being named after a motorcycle could warp a child, but since they were both Harley, maybe it was a family name. She wondered how much fear and pain he'd brought into the garden, and her ears were filled suddenly with the sounds of feathers beating to escape. She was in a flurry of bodies taking off quickly, and felt the searing pain of an arrow through her wing. She tried to gain altitude, but her flight was unsteady, she couldn't maintain it, the ground came spiraling up toward her. She limped along, dragging one wing, and the boy pursued her, shot another arrow . . .

David was standing next to her. "Are you all right, Mommy?"

"Yes. My arm hurts." But already the throbbing pain was receding. How could a dream cause physical pain? She looked at the clock. Either they'd had lunch later than she'd thought, or . . . She noticed the tea in her cup was stone cold. She must have lost track of time.

"Where were you, Mommy?"

"I was right here."

David shook his head. "No you weren't. Was the garden showing you something?"

"No. It wasn't the same. I was in this, not just looking at it. David, can you fly with the birds?"

"No," David said. "Show me."

"It must have been a dream," Annie said, but she inspected her arm for signs of a wound or a scar. There was nothing. But this wasn't the same as with the owl; this had been a vision of the past. The owl had happened while it happened. So there were different kinds of experiences. "I think we should put the bittersweet up now," she said. "Maybe it'll help."

She was perched on a ladder, nailing the twigs and berries above her kitchen door, when she heard Erica's joyful shout at the sight of David.

"It looks good," Mariah said.

"I trust there's no particular way to do this," said Annie. "I mean, it doesn't matter which way the berries go or anything, does it? To make the magic work."

"Not that I know of," Mariah said as Annie came down from the ladder.

"I had a terrible dream about being shot with arrows," Annie said. "And being a bird. I must have dozed off after lunch, and it was . . . I don't know. Maybe I'm cracking up."

"It's understandable," Mariah said. "With these murders in town."

"What have the murders got to do with it?" Annie asked.

"Just that that's how the women were killed. They were shot with arrows, three or four arrows each. And there was a dead bird next to each of them. It makes perfect sense that you'd dream about it."

It made sense to Annie, too, but it came together for her differently. "Come in and have a cup of tea," she said. "There are a couple of things I haven't told you."

Chapter 9

Annie was clearing last year's dead stalks out of the perennial garden when David came rattling up beside her with his wagon.

"Is Dad home yet?" he asked. His face was flushed, and his hair clung damply to his forehead.

"Not yet. You'd beter slow down; you'll be exhausted before he gets here." She looked into the paper grocery bags he had loaded in the wagon. "Not more acorns," she said. "How many are you going to bring home?"

"Mariah said I could have all of them."

"Your room already looks like a little squirrel lives there."

"What's that?" he asked. David pointed to the box sitting beside his mother's trowel.

"Fertilizer. To feed the bulbs."

David snatched it up and ran along the path. "Who wants some?" he asked. The daffodils turned their trumpets toward him and he scattered fertilizer granules into their beds. He got to the end of the path and was about to throw some to a planting of blue-berries, but he stopped. "They don't want this kind. They say it's yucky."

"It's not good for them," Annie said. She paused, trowel in hand, and studied David. "This is just a game, isn't it, David? The plants can't really tell you what kind of fertilizer they like."

David gave her the patronizing look she was coming to know and dread. "Sure they can. That's how I know."

He was right on both counts, she thought. Right about the fertilizer, and how else would he know, if the plants hadn't told him? He couldn't read the instructions.

"Want to see me make it snow?" he asked, handing back the box.

"Not really. I like having spring," Annie said, but he was off, running to the apple tree.

"Watch, Mommy!" He held up his arms and shook them, and the tree shook its branches. Hundreds of petals fell, landing like flakes on the grass, and on David's hair and face. "See, Mommy? Spring snow!"

Annie laughed.

"Do that again, Mommy."

"What?" she asked.

"Laugh."

Oh dear, Annie thought, surprised that her tension had been so obvious. She took David's hand and walked with him along the garden path. "Do you like it here, David?" she asked.

"Yes. It's the best fun I ever had."

Annie anxiously scanned the hedgerow that separated their land from the street.

"Don't worry, Mommy," David said. "The garden will take care of us."

"The garden can't keep arrows out. But that's okay. We have the police watching out for us, and John and Mariah."

David snorted. "The garden's better than them. I'll ask it to keep arrows out."

"I wish I could ask it to do things," Annie said.

"You can, Mommy. Just try." He suddenly stood very still. "Look," he whispered.

A robin had landed about three feet in front of them. It hopped along, cocked its head to one side, searching for worms.

Annie wondered, not for the first time, how much she should tell Mark about what had been happening. He had to travel for work, there was no choice, and she didn't want to make him feel guilty about something he couldn't help.

The robin suddenly thrust its beak into the earth and pulled out a worm. The worm wiggled; the bird flew off.

"I wish I could fly," David said.

"It's not as much fun as it looks," Annie said. "It's mostly work: looking for things to eat, and trying to keep other things from eating you."

"Daddy's home!" David said. He let go her hand and ran toward the front of the house, where their car could be seen moving along the road.

Annie knew Mark would pull into the driveway, so she cut across the back, a shorter distance to where the car would stop. As she came to the edge of the carriage house, she heard the car's tires turning onto their driveway. Then she saw David change direction and cut across the lawn, running toward the moving car. She didn't know whether Mark could see him.

"David, stop!" she shouted.

For an instant she saw his face, alight with smiles for his dad; his small, strong body, running. The car crunched up the drive, a ponderous weight of metal, difficult to stop once in motion, potentially deadly even in the most loving hands. Its path interposed between her and her child and she could not reach him, could only watch the bright, loving, heedless face. An instant of forever, as if somewhere a coin spun, one side bright, the other dark, the coin flipping bright-dark, bright-dark.

David slowed, stopped in time. The car also stopped, with a jolt and a squeal of brakes.

The coin had landed bright side up. Annie began to breathe again. "David," she whispered, as she watched Mark throw David into the air and catch him. "You can't always count on a garden."

Mark took them both out to lunch. "You can behave in a nice restaurant now, can't you, David?" he'd said. David nodded, but Annie had her doubts. Mark had gotten a table by the window, and David was tilting back in his chair and poking at a potted plant.

"David, be careful," Mark said. "What's he doing, anyway?"

"Planting acorns," said Annie.

David, finished at the planter, returned to pushing french fries through the pile of ketchup on his plate.

"Acorns," said Mark. "That reminds me: Did you know he's got bags and bags of acorns in his room?"

"Mariah gave them to me," said David. "To plant."

"He takes them everywhere," said Annie. "He put two in the cement pot of evergreens in front of the restaurant, and another in a crack between the sidewalk and the foundation on our way in." She took a bite of curried chicken salad.

"I thought he was bending over to fix his shoes," Mark said. "Who are you, Johnny Acornseed?"

"I'm David," David said.

A man stopped beside their table. "Mark, Annie, nice to see you." He nodded at David. "How are you, young man?"

Annie looked up, surprised that someone in this town knew them. She recognized Charlie Legere, the banker who'd taken care of the closing on their house.

"Charlie, nice to see you," Mark said.

Charlie smiled and, looking directly at Annie, said, "You have a beautiful family, Mark. Enjoying the new house, Annie?" Then, to Mark: "That's quite an investment property you've got there," he said.

"I know. I've been trying to make Annie understand that," Mark said. "Hey, join us for dessert. Maybe you can explain it to her."

"I don't want to intrude," Charlie said.

"Oh, it's no intrusion. Please do," Annie lied.

Still smiling, Charlie pulled out a chair. Mark ordered coffee and dessert, while Charlie got out a pad and a ballpoint pen. Annie decided she knew exactly why Mark had taken her to a downtown restaurant for lunch. She smiled pleasantly, but was too angry to listen to much of the plan Charlie outlined. She tuned in toward the end of the conversation.

"Of course, we'd prefer to buy the whole property," Charlie said, "but we'd settle for the back half. That hole's not much use to you, and we could bring it up to grade and build there." He finished writing figures and slid the pad to Mark, who looked at it, then handed it pointedly to Annie.

"What would you do with the whole property?" Annie asked.

"Frankly, customer parking is going to be a problem. With half the land, we'd have to blacktop everything around the building. With all of it, we could keep some for landscaping. But I understand you're fond of the house."

"Yes, I am. And of the garden, too."

"It's a very good offer, Annie," Mark said.

"Mommy," David said worriedly, pulling at her sleeve.

"It's all right, David. We're not going to sell."

"Think about it, young man," Charlie said genially. "I bet you could have a new bike, and a nice new house with a bigger room for you."

David stared at him.

"It's out of the question, Mr. Legere," Annie said. "For one thing, it's our home and we don't want to move."

"Annie," Mark said, "it's not like we've lived there for twenty years."

"For another," Annie went on, "I promised Mrs. Avent we'd live in the house. That's why she sold it to us at the price she did, and that, Mark, is why you can smell such a big profit."

"Ada Avent's an old lady," Charlie said. "She doesn't understand business. But I'm sure she wouldn't want you to give up an opportunity like this just because of some sentimental promise."

"Ada Avent understands very well," Annie said. "She told me about your bank. She didn't want to sell to you, she didn't want her home made into a parking lot. And I'm morally obliged to keep my promise to her."

"It was just a verbal agreement, wasn't it?" Charlie asked. "You didn't give her anything in writing?"

"Why don't you build your bank downtown?" Annie suggested. "It's already covered in concrete, and it's dying. The businesses there would love to have you come."

"To stay competitive, we have to go where the people are," Charlie said.

"And kill off that land too," Annie said. "And keep going until everything's covered in asphalt. The world doesn't need another parking lot."

"It needs trees," said David.

"Be quiet, David," said Mark. "Annie, don't get emotional about this."

A look of understanding passed between Charlie and Mark. "Why don't you two just think this over, talk it out," Charlie said. "There's no need to be hasty."

"It's not happening, Mr. Legere," Annie said. "You can take your answer right now. And the two of you can stop being smug at my expense. David's right. The planet's gasping for oxygen, and I'm not going to make things worse by killing a garden."

Mark laughed. "We're not talking about a rain forest here. Just one backyard."

"Can we go, Mommy?" David asked.

"Yes, honey," Annie said. "I'm finished here. I'll meet you at the car, Mark." She led David out of the restaurant, and the last thing she saw before going through the door was Mark look up from paying the bill and turn a puzzled gaze toward her.

"Is Daddy going to sell the garden, Mommy?" David asked.

"No, David. He can't sell unless I sign the papers too, and I won't sign."

They reached their car, and Annie tried to open the door. Locked. She fumbled in her purse for her set of keys, her hands shaking in anger. She found the keychain, tried to insert a key in the door, angled the key wrong, so that it stuck.

"Allow me," said a voice close behind her. A large hand closed over hers, taking the keys. She turned. Harley Baer filled the small space between her car and the next one. He freed the key, then reinserted it into the lock.

"You remember me?" he asked, his hand on the door. "We met at the hardware store."

"Yes," Annie said, her voice less steady than she wished. "You're Harley Baer."

He looked surprised and pleased. "I didn't tell you my name."

"I mentioned you to Mrs. Avent. She remembered you."

Harley smiled. "Didn't know the old lady was in town."

"She's not. We write."

Harley's smile widened, and Annie was furious with herself. "Writing letters about me, are you? That's nice." He looked at David, put his hand on David's head. "Nice little boy," he said, but Annie didn't like the way his huge hand felt the boy's skull. It was too much like the way he'd felt the apple. "What's your name, little boy?" Harley asked.

"David."

"Well, David, don't you let old lady Avent make you any promises. She don't keep them."

David frowned and pulled away from Harley's touch.

"Mrs. Avent said your father worked for her," said Annie.

"I told you that," said Harley. "We was supposed to get that house when she died."

"No," said David. "The garden doesn't like you."

Harley's attention focused on David. Annie edged closer to her car door, to open it, but Harley didn't move out of her way. She had to slide against him to move. "You can move like that anytime you want," he said, but the remark sounded automatic. He studied David.

Annie found his interest in her son far more upsetting than his suggestive remark. "I'd like to go now," she said, her voice ragged.

Harley let out a barking laugh, then looked at something over her shoulder. "Nobody's keeping you," he said, and ambled off.

Annie turned to see what had made him move off. It was Mark, coming toward them from the restaurant. She jerked the car door open and unlocked the back for David.

"Who was that?" Mark asked her. "Was he giving you a hard time?"

Annie could feel her hands shaking, and she didn't much want to talk to Mark anyway. She got into the car and slammed her door shut.

Mark came to her door first and pulled the keys out. Damn, she thought, angry with herself for forgetting them.

Mark walked around to the driver's side and got in. He held the keys out and dropped them into her lap. "Why are you so upset?" he asked.

"Why am I upset? You talk to Charlie Legere behind my back and agree to get me to meet him by pretending to take me out to lunch so he can try pressuring me into selling. And you ask why I'm upset?"

"I didn't pretend to take you to lunch: I did take you to lunch," Mark said, smiling.

"You know what I mean," Annie said. "And it was despicable. And don't try to joke your way out of it."

"I guess it was pretty bad, if you put it like that," Mark said, his face taking on the same look of puzzlement she had glimpsed in the restaurant. "But when Charlie suggested it, it seemed like a really good idea. I can't explain it. Like the right thing to do. And as far as practical financial matters go, selling is the right thing to do. But I still wouldn't try to force you to do anything you thought wasn't right." He put his hand under her chin and looked into her eyes. "You know that, don't you?"

"I hope so," Annie said.

He started the car, then took a deep breath, something he always did when trying to calm down. He looked into the rearview mirror and smiled. "How's it going, Tiger?"

David smiled and growled.

Annie turned to the child in the backseat. "David, how do you know the garden doesn't like him? The garden's not here."

"No, but I am."

Mark turned a bemused smile first on David, then on Annie. "I'll say one thing for you, you sure know how to drive up Charlie Legere's offers. He sweetened it again after you left. We, my dear, could be rich," he said wistfully.

Chapter 10

"I do find it hard to believe you won't even consider this," Mark said in his most irritatingly reasonable tone.

"Can't we just drop it, Mark?" Annie said, and tried not to laugh. She knew it would only make him angry if she laughed, but they were in their bedroom changing into more casual clothes after their lunch out, and there he stood in a dress shirt and a tie, his undershorts, and a serious expression.

"And I don't know why I'm always the one who comes across as being in the wrong. Do you have any idea what excellent financial shape we'd be in if we took the bank's offer?" he said, loosening the tie and jerking it free of his collar.

Annie zipped her jeans, then plunged her head inside a sweater and laughed silently. When she regained control, she pushed her head through the neck opening and looked at Mark. He had put on a pair of workpants and was regarding her with exasperation.

"Well?" he said.

"I'm not going to sell the house."

"Do you have any idea how long I'd have to work to accumulate that much capital? It's not like this was your old family homestead I was asking you to sign over."

"You keep saying you won't force me to sell, but you keep trying to force me to do just that," Annie said. "And I've given you all the reasons I want to stay, and you've given me all the reasons you want to sell, and I don't see any point in going over and over and over the same ground."

"I'm hoping if I drill this into you enough, at some point you will finally see reason," Mark said. He opened the bedroom door, then slammed it shut again. Annie wondered where all this violence was coming from; it wasn't Mark's style.

"Is it your friend from the parking lot?" he asked.

"What?"

"The guy you were so chummy with in the parking lot. Is he the reason you want to stay here?"

"Mark, get a grip on reality."

"He was standing so close you were breathing the same air, and I didn't see you trying to run away."

"He's large, Mark. I couldn't get around him to run away. I expected help in that situation, not accusations."

"He's a big guy. Powerful. Maybe you like an occasional biker type."

Annie controlled an urge to throw something at him. Just then a large black bird landed on the windowsill, startling them. It turned its head to peer at them, then flew off.

"You're just saying this to get me to sell the house," Annie said. "I don't know exactly how you're planning to do it, but I know that's what this is leading up to. It's not going to work." She turned her back on him to pick up a brush and tidy her hair, but she could still see him reflected in the dresser mirror. He looked as though he wanted to kill her. His face looked as though someone else's face were behind it, molding Mark's face to someone else's expression. She didn't know this other person. Her hand shook, and she dropped the hairbrush. "Who are you?" she said.

The illusion faded, as though the controlling face were making a strategic retreat. For the third time that day, Mark looked puzzled. "David's waiting for me. I have yardwork to do," he said, and walked out of the room.

Annie sat down on the bed. The window curtain bellied inward, and a scent of lilac came in on the breeze. She could hear David laughing, could hear bird cries and a sound of wings. She took a deep breath of lilac and resolved not to let him bully her into selling.

What did that mean? As long as she wouldn't sign, he could not sell, so it meant she couldn't let him talk her into signing. She couldn't tell him what had been going on here, about the ladder and the arrows, because any hint of danger was an argument for selling. She felt a rising anger toward Mark, because of the house, because he left her alone so much, because he was no help at all dealing with this Harley person. Because he was so changeable. Her anger was like birds' wings beating inside her body, struggling to get out. She wanted to let fly at him, beak and talons, strike at him, beating wings and all.

David's screams brought her to the bedroom window. She swept the lace curtain aside and saw David standing at the edge of the flower bed.

"Mommy! Mommy!" He looked toward the meadow, then back to her. "They're hurting Daddy!"

She ran down the stairs and out the kitchen door, wings still beating frantically in her head. When she reached the meadow, she stopped suddenly and David came up beside her.

"Make them stop!" he said.

Birds were attacking Mark. Large black birds circled and

wheeled, swooping to strike. Mark was shielding his eyes, but blood dripped from a gash on his forehead. She tried to think the birds away, but another one with talons out struck Mark's head.

"Mommy, make them stop!" David said, clinging to her hand.

"I don't know how."

"Let them go. Just let them go."

She released them then, an act of the will rather than the mind. They flew off, climbing into the sky.

"You shouldn't hurt Daddy," David said.

"I didn't mean to," said Annie.

Mark was looking up into the sky, his arms still raised to ward off attack. When he saw the birds had gone, he got out his handkerchief and wiped the blood out of his eyes. Annie took it from him and held the cloth to the cut.

Mariah came running toward them from the gate in the hedge. She was out of breath when she spoke. "Are you all right? I've never seen anything like that." She looked at the cut on his forehead. "You'd better let John have a look at your head."

Mark seemed dazed. Annie put her arm through his. "John's a doctor," she said, leading him to the adjoining property.

John, wearing a chef's apron, was putting hamburgers on an outdoor grill. His genial expression became professional at the sight of Mark. "What happened?" John asked.

"Bird attack," Mariah said. "A whole flock of crows came swooping down on him."

"Birds?" said John. "Come on inside. I'll dress that for you. When was your last tetanus shot?"

David followed his father and John. Mariah checked the playpen where Erica lay napping in the light shade of the newly leafing oak tree.

"You look like you could use a cup of tea," she said to Annie. "Come on, I can keep an eye on her from the kitchen window."

"Got anything that's good for hallucinations?" Annie asked, following her.

"A hallucinogen? Mushrooms, but I don't know much about those," Mariah said, putting the kettle on.

"I meant to stop them," said Annie.

"Oh. I'd have to look it up." Mariah got a thick notebook with a marbleized cover from the shelf where she stored her jars of herbs and untied the string that held it shut. Loose pages slid out when she opened it. "It's kind of falling apart," she said. "I should recopy it."

"It looks old," said Annie.

"It was my grandmother's. She kept notes on all the herbs she grew, or found wild, and what they were for." Mariah turned pages carefully, and Annie got a glimpse of fading handwriting that was round and legible.

"That's a big book. How did she figure all that out?" Annie asked.

"Oh, she didn't. She got the information from her mother, who got it from hers, who got it from hers. I don't know how far back it goes. Somebody has to recopy it every generation or two, because you can see how the books fall apart when they get used a lot. And it keeps getting longer, because every woman who uses it adds to it. I don't see anything on hallucinations. Who's having them?"

"Me. Birds again. I was upstairs on the bed when David called me, but I'd swear I was inside that flock of birds that was attacking Mark."

"You must have just been dreaming, and the birds got mixed in with the dream because that's what woke you up."

"I'd just had a fight with Mark."

"See? That proves it. That's why you dreamed it."

Annie shook her head. "I wasn't dreaming. I may be going crazy, but I wasn't dreaming."

"Madness," Mariah said, consulting the book again. "There I can help you: hellebore." She turned to the appropriate page. "Hellebore, black. The roots are very effective in curing madness. Pound them to a powder, and take twenty grains mixed with ten of cinnamon. There's a white hellebore, too, but it's apparently not good for much. Oh, terrific: Too much can poison you. The antidote is goat's milk."

"Do you have any hellebore?" Annie asked.

The kettle shrieked, and Mariah got up to make the tea. "You're starting to take all this too seriously," she said.

"What kind of tea are you making?" Annie asked.

"Lipton," said Mariah. "Look, none of this herbal medicine is scientific. There's a lot of superstition, and anecdotal evidence, and no studies that mean anything statistically."

"Don't you believe in any of it?" Annie asked.

Mariah brought a brown earthenware pot to the table and poured two cups of tea. She picked up her cup and drank some before answering. "Some," she said. "Because some of it makes sense. The things I've taught you—peppermint tea for the digestion, and catnip tea to soothe nerves—I know those work, because I've tried them. And the culinary herbs, and how to make chamomile hair rinse and lavender water."

"But you haven't taught me everything."

"I don't know everything. There are things in this book that go back a long way, and that aren't true because the women who wrote them were looking at the world wrong. Like potpourris."

"So? What's wrong about making a room smell better?"

"That's what people use them for now, I know," Mariah said. "But that's not what they were really for, originally. People used to think diseases like the plague were transmitted by air, especially night air. Potpourri has orrisroot in it which, if you read books now, the recipes say is a fixative. But according to my grandmother's great-great-grandmother or somebody before her, orris-root draws poisons to it. That's what the potpourri was for: to draw poisons from the air. But that can't work, based on what we know now about how diseases are transmitted."

Annie shrugged. "So the book's not infallible."

"It could also be dangerous," Mariah said. "If you don't have goat's milk on hand."

Annie laughed. "Do you mind if I read it?" she asked, stroking the smooth paper.

Mariah hesitated. "It's all right, but you'd have to read it here. My grandmother made me promise so many times never to let the book out of my possession, I would have a crippling attack of guilt if I ever let anyone borrow it."

"I understand. It's irreplaceable. I'd feel the same way. Is it all right if I copy some of it?"

"Oh, sure. It can be quite interesting. Like strawberries: They were used medicinally for people with loose teeth and spongy gums before anybody ever heard of vitamin C or scurvy. But you've got to promise me you won't do anything risky. Herbs can be poison-ous."

Annie smiled.

"All mended," said John, coming into the kitchen followed by Mark. "I prescribe a beer for the patient, and one for the doctor."

Annie looked at Mark's bandaged forehead. She went over to him and kissed him contritely. He put his arm around her. "Is there going to be a scar?" she asked John.

"No, I don't think so," John said. "It wasn't that deep once we got it cleaned up. I did want to make sure it was clean, though. Birds' feet are dirty things." He opened the refrigerator and reached for the beers. "Ladies?" he asked.

"We'll finish our tea," Mariah said.

John handed Mark a bottle and opened one for himself. "It's

funny," he said. "But maybe this bird thing is specific to this neighborhood. I was telling Mark, I grew up around here, and I can remember a bird attack before this, when I was a kid. Happened on Mrs. Avent's property, too."

"John, that must have been thirty years ago," Annie said warningly. She nodded toward David.

"Huh?" said John. "Oh. Right. Hardly a big trend. Nothing to worry about, David."

"My mommy wouldn't hurt me," said David.

"Right," John said, and winked at Annie. "Your mommy will keep you safe from bird attacks. Now let's go cook some hamburgers."

He went out with David, and Mariah followed carrying a platter of raw meat patties.

"You're quiet," Annie said to Mark.

"It's been a hell of a day. Friends?" he asked, pulling her closer.

"Friends," she said. "Does your head hurt?"

"It's not too bad. I'm not looking forward to going to work, though, and explaining I got beaten up by a crow. Come on, let's go be company. At least we don't have to worry about another bird attack for the next thirty years. There's comfort in that."

Annie didn't quite agree with that assessment. She supposed it could be worse: What if they lived in a jungle, and instead of birds, she identified with cats? But she kept the observation to herself and just smiled.

"Maybe I should buy a rifle," Mark said.

Annie pulled away from him. "No."

"Don't I deserve revenge?" He smiled. "Come on, let's join the party," he said, and walked toward the others.

Annie watched him go. She felt frightened for the birds, and for herself.

Chapter 11

The wisteria was in full bloom, a waterfall of flowers cascading down the front porch. Annie stroked one of the purple clusters and watched it flow along her hand, then ripple back into place.

"Impressive," Mark said, coming up the steps to where she stood. "Too bad it only blooms for a couple of weeks."

"If it bloomed much longer, you'd stop looking at it," Annie said.

Mark put his arms around her and she leaned against him. "I've got the car loaded," he said.

"Okay."

"Look, why don't we plan on going out somewhere when I get back, just the two of us? Dinner, dancing, whatever you want. Mariah's got a kid, she should be able to recommend a sitter."

"Is Mr. Legere going to just happen to show up at the same restaurant?"

"You're never going to let me forget that, are you? I'm sure he and his wife must be a fun couple, but no, he won't be there. I still think . . ."

She pulled away from him.

"All right," he said. "Let's not argue about it now. I want to say good-bye to Tiger, and then I'm off to Denver. You two ought to come with me on some of these trips."

Annie felt the plants were upset by this suggestion. She could not leave now, in the middle of spring planting, but knew her feelings tied to the garden would become another argument for selling. "We'll see," she said.

After Mark had gone, Annie took David out to the vegetable garden.

"Let's see if the carrots are up," she said.

"Okay," he said. "I made the lettuce striped."

"Striped?"

"Red and green."

"Oh, that's just the way that kind grows, honey," Annie said. "It's supposed to be red, but it's always got some green mixed in with it. You didn't do that."

"I made it striped," David said.

When they rounded the corner of the carriage house, she saw that he had indeed made the lettuce striped. Each leaf was patterned in neat bands of red and green. She looked around, wondering what other eerie surprises might be in store. "Did you do anything else?" she asked.

He pointed. "I made the carrots grow faster. I made them sweeter."

Where she had planted seeds two weeks ago, there were now rows of baby carrots, big enough to eat.

"And I didn't let the spinach grow at all," David said.

"Your father likes spinach. It's his favorite."

"It's yucky and he makes me eat it."

"That still wasn't very nice."

"I didn't stop it very hard. You could make it grow, Mommy."

"I don't much like spinach either. But you'd better not do anything to my broccoli." She inspected the broccoli row. By bending down, she could just make out the newly sprouted seedlings. Right on a normal schedule. "No, I guess you didn't."

"You could make it grow faster, Mommy. It's not hard."

"Not hard for you. It's impossible for me."

"No it isn't. Try."

"David, I can't."

"Try." He took her hand. "I can't do the birds," he said. "It's easier than the birds. Try."

She looked at the broccoli with him, playing the game to keep him happy. His hand was small inside hers, and warm, and she was thinking about that, not the seedlings, when she felt a tug, as though part of her consciousness had slipped its moorings and was moving away. She wasn't inside the small green plants exactly, not the way she could be inside the birds, but a thread led from them to the other plants, the grass, the apple tree. A network of communal life, and she could feel herself being drawn into it on a very strong current. She grew frightened and pulled back while she still could, letting go of David's hand and the garden at the same time.

"You're getting it, Mommy," David said. "But you forgot to make the broccoli grow."

Annie knelt down and looked into his face. "Doesn't that frighten you, David?"

"No. The garden won't hurt me. It makes me safe."

His face seemed the same little boy's face, the same eyes ready to show delight or hurt with a small child's vulnerability. But he could do these things: How was that changing him? "Does it make you a plant?" she asked.

David laughed. "No," he said. "That's silly. Come on, I'll show you my garden."

He took her to the outside corner of the greenhouse, where the potting table was. Clay pots and broken shards lay about, and spilled potting soil and sand. She thought he'd just been digging over here, but the rows of seedlings were evidence of other activity.

Annie frowned. "What are they?"

"These are radishes. I tried to make them be potatoes, but they came out funny." He pulled one out, exposing a lumpy, reddish brown mass at the end of a misshapen leaf and stem. "I didn't have potato seeds," he said. "Those are beets. I tried to make them grow into candy, but they go all soft. And these are acorns. That one's supposed to grow apples, and that one's supposed to grow cherries, and that one's supposed to grow bananas. They look funny, don't they?"

Annie shuddered. "They're all perversions, David."

"What's that?"

"Bad things. You tried to make them grow against their nature. If you want to make the carrots grow into bigger, sweeter carrots, that's fine, because they're still carrots. But a radish is never going to be happy trying to be a potato."

"That's what the apple tree says."

"It's a very smart tree," Annie said, feeling ridiculous because she was pleased to be told that a tree agreed with her. "Why don't we pull all these things up and put them out of their misery?"

"Okay." The radishes and beets came out easily enough, but Annie had to use a trowel on the acorns.

"Look at the taproot on these things," she said. "They sure send it down fast." David nodded, and together they tossed the

86

plants onto the compost pile. "You're not going to do anything like this again, are you?" Annie said.

"No. But can I grow square tomatoes for Daddy? He wants them to fit his sandwiches better. He always says it."

"Yes, he does. Okay, but not too square. Don't make them perfect. It would just upset him if he knew how you were doing it."

"Don't tell him," David said, admonishing her with an earth-covered finger. "It's a surprise."

"I won't tell," Annie said, but she was distracted by a change in the notes of birdsong around them. She looked up to see sparrows circling excitedly, flying to the front of the house and coming back to twitter importantly on the branches of the nearby fruit trees.

"What, Mommy?"

"I think somebody's here," Annie said, brushing the dirt off her hands. She walked quickly to the front of the house.

Harley Baer was at the garage door, rattling the handle and peering through the glass.

"Did you want something?" Annie asked.

Harley turned slowly, and David came up beside his mother.

"Go onto the porch," Annie said softly to David, and he faded into the safety of the wisteria.

"I'm thinking of renting the apartment," Harley said, indicating the upper level of the garage.

Annie didn't believe him. "It's not for rent," she said.

"Good income property like that? You should. Door's locked, though. You want to open it for me so I can take a look, see what condition it's in these days?"

"No. It's not for rent."

Harley's expression became crafty. "Let me talk to your husband," he said.

"He's not here now," Annie said, and immediately could have kicked herself.

"Left you alone again, has he? You and the boy? Hey, David, you like the place?" He stepped toward the house, but the smirk left his face when he tripped on a root that had suddenly moved into his path. Annie looked at David, who was studying the view from the porch steps with an exaggerated air of innocence.

"Shit!" Harley said. He managed not to fall, but came down hard on his left ankle in order to keep his balance.

"I think you should go now," Annie said.

"Yeah," Harley said. His grimace of pain was replaced by a look of plain hatred, and Annie wondered why he disliked her so much on such short acquaintance.

"How come old lady Avent gave you this place?" he asked.

"She sold it to us. She wanted to move into a nursing home."

"For the price you paid, she gave it to you. She should have given it to my dad and moved into a nursing home twenty years ago. She owes us."

Annie shrugged. "I wouldn't know about that," she said.

He looked at the house, the grounds, and the hatred didn't leave his face. Maybe it wasn't all directed at her. "This is a powerful place," he said with his air of knowing something no one else did. "Powerful. Old lady Avent thought she knew, but she didn't know shit. Not her. If it was mine, I'd let them make the whole thing into a parking lot. Pour asphalt over the whole thing." He waved his hand in an expansive gesture, but stopped and gave a sudden cry of pain. His hand had gotten tangled in the thorns of the rosebush that grew around the house. He pulled himself free and stepped back, looking thoughtfully at the bush, then at Annie.

"Witch!" he muttered, or maybe it was "Bitch!" He walked down the driveway, his limp improving as he went, then looked over his shoulder at Annie. "You bought more than you know," he said.

David came up softly and put his arm around his mother. She

rested her hand on his shoulder, and they watched Harley lumber off. How did Harley know about the bank's offer?

"I didn't scratch him with the thorns, Mommy," David whispered.

"I know," Annie said. "Neither did I."

Chapter 12

Mark came home briefly at the end of the week, and David was not happy that his parents were going out without him on the one night his dad was home. Pouting, he slouched against the doorjamb of their room and watched them get ready.

"You'll be in bed in an hour anyway," Mark said. "Be fair. Think of all the things I did with you today: Didn't we play catch, and go for ice cream, and paint the posts on the tennis court? Next time we'll put up the net."

David slid farther down into his pajamas, so that the legs wrinkled up and his toes strained against the pajama feet.

Mark put his hand under David's chin and raised it. "Hey, Tiger. I have to spend some quality time with Mommy," he said, and winked. Then he went to the vanity where Annie was putting on mascara and leaned on the back of her chair. "Am I supposed to pick this sitter up?"

"No, she only lives on the corner. She's walking."

"No drive across town late at night to take her home? Sounds great."

"Mariah says she's a good sitter ... reliable, likes kids. She also says she's nosy, so if you have anything incriminating in the house, lock it away."

"What?" said Mark.

"You can't expect perfection for three dollars an hour," Annie said, and laughed at the shock on his face. "Relax. Mariah just said she tried on her clothes and makeup. She's fifteen, I guess she still likes to play dress-up. At least David likes her: He played with her next door while she was sitting Erica."

"That was a sitter?" David said in disgust. "I thought she was just a girl."

Mark laughed. "Did she charge you for that?"

"No. She suggested it, so David would know her."

"She can't be all bad," Mark said. The doorbell rang. "There she is. Come on, kid, let's throw you to the sitter." He casually tucked David sideways under one arm, and went downstairs with him. David shrieked happily.

"Her name's Tiffany," Annie called after them. She returned her attention to the mirror and finished putting on mascara. The room was quiet without David and Mark, quiet enough so that she could hear a faint tap-tapping at the window. She set the mascara brush down, pushed the curtain aside and raised the sash. The reason for the sound was immediately apparent: Seed pods were falling from the maple tree, hitting the glass and the windowsill.

Annie leaned out and looked at the tree outlined against the twilight sky. "Did you want something?" she asked.

The tree released a flurry of seedpods, which came pinwheeling down around her, sifting into the room.

"Is something wrong?" she asked it. There must have been a wind, Annie thought, although she didn't feel one, because the tree shivered and a vortex of seed pods came down like little helicopters and swirled along the driveway. Annie shivered too.

"I'm just going out for a few hours," she said, just in case all this was real. "Take care of David for me."

Some clouds must have cleared the sun just as it set then, because Annie felt a sudden, warm glow from the tree. Reassured, she closed and locked the window.

"Now I'm talking to trees," she said. "And myself." But they were going to have a good time tonight, and she refused to let anything upset her. She grabbed her sweater from the foot of the bed and went downstairs.

Tiffany was in the hall, flirting with the men. Annie smiled. "Did Mark give you the phone number of the restaurant?" she asked.

Tiffany looked up. She wore her hair piled up and pushed forward in a blonde, frizzy mass, and since her eyes were heavily ringed in black liner and violet mascara, the effect was a bit like a young raccoon peering out of the forest. She smiled and nodded, and the chime of little bells came from the single earring that dangled from her right ear.

"All set," she said. "I brought some tapes, if it's all right with you for David to watch them."

Annie checked the titles: *The Little Prince.* "Fine," she said, and handed it back to Tiffany. *Sleeping Beauty.* "Also fine." The third was *Attack of the Killer Tomatoes.* "Not this one," she said. "I don't want to give him ideas."

"What?" said Tiffany. "He won't get bad dreams. It's not a scary movie."

"No," Annie said. "This is not a movie for David."

Tiffany shrugged and blew a bubble with the wad of gum in her mouth.

David was clearly fascinated. "Wow," he said softly.

Tiffany popped the bubble and sucked it back into her mouth. "Don't you know how to do that? I'll teach you," she said, taking a pack of gum out of her purse. "If it's okay with your mom." She looked at Annie. "It's sugar-free."

"That's fine," Annie said. "Just don't let him fall asleep with it in his mouth. And Tiffany, I don't mind if you play with my makeup as long as you don't leave a mess."

Tiffany tossed her head and the little bells on her earring tinkled. "I just did that once. Mrs. Fenton had a new shade I wanted to try. I've bought my own now," she said with a quiet but prickly dignity.

Annie felt sorry she'd mentioned it. "There's plenty of food in the kitchen, just help yourself. David will probably want some cocoa later."

"We'd better be going," Mark said, opening the front door. He looked at Tiffany with a puzzled expression. "You must have lost an earring on the way over. We'll look on the path for it."

Annie intercepted the offended expression Tiffany threw Mark's way. "It's the style," Annie said, poking her elbow into his stomach. "Give me a kiss bye-bye," she said to David, who was already intent on learning a new skill. He gave her a hurried, bubblegum-scented kiss, then turned his attention back to his instructor.

Mark led her out into the wisteria-scented air, closed the door, and burst out laughing. "That's quite a sitter you got for David. Do you think he can handle her?"

But Annie had gone to the edge of the porch where she stood looking out into the night. Were the shrubberies just naturally thick with shadows, or were they trying to warn her of something? "I don't think we should stay out late," she said.

Mark was still chuckling about the baby-sitter. "Smart decision," he said, and walked with Annie to the car.

The restaurant Mariah had suggested was called The Country Kitchen, and its menu featured roast pheasant under glass, duck à l'orange, sauerbraten, five kinds of quiche, pecan pie, and enough flambé main courses and desserts to keep their fire insurance premiums high. The decor was wood paneling and hand-hewn beams, with a walk-in fieldstone fireplace in the main dining room. There was no fire due to the summer weather, but soot marks could be seen plainly behind the floral arrangement that filled the hearth.

Mariah had made their reservations, and with a doctor's wife's influence had gotten them a choice table with a view of the lake. Stars were out, and the moon shone, reflected in the water. Annie looked from the moon that quivered in the water to the one that hung still in the sky, and realized with a feeling of unease that it was full. But the scene was peaceful, brought to human proportions by the string of house lights that marked the lakeshore.

"They have a fancy menu for a place called The Country Kitchen," Mark said.

"They don't say which country," Annie said. "Maybe they're trying to be all of them: They seem to have everything but sushi."

"I think I'll have a steak," Mark said.

Annie decided on a seafood pasta salad, and Mark ordered the food plus a bottle of Liebfraumilch. Annie unfolded the heavy linen napkin and peeked into the bread basket.

"Mariah says to be sure and try the muffins," she said, taking one from the basket. She split it open and a fragrance of nutmeg rose from the interior.

"Does Mariah supply this place with their herbs?" Mark asked, nodding toward the bunches of plant materials that hung from the beams near the hearth.

"Yarrow, celosia, lunaria. Just decorations," Annie said. "None of those are for cooking."

"You're becoming quite the expert," said Mark.

Annie shrugged. "It rubs off."

The wine arrived and Mark poured them each a glass. "Not that Mariah isn't nice," he said, "but she is a little strange."

"No she isn't."

Mark leaned forward with a mock serious expression and said confidentially, "I've heard she's a witch."

"Who told you that, Charlie Legere?"

Mark sat back and smiled. "Several people. It's common knowledge. You should get out more, meet other people."

"I've met the paperboy and a very old gentleman in the hardware store. When the world was built, I think he was around to sell the nails that hold it together, and I don't think he's approved of anything that's happened since. Oh, I've met the paperboy's dog, too."

The waiter set their food in front of them.

"Looks good," Mark said, picking up his knife.

"Anyway," Annie continued, "it's hard to get to know people when you have no car."

"Exactly," Mark said. He took something from his pocket and held it out to her.

"The car keys," she said as he dropped them into her hand.

"Do you know what that means?" Mark asked.

"You're planning to drink too much and you want me to drive home?"

"No. Of course not. It means I'm giving you the car. I'd have given you your own set of keys, but you already have your own set of keys, so I'm giving you mine. This is just symbolic."

"I don't understand this," Annie said.

"I've talked the company into providing me with a car. That means I can leave ours home with you."

"Oh," Annie said.

"The Y has mother-child swimming classes. David ought to learn. And there's a half-day preschool we should look into. So what are you going to do first, something constructive, or just go shopping?"

Annie looked thoughtfully at the lake. The keys felt cold in her hand, but familiar. "I think I'll drive out and visit Mrs. Avent," she said.

There was a brief pause in the conversation at this, but Mark let it pass without comment. Instead he changed the subject to a discussion of whether to paint or paper the downstairs rooms. Annie smiled, appreciative of his efforts to be good.

It was about halfway through the main course, when he re-filled their glasses, that she had the first sensation of wings. The owl was flying, distracting her. She pushed it aside, concentrating instead on Mark.

"... really ought to strip the paint off the banisters, but it'd be a hell of a job," he was saying.

The rush of feathers grew louder, more insistent. The owl was trying to show her something. She fought to listen to Mark, but she could hear the wind and, while she saw Mark across the table, she also saw an aerial view of their house as the bird circled, calling her attention to something.

"You're quiet tonight," Mark said, looking at her carefully.

There was a figure moving along their property line, on the outside of the hedge, on the sidewalk.

"Are you all right?" Mark asked.

"Maybe we should go home," Annie said.

"Why? Don't you feel well?"

"I'm fine. It's just ... It's like I'm flying over home, and I feel something's wrong."

Mark laughed and moved her glass to one side. "I think I'd

better drive." He pocketed the car keys and signaled the waiter. "Two coffees, please. And we'll try the pecan pie."

Annie sipped her coffee and told herself she hadn't seen any real menace, just someone on the sidewalk. It could be anyone, probably just one of the neighbors going to catch a bus. But it wasn't until they pulled into their driveway that the double image receded, and the feeling of being in both her own body and the owl's faded from her mind.

They found Tiffany in the living room watching MTV with a schoolbook propped up in her lap. "Hi!" she said, looking up when they came in.

"Everything okay?" Annie asked.

"Sure. He was real good," Tiffany said, snapping her book shut. She got up and turned off the television. "He's got quite an imagination. You should have heard all the things he was telling me he does with the plants."

"That's our boy," Mark said, taking out his wallet and paying her. "Think you can stand staying with him again, if we need a sitter?"

"Sure," Tiffany said. "Thanks. I'd better be getting home." She gathered her books and dumped them in her bag.

"Mark, I think you should walk Tiffany home," Annie said.

"Oh, that's okay, Mrs. Carter. It's only to the corner."

"I know, but with all that's been going on, I think we should make sure you get home safely."

"I agree," Mark said. "Tell you what, I'll walk you to the sidewalk and just watch till you get home, how's that?"

"All right," Tiffany said, with an air of humoring the grown-ups.

Annie watched the door close behind them, then went upstairs. She felt better about the situation, with Mark seeing the girl home, although whoever had been by the hedges was probably long gone. She checked on David, found him safe and asleep, then went to her own bedroom, where she turned on the light and kicked off her high heels.

She opened the window, then held on to both sides of the frame and looked out into the night. It was nice having an old house with generously-sized windows and deep sills. The night air was warm and humid, and she wondered if it was too early in the season for a thunderstorm. She could hear the dry patter of maple seeds falling, although she couldn't see them. The tree seemed jittery; the frequency of the clicks the seeds made increased. The tree seemed to be warning her of something. Still holding on to the window frame, she leaned back inside the room. Maybe she should check on David.

A sudden pain in her hand made her gasp. An arrow had struck her hand and, through her hand, the window frame. Blood flowed warmly down her arm. If she hadn't moved, it would have struck her chest. She was suddenly aware of herself standing in the lighted window frame, still a target, and whirled aside so that she was protected by the wall.

She had to get her hand free, had to pull the arrow out. She tried to reach it with her free hand, but couldn't without standing in the window. Now that her arm was at a different angle, blood flowed down the window frame and dripped from the sill, and she knew she had to stop it.

Mark should be home soon. He could pull out the arrow, get help. How long would it take him to see the sitter home?

Her hand hurt like hell. She couldn't wait for Mark.

The light switch. It was in this wall. If the room were dark, the archer couldn't see her to take aim. She stretched her right hand toward the switch, and almost touched it. She stretched a little more. This made the hand with the arrow in it move, and she nearly passed out from the pain.

Blood was collecting in a pool beneath the window. Her blood. She'd just have to risk it. She turned to the window, grabbed the arrow, and pulled. It came free of the wood but not her hand, and she sank to the floor just as another arrow hit the frame near where she'd been standing.

Annie drew a deep breath, then pushed herself along the floor with her feet. When she was near enough, she reached her right hand up to the switch and turned off the light. There. She sat in the darkness, breathing shallowly and gathering strength. She knew she had to do something about the arrow, which was still in her hand, and the blood, which was pouring out of it. But she felt safer in the dark, and her heart beat more slowly.

She stood up and made her way into the hall, where there was light but no open windows. She looked at the arrow. Wooden shaft, nasty triangular point covered with blood. It would do more damage being pulled back out. But since it had gone clear through, she could cut the shaft and not have to pull it back out.

But with what?

Pruning shears. In the kitchen. She made her way downstairs, stopping on the way to grab a towel from the bathroom to try to catch some of the blood. The hand didn't hurt so much now, not unless she moved the arrow. That surprised her. The pruning shears should be in the second drawer of the cabinet, and she was thankful to find she'd remembered to put them back after the last time she'd used them. She held them to the arrowshaft, and wondered how much it would hurt if she bent the arrow while cutting it. There was no way to hold the arrow still without another pair of hands. Where was Mark when you needed him?

She cut the shaft, and the feathered end went clattering along the floor. She pulled out the shorter piece, and then the worst was over. She ran cold water over her hand, trying to stop the blood. The flow cleaned the blood off her hand, her arm, off the arrowhead lying in the sink. There was something odd about the arrow-head. She picked it up.

It was made of stone. Somebody had shot her with a stone arrowhead.

Mark came in. His face wore a pleasant expression, which faded as he took in the bloody towel on the table, the red splatters on the sink, and Annie standing there turning clear water to pink.

"What the . . . What happened?" he said.

Chapter 13

The emergency room didn't look busy. At least, the staff wasn't moving as though there were any emergencies, and Annie saw the effect this had on Mark, who was always outraged if other people didn't panic when he did.

"I'd like some help for my wife," he demanded before the nurse doing paperwork behind the counter had had a chance to look up. She wore glasses, Annie noticed, with one of those strings around the back to keep them from falling. Annie wondered if it got tangled with the stethoscope she also wore.

"What seems to be the problem?" she said, putting down her pen.

"Dr. John Fenton is supposed to be meeting us here," Mark said. "I called his service and told him to meet us."

The nurse looked at something on her desk, then back at Mark, and the string from her glasses swayed with the movement. "Dr. Fenton isn't on call tonight," she said.

Mark exploded. "What's wrong with this place? Do you

know how far my wife had to walk from the parking lot? Don't they give you any courses in dealing with sick people?"

"There's space reserved for injured people to come in right through those doors," she said, her voice controlled but her glasses-string quivering.

Annie suddenly felt tired, and David's clinging heavily to her good hand wasn't helping. "Let's go sit down," she said to him.

"Why is Daddy mad?" he asked.

"Because he's upset." Annie raised her free hand in its blood-stained towel to get Mark's attention. He didn't notice, but the nurse clearly did, and said something to a black man who was sitting at a computer terminal, his back to the situation. He swiveled around and the nurse resumed dealing with Mark.

Annie tuned the whole thing out and found a seat. Let somebody else calm Mark down; she didn't have the energy. She'd used it up trying to keep his mind on the road driving over here.

"What's the trouble?" a deep voice asked. Annie looked up and saw the black man standing there. He was over six feet tall, and his white uniform was bright under the fluorescent lights. She could feel David huddle closer to her.

The man hunkered down so he was on eye level with David, and smiled. "Something happen to your mama?" he asked.

"She got shot," David said.

"Shot?"

"With an arrow," said Annie.

"Is it still bleeding?"

"I don't think so. I don't know, I get it to stop, then it starts up again," Annie said.

"We'd better have a look at that." He smiled at David again. "What's your name?"

"David."

"I'm Dr. Carl Smith, but you can call me Carl," he said, shaking David's hand. "I'm going to take your mama to an examining room and see what I can do to fix up her hand. Could you do me a big favor and wait out here with your dad?"

"No," David said, and tightened his grip on Annie.

"You're not going to cry, a big boy like you, are you?" Carl asked.

"Yes," David said.

"He won't be any trouble," Annie said.

Carl sighed. "I hate it when kids cry. All right. I guess you can come with us." He helped Annie up. "Do you want a chair, or can you walk?" he asked.

"I can walk." She looked at Mark, who was going through his wallet, probably looking for his Blue Cross card. There was a clipboard full of papers on the counter in front of him.

"Your husband can do the paperwork," Carl said.

"Oh good," Annie said, and Carl laughed at the relief in her tone. "Well, he's better if there's something he can do," she explained.

They went into an examining room, where Carl unwrapped the towel and cleaned the blood away to get a better look at the wound.

"It's still there," David said, and Annie could feel the tension in his grip lessen.

"What is?" she asked.

"Your hand. I thought it got shot off."

Annie smiled. "No. It's just got a hole in it."

"It sure does," said Carl. "How'd this happen?"

"I was standing at my bedroom window and somebody shot an arrow at me. It went through my hand."

"You have it with you?"

"In my purse. David, could you get the arrow for me? It's wrapped in a paper towel.

"Must be a small arrow," Carl said, looking at the size of her purse.

"I had to cut it to get it out," said Annie.

"You did that yourself?" Carl said.

David carefully unwrapped the two pieces of the arrow. The point and shaft were bloodstained; the feathered end still clean.

"Nasty," said Carl. He looked at the arrowhead in silence, his expression troubled. Then he made a visible effort to put aside whatever was bothering him. He returned his attention to Annie. "You're going to need a tetanus shot, if you haven't had one in the last five years." He picked up a clipboard and wrote while he talked. "I'm sending you to X-ray, and I want a plastic surgeon to look at this."

"I'm not worried about a scar on my hand," Annie said.

"We need him to repair the tendon damage."

"Oh," Annie said. "Will I have the full use of my hand again?"

"I don't see why not." Carl pointed to the arrow. "Better hold on to that."

The nurse brought Mark into the room then. "There you are," she said to Carl. "I have some releases for Mrs. Carter to sign."

Carl held up his hands defensively. "Just looking. Haven't started any treatment yet."

"You people would let my wife bleed to death while you did the paperwork to make sure you wouldn't get sued," Mark said.

David whimpered and moved closer to his mother.

"Mark," Annie said, "just calm down. It's okay, David, I'm not bleeding." She signed the forms and gave them to the nurse. At the same time Carl, his face bland, gave the prescription he'd written to the nurse, whose expression clearly said, "I knew it."

Mark looked at Annie. "You're not very upset about all this," he said accusingly.

Annie ignored him.

"Someone will be along shortly to take you to X-ray," the nurse said.

They were waiting in X-ray when the policeman came. He was a young man, in uniform, and he was intensely serious. His ears stuck out from his close-cropped head.

"Mrs. Carter?" he said. "State Trooper Keene. I'm here to investigate the shooting incident."

"Shooting incident?" Annie said.

"Dr. Smith reported you'd been shot with an arrow."

"Do you have to bother her with this now?" Mark said. "Can't you see she's in pain?"

"Sorry, ma'am," Keene said, "but in this particular case, we like to follow leads while they're fresh." His face remained pale, Annie noticed, but his ears had turned crimson.

David looked closely at the trooper's holster. "Is that a real gun?" he asked.

"Why this particular case?" Mark asked, puzzled, but Annie understood.

"Sir, could you take the little boy for ice cream or something, while I talk to your wife?"

Mark looked at Annie doubtfully. David frowned.

"Let him plant acorns in the front lawn," Annie said.

"It's dark out," David said.

Annie sighed.

"Come on, Tiger, let's check out the gift shop." Mark took David's hand. "Five minutes," Mark said over his shoulder as he led David away.

Keene got out his notebook and pencil.

"You mean because of the murders," Annie said. "Because they were done with arrows. That doesn't mean there's a connection."

"Did you happen to keep the arrow, ma'am?"

"Yes," Annie said. She fumbled in her purse and gave it to him. "Is it the same kind?"

"I'm not supposed to give out information about the investigation, ma'am."

"If a stone arrow was used in the murders, it could mean a murderer is shooting at me," Annie said. "I think I have a right to know that."

Keene's ears deepened in color. "It's the same, but don't tell that to anybody. Do you have any enemies, ma'am?"

"No. I'm just a housewife, and I haven't been in town very long."

"Does your husband?"

"No."

"Where was your husband when this happened?"

"He was out watching the baby-sitter walk home, to make sure she got there safely."

"So he wasn't with you?"

"No."

"You say you haven't been in town very long."

"We just moved here a few months ago."

"But your husband lives with you."

"Yes. Mostly. I mean, he travels a lot. For his work."

"You two getting along okay?"

"Of course we are. My husband did not shoot me with that arrow."

"How do you get along with the neighbors?"

"Fine."

"Nobody suspicious hanging around, nothing like that?"

Annie hesitated. "No," she said.

"Have you and your husband quarreled lately? Because in most of these cases, we find it's a husband or a boyfriend. He probably didn't mean to shoot you, but maybe he wanted to frighten you and he hit you by mistake. A lot of times, when that happens he'll overreact out of guilt, give the hospital staff a hard time."

"Mark doesn't even know how to use a bow and arrow."

"So you haven't seen anybody shooting arrows?"

"Oh," said Annie, remembering. "Not lately, but the first week we moved in, somebody shot an arrow past me into a tree. But that was a metal-tipped arrow, so it wouldn't be the same person, would it?"

"Could be he's just getting deeper into his hobby," Keene said. "Are you sure you haven't seen anyone suspicious in the neighborhood lately? Because when I asked that, you seemed to hesitate, like you were thinking about somebody."

"No. Well, there's this one man who used to live in the carriage house. But he hasn't done anything."

"Do you know his name, ma'am?"

"I don't want to get anyone in trouble with the police when I haven't really got anything bad to say against him."

"But he gives you a bad feeling."

"Yes."

"We'd like his name. We're going very easy with this. The last thing we want is to accuse the wrong man. But three women have been killed, and we're asking for all the help we can get."

Annie sighed. "I'm not accusing him," she said.

"I understand that. Don't forget, we know things you don't. This could help us tie things together."

"His name is Harley Baer. But you won't tell him I told you?"

"No, ma'am. This is my responsibility. It's interesting you're afraid for him to know."

"It's probably all just some psychopath," Annie said.

"That's right, ma'am."

"Anyway, how could Mark be involved? We just moved here three months ago."

Keene put away his notepad. "That's about when the murders started, ma'am," he said.

Chapter 14

It was past midnight when they got home from the emergency room. David was asleep, and Mark draped the child over his shoulder and carried him to bed. Annie followed the trail of blood she had left on the stairs and hall to her own room. The floor by the window was a mess, and so was the wall. She'd clean it up tomorrow.

She kicked off her shoes and let her dress drop to the floor. It was ruined anyway. Deciding her slip would do for a nightgown, she slid between the sheets and tried to find a comfortable position for her injured hand.

Mark came in. His face was pale, with a stubble of beard growing in, and he had dark circles under his eyes.

"You look wiped out," she said, but he was staring at the bloodstains. After a moment he turned to her.

"Your painkillers," he said, taking a vial of pills out of his pocket. "Do you want one now?"

"No. The stuff they gave me at the hospital hasn't worn off yet."

He set the pills on her nightstand, hung up his jacket, and went into the bathroom. Annie looked at the label on the vial: Tylenol with codeine. Mark came back with a glass of water and set it beside the Tylenol. "You might want it later," he said, and left the room, rolling up his shirtsleeves as he went. He came back a few minutes later with a bucket of water and some rags, and set to work scrubbing away the blood.

"I'll do it tomorrow," she said, from a vague feeling she ought to be cleaning up her own mess. "Do you really have to leave tomorrow?"

"I'm putting the trip off for a day. We'll see how you feel in the morning. Don't worry about anything," he said, wringing pink water out of the cloth and into the bucket. "I don't think we want this to be the first thing we see when we wake up tomorrow."

Annie rested her head on the pillow and watched him. The activity was just irritating enough to keep her from falling asleep, but he was right: She didn't want to see the traces of her ordeal by morning's light, either.

Mark moved the curtain aside to scrub the window molding. He saw the second arrow then, imbedded in the wood, and pulled it out. "Hunting arrow," he said.

Annie frowned. "How do you know?" she asked.

"The tip. It's triangular, with barbs on the sides so it won't fall out. Target arrows are just a point, so they'll pull out easily. Although I've never seen a stone target arrow."

"I meant how do you know about arrows?"

"Archery was my sport in college. We all had to have a sport, and that was mine."

"You never told me that."

He shrugged and dropped the arrow into the wastebasket. "I wasn't any good at it," he said, and recommenced scrubbing. Finally he dropped the rag into the water and said, "That's the best I can do." He got rid of the bucket, then climbed into bed beside Annie and turned out the light.

Annie turned onto her right side and rested her injured hand on the edge of the bed.

Mark reached over and lightly massaged the back of her neck. "You okay?" he asked.

"Yes. I just don't want you to roll over onto my hand," she said.

"I hate hospitals," Mark said.

"I know." Annie wondered if the trooper would check out Mark's background. If he found out about the archery thing, he'd think she'd been lying. "I wonder how the police will feel about your cleaning up the blood," she said, it having suddenly occurred to her that Mark had destroyed evidence.

"To hell with them," he said. Then exhaustion overtook them both, and within minutes they were asleep.

Annie woke in darkness, still tired and wanting to sleep, but dragged to consciousness by the pain in her hand. She remembered the doctor's words when she'd told him it didn't hurt. "It will," he'd said, insisting she take the prescription. She reached for the Tylenol and knocked over the water glass.

"Damn," she said. She could hear the water spilling onto the floor. She got out of bed, found her ruined dress, and used it to soak up the water. It was a rag now anyway.

Her hand was unbelievably painful. And stiff. And the night air had turned cold. The sound of Mark's breathing told her he was deeply asleep. There was no point in waking him. She put on his terrycloth robe, which he always left lying at the foot of the bed, dropped the Tylenol into its pocket, and slipped out of the room as quietly as she could.

Moonlight filled the hallway. She went down to the kitchen through a black-and-white world, moving through the spoked shadow of the banister and avoiding the patches of blackness that might hold nothing or anything. In the kitchen, she turned on the burner under the kettle and the gas flame became the brightest spot in the room. Tea might help. Or cocoa. She opened the refrigerator and searched the brightly lit interior for juice with which to take the pill, then took the container out of her pocket.

The vial had a childproof cap. How did they expect her to get the cap off with one hand? She'd have to wake Mark.

Catnip tea would probably work better than Tylenol anyway, she thought. Fresh catnip from the garden. Would the moon be bright enough, or would she need a flashlight? And was it safe? Surely the garden would warn her, as it had earlier. She had only to trust it. She stepped out onto the back porch.

Moonlight softened the darkness with a diffuse, quicksilver brightness that stopped at the threshold of color. Each leaf hung still in the windless air. The silence was intense. Annie listened for crickets, frogs, a nightbird, but heard only her own heart. The garden was watchful, and held her safe.

She stepped onto the garden path. The bricks were warm under her bare feet, and she followed them to where she knew the catnip grew. It was already two feet tall, with shaggy leaves: the wild catnip that Mariah had given her, saying it was stronger than the cultivated kind. She reached for what she thought was the right plant, crushed a leaf, and knew from the minty, woodsy scent with its undertone of the forest floor that she had found it.

She looked up at the moon, so intense it seemed white-hot, but clearly marked with dark craters and fracture lines. She could make out jagged teeth along one curving edge: the mountains of the moon. In the darkness around it was a haze of stars.

Her unbandaged hand still on the plant, she wished there were a way to make the catnip yet more potent. Anything seemed possible in this moonlight. She could sense the movement of juices through the plant, the slow action of its cells. The pain in her hand made her long for daylight, which always brought some kind of balance. But it was hours off, and she released the plant's ability to produce the chemical she wanted, and to move the distillation all to one stem. She knew this was happening through a sense that underlay all her others, and when the stem was ready, she grasped it unerringly, broke it off, and took it into the kitchen.

The kettle was boiling. Averse to turning on the bright ceiling fixture, Annie again opened the refrigerator and set up her teapot by its light. When the tea was brewing, she closed the refrigerator again and sat down at the table.

She poured herself a cup of tea. The steam that rose from it was strongly herbal, and as she sipped she could feel the pain in her hand recede. She'd proved David right, anyway: She could alter the plants.

She finished half a cup, and the world unfolded around her like a night-blooming flower. The air became warm and heavy, soft with drooping mosses. Lichens glowed with cold light, and phosphorescent moths illuminated the darkness with their blue-and-green wings, signaling to each other. A spider, each limb veined with red fire, picked its way along an invisible web. The underbrush rustled, and unfamiliar cries sounded, sometimes in long trills, sometimes cut suddenly short.

The darkness softened as dawn came sifting through the canopy of trees. Mist rose from the rain forest floor, and orchids, clinging to tree branches, presented dawn with its own colors. Birds chattered expectantly.

The sun rose, and Annie was flying with a flock of parrots into the dazzle of its rays. Red and yellow and green they flew, with a quick beating of wings, straight up through the protecting trees and into the blue sky.

The forest lay green beneath them: Green was everywhere, unbroken, stretching from the horizon to the mountain whose top almost touched the sun. They flew to the mountain, rising into cooler air, until they could see to fly past it.

Beyond the mountain, the land changed to desert. The green sea was gone, replaced by mud and stumps and fires whose smoke columns pointed to the sky. Yellow bulldozers sat waiting for the day's work to begin. Annie could see the shapes of men emerging from tents into the desolation they had created.

The flock of parrots screamed and wheeled back toward the forest. They circled the mountaintop, flying close to a man who stood watching them. He had dark hair and skin, and a sloping forehead. He wore a cape of parrot feathers and there were jade studs in his ears. He carried a bow, and this he raised, aiming his arrow into the flock of birds. Annie could feel his gaze on her, could see the arrow pointed directly at her. The other birds were oblivious to the danger he represented, but she screamed and flew toward him, attacking the bow.

Startled, he failed to release the arrow, and instead lowered it. The beat of wings was all around them. He looked at Annie among all the multitude of other parrots. She felt he wanted something from her.

The sound of wings retreated. Annie breathed deeply. She was sitting again in her own kitchen, with the morning sunlight streaming through the window. In the sunlight, formed by the sunbeams themselves, stood a Mayan figure in a parrot-feather cape. He looked at her.

"What do you want?" she asked.

He grew transparent as she watched, became a spangled cloud, and disappeared, leaving her with the kitchen and the sunlight, both empty.

Annie touched the table in front of her and found it reassuringly solid under her shaking hand. The catnip tea, long cold, she poured down the sink, but the catnip stalk still had more than half its leaves. It was worth saving and using more sparingly. She hung it on the wooden drying rack, then looked for something to tie to it to mark it as different from the other catnip.

There was nothing in the odds-and-ends drawer, but when she turned toward the table she saw just the thing lying on the floor where her visitor had been: a feather. She picked it up and tied it to the catnip. A bright, iridescent green feather. A parrot's feather.

If she'd been hallucinating, she'd sure done a bang-up job.

Chapter 15

"Annie?"

Annie looked up to see Mariah standing outside the kitchen's screen door.

"Come on in," Annie said, closing her cookbook.

"I brought you some strawberries. Just picked them this morning," Mariah said. The fruity smell of them came into the kitchen with her. She set the basket on the table and looked at Annie's bandaged hand. "I'm sorry about your hand."

"How did you know? It only happened last night."

"John called his service this morning and got Mark's message, and then he called the hospital to find out what had happened. The service really should have beeped him, but I guess they told Mark the doctor on call would take care of it, and they thought that was enough."

"It was enough. It needed a plastic surgeon anyway, so all John could have done was call one."

"We heard Mark was upset."

"He lived through it," Annie said.

Mariah looked at Annie's injured hand again, and said, "Do you have a colander? I'll hull these for you."

"Thanks," Annie said, getting one from the cabinet. "I've been looking for recipes for one-handed cooks, and I think what you do is use your good hand to dial the phone and order a pizza. Where's Erica?"

"With Mark and David. They were walking to the corner for ice cream, and they took her along. She's riding in David's wagon," Mariah said, hulling berries deftly. "Do you feel all right about being alone here?"

"Oh sure. The police have stepped up their patrols. And besides . . ." She wondered how much Mariah would believe about what had happened last night. Maybe if she approached the story through Mariah's interest in plants. The catnip was an important part of it. "Your grandmother's book is fascinating. But I was wondering, how come it came to you? Were you the only grandaughter?"

"No. I have four girl cousins."

"I can see why she'd give it to a girl, and not a grandson, because the book has always been kept by women. But why you in particular?"

Mariah's expression grew distant as she searched her memory. "She said I was talented. That's the expression she used. I think she really gave it to me because I was the only one who took an interest in plants."

"And your cousins didn't mind?"

"Oh, didn't they? They were furious. They always thought I was her favorite. And they said I was a witch. That's when my mother . . ." Mariah's voice trailed off, and Annie waited in vain for her to continue.

"Anyway, I'm glad you let me make a copy," Annie said.

"No problem," Mariah said. There was a brief silence broken only by the plunk of strawberries hitting the metal colander.

"Did she ever do anything with it?" Annie asked.

"Do anything? I don't know what you mean."

"With the information in it. Did she use the herbs for any of the things they're supposed to be good for?"

"I suppose so. Some," Mariah said evasively. "She died when I was pretty young. You know, I really don't like the idea of this guy shooting arrows in the neighborhood. Even if it's not the murderer and it's just some fool kid, it's gone too far."

"Yes."

"There must be something we can do."

Annie smiled. "David's making the hedges grow thicker, and the tree branches interlace more. And I'm listening carefully to whatever warnings the garden gives me. It's pretty good about knowing when there's danger."

"I meant something real," Mariah said. "Maybe we should start a neighborhood watch program."

"We could do that." Annie looked at her bandaged hand. "I was thinking of trying a poultice of tansy to make my hand heal faster. Or maybe yarrow. Which would your grandmother have used?"

"Yarrow. But she'd tell you it wouldn't actually work."

"But why? Why keep this book generation after generation if you don't believe it works?"

"She wouldn't have wanted people to think she was a witch."

"People don't believe in witches anymore," Annie said.

"You'd be surprised," said Mariah, brushing the pile of hulls into the trash. Her fingers were stained red.

"Was she?" Annie asked.

"No." Mariah took the colander to the sink and ran cold

water over the berries, then left them to drain and sat at the table opposite Annie. "Why do you keep going on about this?"

"Because something odd's happening, and I think something odd happened back then. It's the way you don't want to talk about certain things about your grandmother."

Mariah stared at her fingers, and tried to wipe the berry stains off with a paper napkin. "People said she was a witch. At least, the neighborhood kids did. She'd take me out gathering herbs . . . there were more meadows and woods around then, and she didn't try to grow everything herself. But my cousins got the kids started calling us both witches, so my mother wouldn't let me go anymore."

"So what's upsetting you?" Annie asked.

"Damn," said Mariah, throwing the napkin down. She went to the sink, moved the berries aside, and washed her hands. She dried them carefully, saying, "It was the way she died. The kids ganged up on her, shouting. They threw stones. I don't think they really meant to hurt her, but she was old and frightened and she had a heart attack and died. I remember it like I was there, but of course I wasn't. My mother had stopped me from going. Maybe if I had been there, it wouldn't have happened."

"How old were you?"

"About ten. I still dream about it sometimes."

"Do you dream about the Indian?" Annie asked, not sure herself what prompted the question, but feeling an urgency about the asking.

Mariah looked startled. "What Indian?"

"Like a Mayan, medium height, wears a feather cape. Sloping forehead and a big nose."

"Yes," Mariah said. "That's a pretty good description of him. Except he seemed more glamorous to me than you make him sound." She paused and Annie waited. "My grandmother said there was an Indian there that day. She talked to me before she died, I think. She said an Indian pierced her through the heart."

"Was she shot with an arrow?"

"No. It was a heart attack. But I remember her telling me about the Indian, and the memory is just as real as anything from my childhood. But she couldn't have told me, because she died under the tree with those little shits throwing rocks at her, and I wasn't there."

"I saw the Indian last night," Annie said. "He had an arrow pointed at me, but then he changed his mind and lowered it and didn't try again."

Mariah took a deep breath. "None of this is possible," she said. "Last night. What kind of painkillers did they have you on?"

"They had me on Tylenol 3, but I didn't take it. I had catnip tea instead."

"That explains it, then. You were tired, and overwrought, and maybe you brewed it too strong. It's no wonder you're seeing Indians with all these arrows flying around."

"What about your grandmother's Indian, and your remembering what happened when you weren't there?"

"That's not possible either. I must have dreamed it." Mariah looked out the window toward the road. "The ice cream foragers ought to be back soon. Too bad I didn't think to tell Mark to pick some up to go with the strawberries. Look, Annie," she said, dropping the curtain's edge, "is Mark going on the road again? Because when he goes, John and I think you should come stay with us for a few days."

"I'll be fine. He's leaving tomorrow, but I'm okay here. Really."

"Not really. You have one good hand and a five-year-old boy to look after."

"I sleep better in my own bed, Mariah, but thanks anyway."

"I think it would be better . . . I don't . . . Look, I don't want to upset you, but you know Carl, right? Well, you met him last night, anyway. He's really upset about these murders. He was at the hospital when they brought the first girl in, even though it was too late to do anything for her. When the second one was killed, he put up a map and people have been putting little information flags on it, like where the bodies have been found, where the victims worked, lived, that sort of thing. Almost like a game. It turns out all three bodies have been found within a mile of each other, and if you connect the points you get a triangle with this house at the center."

"That doesn't mean anything," Annie said.

"Carl was telling us because of course our house is at the center, too, but John and I think it's really your house, because of last night."

"I can't leave the house," Annie said.

"I think you should. Last night was only the first night of the full moon. More could happen."

"I'm stronger if I stay at the house."

Mark opened the kitchen door and ushered in two ice cream—smeared children. "Wet towels for everyone!" he said.

"I had chocolate," David said. "Erica had strawberry."

"So I see," Mariah said, wetting a towel and cleaning their faces. "Mark, I'm trying to talk your wife into staying with us while you're gone."

"Good idea," Mark said.

"It's nice of you, but no," Annie said. "You know, if the murders have been in this general area, I'll bet it's because of the bus stop. Three lines cross here, don't they? All those transfers. I'll bet he picks them up at the bus stop."

"You know, that makes sense," Mark said. "I wonder if the police have thought of it. I'm going to phone Keene now and suggest it." He went into the hall, and Annie watched the door swing shut behind him.

"You don't believe a word of that, do you?" Mariah said.

"I'm more secure here," said Annie.

Mariah looked pointedly at Annie's injured hand. "Sure you are," she said.

Chapter 16

 In the late afternoon, when Annie's hand began to hurt, she got the pruning shears and a basket to harvest yarrow for a poultice. The yarrow grew at the back of the perennial garden with the other tall, invasive plants, and the best way to get to it was from the meadow, but it would be quite a sprint back to the house, and with very little cover. She stood in the doorway, considering the open, sunlit field and the shadows that stretched from the hedgerows.

"Are you going out or not?" Mark asked. He had come up behind her, and stood with a can of charcoal lighter in one hand and a box of matches in the other. "You're getting to be like a cat: always wanting to go out, and not able to make up your mind once the door's open."

The garden seemed serene. Annie went out, and Mark, following before the door could close, walked quickly to the barbecue.

Annie went into the meadow. The grasses had grown in the last few days, and many were going to seed. Cornflowers bloomed, and daisies, and the wild strawberry plants were red with tiny fruit. She set her basket down by the yarrow and looked at the grasses, golden in the afternoon light, motionless except for the bobbing caused by an occasional bee working late hours.

There was no reason for alarm. She cut fronds of yarrow and trimmed them to the size she needed before dropping them into the basket.

David popped out from behind a stand of tiger lilies. "Hi, Mommy!"

"Oh! Hi, sweetie. I thought you were helping Daddy. What have you got all over your face?" she asked, noticing a stripe of red that glowed across his nose and cheek. She dropped the pruning shears into the basket.

"Nothing."

Annie reached for him and ran her finger along the streak. A powdery red substance rubbed off, and she held her finger up for him to see. "Lily pollen," she said. "It looks like war paint."

"Wow!" said David. He touched a lily and brought his hand away dusty with pollen, then put finger smudges on her cheek. "Now we're both Indians," he said.

Annie frowned. "I thought your dad was looking after you."

"He's busy. The garden's looking after me."

"Does the garden warn you if there's danger?"

David shrugged. "It just looks after me."

Annie turned toward the house, intending to signal Mark that David was with her, but Mark was nowhere in sight. "Your father's going to be worried," she said.

"No he's not. I just get in the way."

"You don't get in the way," Annie said, hugging David.

"Yes I do."

She tickled his belly and he giggled. "Well, sometimes. But we like having you around anyway." She tickled him again and he laughed.

Suddenly the nearby leaves quivered in warning, and the hedgerows took on a defensive posture. David gasped as though someone had thrown a bucket of cold water on him. The garden clamored of danger—but from which direction? Where could they go for safety? The house seemed impossibly far away.

She could feel the pine tree calling them. She grabbed David's hand. "Come with me. Run!"

They pounded across the meadow. The shadows of the trees and plants had stiffened with urgency. David fell, and Annie stumbled, then snatched him up and ran for the safety of the tree. The tree lifted its lower branches for them, and Annie thrust David underneath and then rolled in herself just as a flock of birds burst into the meadow, chattering and swooping in alarm. The tree lowered its protective branches and Annie and David, breathing heavily, rested in the circular, rock-walled room the tree concealed. The ground was soft and fragrant with pine needles.

David caught his breath first. "There's something bad out there," he whispered.

Annie nodded.

The birds called their shrill warning, the sound coming excitedly from all parts of the garden. Annie knelt by the wall and found she had a limited view of the meadow, just what she could make out at ground level from under the tree branches. David came next to her, got a toehold in the rocks, and pulled himself up high enough to see out as well.

The birds grew louder. They were out of sight, but they sounded like they were alighting high in the pine tree, ready to swoop or fly off at any moment. Annie was tempted to try to join them to see what was going on, but she had never flown with the birds at a time of her own choosing and didn't know if she could. There was David, too. Could she count on being able to split herself so she could be with him and the birds at the same time?

While she hesitated, the birdsong crescendoed alarm.

"Look, Mommy," David whispered, pointing.

The grass was moving. No, not all of it, and not from the wind. Something was coming toward them through the grass. She put her finger to her lips and David nodded his understanding. They watched in silence as the rippling motion advanced and a pair of jean-clad legs ending in sneakers appeared. From behind these came another pair of legs, and the two people stopped, apparently conferring. The second pair of legs, a man's legs, were bare, but on his feet the man wore calf-high boots of sleek, spotted fur that laced up the front. Annie thought they looked a little like gladiator's boots. Then the bottom part of a bow appeared in her line of vision, as one of the men rested the end of it on the ground. She couldn't see enough of the figures to tell which of them held the bow.

Which way would they go?

"David," she whispered. "If they look under the tree, I'm going to run out. You stay here, okay? And hide."

"No, Mommy," he said, but she put her fingers to her lips again and he was quiet.

It was pleasantly warm under the tree, the scent of the pine needles enticing. Annie could feel her eyes closing. No, she thought, fighting off sleep, knowing the tree wanted her to stay under cover. She'd have to draw them off if they came to where David was.

The men turned, apparently attracted to something on the other side of the meadow. They walked purposefully toward it. The grass closed behind them.

David giggled.

"What did you do?" Annie asked him.

"I made the hedges move. He thinks we went out into the street."

"That was smart," Annie said. "Could you tell which of them was holding the bow?"

David gave her a puzzled look. "There was only one," he said.

"Two."

"One."

"What did he have on his feet?"

"Sneakers."

"You didn't see the one with the fur boots?"

"Fur boots?" David said incredulously.

Odd, Annie thought. Maybe it was the angle David was looking from. Maybe the spotted boots had blended into the grass for him. "But you did see the bow?" she asked.

He considered this. "I don't remember."

There was a great flutter of wings then, as the birds flew out of the pine tree. Their cries diminished in intensity as they dispersed. The meadow became quiet, the silence broken only by an occasional conversational chirp.

"I think they're gone," said David.

Annie listened. She could feel the relaxation all around. "Yes," she said. "We'd better get back to the house."

They walked across the meadow. The sun had fallen behind the hedgerows, and the sky had dimmed. Annie picked up her basket of yarrow on the way, and they found Mark standing by the barbecue and staring into a stoneware bowl.

"How long to dinner, Daddy?" David asked.

"Hmm? It'll be shorter if you go in and get the hamburger rolls for me," Mark said.

"Okay." David trudged into the kitchen.

"There were two men in the meadow just now," Annie said.

"It doesn't surprise me," said Mark. "I found a dead bird with an arrow through it out front. And this."

He held the bowl toward her and she looked at the contents. Something small and glistening, from the inside of an animal.

"The bird's heart?" she asked.

Mark nodded. "The bird was slit open, and this was beside it. Disgusting."

"You saved the bird for the police?" Annie asked.

"Yes." He looked at the contents of the bowl again, then suddenly dashed it onto the fire. The heart hit the white charcoals and sizzled, then sent a thread of smoke into the sky as it burned up.

Annie watched the smoke rise and wondered what god would accept the sacrifice.

Tranquillity settled over the garden with the twilight. Mark had called the police, who told him they'd pick up the evidence when they came by on patrol.

"I think they're getting bored with us," Mark said.

"Did you tell them about the two men I saw?" asked Annie.

"They said they'd make a note of it."

"I'm hungry, Daddy," David said.

Mark cooked hamburgers and they ate under a violet sky. The trees invited the birds to settle for the night, and told Annie all was well. Stars appeared in the sky, and fireflies imitated them in the garden. Laughing, David ran after the insects, who always disappeared before he could catch them.

"I wish I didn't have to leave," Mark said.

"We'll be all right," said Annie. "By now the entire neighborhood is taking turns watching this house, and the police are driving by practically every half hour. Plus the trees are watching out for us."

128

"Yeah, right," said Mark.

"Everything's fine," Annie said with conviction. Then she noticed that the full moon had risen, and she shivered.

"Sure you're okay?" Mark said.

Annie nodded. The birds were quiet, but the crickets had begun their evening concert. She saw one bird flying late to its nest, then realized it wasn't a bird but the flittering shadow of a bat against the darkening sky. The mood of the garden was comforting, and she felt secure knowing it was going about its regular evening schedule. So long as crickets sang, what could be wrong?

After dinner, Mark put David to bed while Annie made a poultice for her hand.

"Is that going to smell?" Mark asked, coming into the kitchen just as she was wrapping strips of cotton rag around her hand which was covered with the mealy yarrow mixture.

"Not any worse than Vicks, and not as bad as that liniment you use when you get overcompetitive with your sports buddies."

Mark sighed. "I haven't done that in a while."

"You should get to know some of the men in the neighborhood. John plays tennis," Annie said.

"The tennis net! I forgot to put up the tennis net for David. I'll have to do it next weekend."

"I think he's a little young for tennis anyway," Annie said.

They locked up the house and went to bed. Annie listened as she drifted into sleep, and heard crickets and rustling leaves and one nightbird, but no sounds to alarm her. She planned to sleep with part of her mind alert to danger, but she quickly fell into a deep sleep and when she woke, it was morning. The sun was bright, the birds clamorous with joy, the garden full of well-being. Mark slept quietly beside her. She slipped into jeans and a sweatshirt, then went down the hall to check on David. He, too, was sleeping. Annie smiled. She'd found the key to their survival.

She went into the kitchen and made coffee, then took a mug out to the porch with her. The floorboards, shaded by the wisteria vines, were smooth and cool under her bare feet. Beyond the vines, the world burst out in Technicolor, new and safe and hers.

The paper lay on the top step, and she sat beside it, stretching her legs into the sunlight. She unfolded the newspaper and looked at the front page.

The archer had struck again last night. A woman was dead not three blocks from here, the body not even hidden. The paper hinted at mutilation without saying what had been done. Annie supposed the police were holding that information back. Her own guess was that the woman's heart had been cut out.

She didn't want to read any more. This murder saddened her. She let the paper drop to the porch floor and thought about the woman she didn't know, who probably had no idea she was going to die, no chance to defend herself. Surviving the night no longer seemed such an accomplishment. Having established one fortified place wasn't enough.

She thought of the Indian, and wondered who he was. She'd accepted a lot of strange things lately, without knowing much about them. It was time to learn.

Chapter 17

 Mark was running late. Annie watched him hurriedly fold shirts and pack them into his suitcase, and she knew they'd be wrinkled when they came out, but it wasn't a job she could do for him with one hand.

"Ties," he said. "Where are my ties?"

She opened his closet and gave him three that would go with either of the suits he was bringing.

"My blue suit has to go to the cleaners," he said. "And I think the tweed has to be picked up. Ticket's in the pile of stuff on my dresser. You can do it this morning when you're getting the car inspected."

"I'm getting the car inspected?"

"I made an appointment. Didn't I tell you?"

"First I heard of it," she said while he closed the suitcase.

"It's on the calendar," he said in the aggrieved tone of one who's in a hurry and can't be expected to do everything. He carried his suitcases down the stairs and shouted, "Tiger! Come say good-bye to Daddy!" before going out the front door.

David burst out of the library and ran after Mark. Annie followed both of them to the car and waited to say good-bye while Mark loaded his luggage.

"They gave you a nice car, Daddy," David said, climbing into the driver's seat. "It smells good."

"New-car smell. Nothing like it," Mark said, slamming the trunk closed. He came around to the driver's side.

David gripped the steering wheel and grinned. "Can I drive, Daddy?"

"In sixteen years," Mark said, bending down to kiss him. "Out you go." He tried to pick David up, but David clung to the steering wheel.

"Try eleven," said Annie.

Mark did some quick mental arithmetic. "You're right. Eleven. Just eleven more years and he'll be driving."

David beeped the horn.

"Okay, David, Daddy has to go."

"Can I come?" David asked.

Annie was looking at the knob of the door that led to the apartment above the carriage house. "Were all these scratches always on this doorknob?" she asked.

"What?" said Mark, coming over. "Looks like somebody's been trying to break in." He tried the door, found it locked. "Maybe the Tiger did it playing some game. I don't understand half the things he's into around here."

"I don't suppose you would," said Annie. "David, did you scratch this doorknob?"

"No, Mommy."

"Mention it to the police next time you talk to them," Mark said. "Now could you please take David? I really have to leave."

"Why don't you take him for a ride around the block if he'll promise to get right out when you get back?"

"I'm running late already."

"By the time you slow down to spend time with him, you might be watching him drive off."

Mark sighed and went back to the car. Annie went into the garage for the key to upstairs, and when she came out, Mark was in the driver's seat with David beside him. "We'll be right back," Mark said, starting the car.

Annie waved to them, then unlocked the carriage-house door. She hadn't been up to the apartment since they'd moved in, but she remembered it as slightly shabby and quite empty. She went up the stairs, which led directly into the living room.

It was uncurtained, and sun streamed in through the windows facing the road. There were dust motes in the sunbeams, and dust on the linoleum-covered floor, and marks in the dust: several sets of footprints. Near the windows, she found tracks that looked like the struggle of something feathered. But how recent were all the marks? They could be hers, Mark's, and the real-estate man's footprints, and surely he would have been showing the house to other prospective buyers. What looked like signs of a struggle could have been somebody dropping something and picking it up, couldn't it?

The doors to the other four rooms were open. The bathroom was dark and windowless, and when she flipped the light switch, nothing happened. The apartment's electricity was separate, and they hadn't had it turned on.

The kitchen was small, and contained a sink and stove with a short counter between. There was an empty place where the refrigerator should be, and the window over the sink was shadowed by a closed venetian blind. A clutter of small items lay on the counter.

Annie checked the two bedrooms, which should have been fairly well lit because they had windows facing the garden, but overgrown shrubbery obscured the light. Both rooms were empty, and she was about to leave when she realized she hadn't checked the closets.

She opened the closet of the larger room and found several wire coat-hangers and a white sock.

She opened the closet of what would have been the child's bedroom, and found an unstrung bow and a quiver of arrows. She couldn't recall if it had been there when they'd first looked the house over. She didn't remember looking in the closets then. She took an arrow from the quiver. It was a hunting arrow with a stone head. The feathered shaft wasn't dusty, but the closet was much less dusty than the room.

What had been in that clutter in the kitchen? And why was clutter there, when the place generally was so empty? She went back to the kitchen, opened the venetian blind, and in the sudden light inspected the objects on the counter: a dirty plate and glass, a crumpled paper bag, a box of matches, and a candle stuck to a saucer. The candle had been partly burned down. Someone could have been in here, could have burned a candle for light because the power was off, but why? And when? She looked in the one cupboard and found a few mismatched pieces of china and another glass like the one on the counter. She tried the faucet of the sink, but the water was turned off. Annie found it all puzzling.

A car horn beeped close to the building, and she jumped. David and Mark must be back. She hurried downstairs and let the door lock behind her.

David got out of the car and walked slowly around it.

"Here he is at last," Mark said through the open driver-side window. "Now I've got to get on the road."

Annie leaned down and kissed him good-bye. When she straightened up, David was standing beside her eating an ice cream cone. "He just finished breakfast," she said.

"Peace at any price," said Mark, putting the car in gear.

"Mark, I went into the apartment . . ." Annie began.

"Tell me about it later. I really have to go," Mark said, and drove off.

"I want to go in the car with Daddy," David said.

"You can go in the car with me. We have lots to do."

"Shopping?" he asked suspiciously.

"Yes."

"Can I buy a toy?"

"You already have ice cream. How much do you expect to get out of this day?"

"A toy."

Behind the wheel, Annie was pleasantly surprised by how little it hurt to use her hand. She was backing out of the driveway when Mariah pulled up at the foot of it and beeped her horn lightly. They both stopped their cars, and Annie leaned out her window while Mariah got out and talked over the top of hers.

"I see you've got wheels!" Mariah shouted over the noise of the engine.

"Yes. And the first things I get to do are go to the dry cleaner's and have the car inspected. Aren't I lucky?"

"That's the kind of luck I always have," said Mariah. "I was going to ask if you wanted to come to the mall with me. I have to pick up a bathing suit for Erica, and I thought we could have lunch and let the kids ride the carousel."

"Can we, Mommy?" David said, but was immediately distracted by the sight of the mailman coming up the path. "The mail! I'll get it." He unbuckled his seat belt and scrambled out of the car, leaving the door open.

"Sounds good," said Annie to Mariah.

"Better than waiting around while your car's being inspected. Where are you having it done? Grady's?"

"Yes."

"I'll meet you there."

Mariah drove off. Annie waited while her passenger climbed back into the car.

"Here's the mail, Mommy," David said, handing her two letters and a department-store flyer as though they were of the utmost importance. He reached over and slammed his door shut.

"Thank you," said Annie, putting the mail on the seat between them. She pulled his seat belt across and buckled it.

"I'm going to be a mailman when I grow up," David said.

Annie drove to the dry cleaner's first, anticipating difficulties because it was right next door to Mark's favorite ice cream store. When she parked, David got out eagerly and hurried toward the Ben & Jerry's, but he stopped at the planter outside it.

"Look, Mommy!"

Annie went over. Among the petunias was one large-leaved oak sapling. "Yours?" she asked.

"Mine," he said, patting the leaves.

"Very nice," Annie said, wondering how long it would be before somebody weeded it out. "Let's go into the cleaner's now." She was surprised when he went along docilely. "Thank you for not pestering me for ice cream," she said, holding the door open for him.

"I just had ice cream," he said virtuously. Annie handed Mark's suit over to the boy behind the counter and waited while he found the cleaned suit.

"Besides," David said, leaning against the counter and looking up at her appealingly, "I like soft ice cream."

Annie laughed. "Oh, David!"

"Can we get soft ice cream?"

"David, you are going to turn into an ice cream cone."

She paid for the cleaning and they left. At the corner, they were stopped by a red light, and Annie glanced down at the mail. One letter had URGENT! preprinted all over it, so she knew it was trash; the other was from their bank. She opened the one from the bank.

It was a mortgage delinquency notice. Apparently Mark hadn't paid the mortgage, and to reinstate the loan he had to send—the car behind her honked its horn—he had to send the regular payment plus a fine. . . .

"Mommy, the light's green!" David said.

Several cars behind her were honking now. Furious with Mark, she dropped the letter and drove on. What kind of game was he playing? Was this some way of trying to force her to sell?

She found Mariah waiting at the garage. Annie shoved the letter into her purse before handing the car keys over to Grady and getting herself and David into Mariah's car. She tried to push the bank to the back of her mind: This was something she only wanted to take up with Mark.

"To the carousel!" said Mariah.

"Yay!" said David and Erica.

At the mall, the children led the way to the carousel. David climbed onto a white horse that went up and down, and Mariah strapped Erica to a stationary pink pony, then sat beside Annie to watch the ride.

"You're quiet today," Mariah said.

"Am I? Sorry. I guess I have a lot on my mind. You heard about that woman who was murdered?"

Mariah nodded. "We could see the police cars and the ambulance from our front porch. I don't know why the police don't do something."

"I think we should do something," said Annie.

"The whole neighborhood's on the alert," Mariah said. "Anytime a stranger walks away from the bus stop, somebody calls the police. Now we've got sightseers coming in to look at the spot where the body was found, and I think the police are getting sick of being called. You know what's strange? Our paperboy lives next to the lot where the body was found, and anytime somebody wearing boots goes there, his little dog goes berserk. Jeremy says the dog was barking the night it happened, too."

"Maybe the dog saw something," Annie said.

"That's what I think," said Mariah. She waved as Erica flashed by, shaking her pony's reins. David was behind her, contentedly going up and down.

"It's time we did something more," said Annie. "Do you know of any plants that help you see more clearly? I mean, that enhance psychic ability?"

Mariah looked startled.

"Or that ward off evil. That kind of information was conspicuously absent from your grandmother's book, considering how far back it goes."

"Annie, that's just superstition."

"Because whatever plants you can come up with, I can make their properties stronger," Annie continued. "Look." She unwound the gauze bandage she had wrapped around her hand.

"Oh, how is your hand?" Mariah said. "I should have asked before."

"Good. It's healing fast. I've been using yarrow poultices on it."

Annie showed Mariah her hand. The wound had closed completely; an angry red scar marked where it had been.

"That's impossible," said Mariah.

"I enhanced the healing properties of the yarrow before I used it."

Mariah gazed off into the distance. Erica rode by, waving happily, and Mariah gave a weak smile and wave in response. David seemed to be looking at something behind Annie and Mariah.

"Don't tell John," Mariah said. "But there is a coda to the herbal medicine book. It gets into more arcane matters. My grandmother didn't believe in it, but she thought the information should be preserved. It tells us something about the past. I'll get it out for you."

"Thank you," Annie said. "But are you sure your grandmother didn't believe in it? You sound doubtful."

Mariah glanced at Annie's hand, then shook her head. "I don't know. When I think back, it's always my mother I remember saying that my grandmother didn't believe."

David rode past and he waved to Annie, then pointed for her to look behind her.

Annie turned. The mall was behind them, two stories tall with shops all around the center walkway. She and Mariah sat at the edge of a planted area where palms and bromeliads soaked up sun beneath a skylight. Intermixed with the semitropical foliage were several sturdy young oaks. They blended in well, and Annie supposed the maintenance staff just didn't know what the trees were or that they didn't belong.

The carousel stopped and Mariah went to retrieve Erica. David rushed to Annie.

"Look, Mommy," he whispered, pointing.

"I see," she said. "They're doing well."

"They like this soil. It's not deep enough, but I told them they could go down as far as they liked."

"Won't they crack the foundation?"

He gave her a blank look.

"The cement under the building."

"Oh no," he said, shaking his head. "There isn't any cement under the plants."

That's a cost-cutting measure the mall owners may regret, she thought.

"They need to go deep to be strong," David said.

"How tall did you tell them they could grow?" Annie asked.

"All the way up," David said, standing and reaching his arms straight up. "And through!"

Annie looked at the skylight.

"I put some at the other end, too," David confided.

Annie thought: Well, it's a good thing oak trees grow slowly. The owners had years to figure it out. She sure didn't want to be the one to try to explain it to them.

Chapter 18

The day after Annie got the car inspected and the other errands out of the way, she finally got around to doing the first thing she'd wanted to do when Mark gave her the car keys: visit Mrs. Avent. She and David were just about to leave when the phone and the doorbell rang at once. Annie picked up the phone, said hello, and, carrying the phone with her, went to answer the door.

"I got your message to call," Mark said from the other end of the telephone connection. "What's wrong?"

Annie looked through the narrow window beside the door and recognized Trooper Keene. "Hold on, the policeman's here," she said, opening the door. She smiled at Keene, said, "I'll be right with you," and motioned him toward the library. He nodded and when, followed by David, he had gone inside, Annie quickly sat on the stairs and spoke into the phone with quiet intensity, not wanting to be overheard.

"Mark?"

"Has something happened?" Mark asked. "I got a message to call home, it was urgent."

"Have you paid the mortgage? The bank sent us a delinquency notice."

"That's your idea of an emergency?" Mark said. "I thought something terrible had happened to you or David."

"I didn't say it was an emergency, I just said I had to talk to you. I couldn't get through to you yesterday."

"I was at the plant till late. We're having problems with the equipment."

"The bank is threatening to foreclose."

"They won't foreclose because we're late with one payment."

"They say they will. Why didn't you pay them?"

"I guess I forgot. I've been busy lately."

"Mr. Compulsive forgot something to do with finances? You expect me to believe that? I don't appreciate your playing these games, Mark."

"What games? Look, I've got a list of problems here that's going to keep me hopping till next week. I'll take care of the bank when I get home. Or if you're that worried about it, pay them. You know where the checkbook is. Write out a check and put it in the mail."

"I don't know where the mortgage coupon book is."

"Top right-hand drawer of my desk. I can't believe you're making such a big thing out of this. I've got to get back to work. I . . . What do you mean by games?"

"I know you want to sell the house to the bank. Could this be some way of trying to finesse me into doing it?"

"Annie, I want to sell to the bank for a large profit, not give the house to them for the price of our mortgage."

"Oh," Annie said. Mark was silent. "I'm sorry," Annie said.

"That's okay," Mark said, and she was surprised that he had

shifted to a much more serious tone. "What exactly was in the notice they sent?"

"I don't have it in front of me, but it was to the effect that our payment was delinquent and they had the right to foreclose, but they would consider reinstating the mortgage if we paid them right away, something like that. And there's a penalty." She waited for Mark to speak.

"Annie, listen carefully," Mark said at last. "I want you to write out a check for the mortgage plus penalty, and I want you to take it to the bank with the coupon and a xerox of the letter. Keep the original. Can you do that today?"

"Sure," Annie said. "But why?"

"And get a receipt."

"Why?"

"So we have some proof they received the payment. I'm not playing games here, but I think the bank might be."

"Oh," Annie said.

"Don't worry about it," Mark said. "But it's better to be careful. Now I've really got to go. I'll call when I have time. Love you."

Annie heard the sound of his hanging up, followed by the line going dead. She hated when he hung up like that, without the warning of a good-bye—the sound hurt her ear, but he always did it when he was busy. She couldn't say she felt any less anxious for having spoken to him, but at least she had less of a feeling he was in league with the bank. But Keene was waiting and there wasn't time to think about this now. She put the phone down and went into the library.

David and Keene were seated at the library table. David wore Keene's state trooper cap, and Keene was paging through the old photo album, which she had left out. They looked up when she came in.

"This is nice," Keene said. "It's all old pictures of this house, isn't it?"

The trooper was momentarily without his official formality, and without it he seemed to Annie little more than a boy. She wondered suddenly why he had become a policeman, guessed that the motive would have been some form of youthful idealism. She smiled. "Yes. The woman who owned the house before us gave it to me."

"If I ever buy a house, I'm going to do this." Then, standing and assuming his usual deadpan seriousness, he said, "But I'm here on official business. I understand you had a break-in, ma'am?"

"I'm not sure. I think so. In the carriage house." When they both started to follow her, she said, "David, you stay here. And stay clean; we're still going out."

"I want to come."

"No," Annie said. "It's too dusty up there. I won't be long. Now give the trooper back his hat, and wait for me like a good boy."

David handed over the hat, then slumped into a chair. As she left, Annie could hear him saying, "I'm bored."

Annie went down the path to the carriage house. On her right the lawn lay open to the sun, open to the street. She felt exposed to danger, and stopped abruptly, causing Keene to bump into her.

"Excuse me," he said.

"It's my fault," Annie said, doing a quick scan. She'd been careless to assume she was safe because a policeman was with her. Luckily everything seemed all right. She continued along the path.

Before unlocking the door, she showed Keene the scratches. "It looks as though someone were trying to break in," she said.

"Pretty clumsy for a professional," he said. "The little boy seems anxious to play up here. Could he have been trying to get in?"

"David doesn't know how to pick a lock."

"They see all kinds of things on television."

Ignoring this, Annie led the way upstairs. Keene shook his head when he saw all the tracks in the dust.

"How many people have been up here?" he asked.

"I don't know. The house was on the market, the realtors would have brought . . ." Keene shook his head again. "What about these marks? This looks like there was a struggle," Annie said.

"Ma'am, that could be anything."

She showed him the dirty dishes and the partially burned candle. "Someone's spent time up here," she said.

"Probably the little boy. Kids like to have clubhouses, secret places, that sort of thing."

"David is five years old. He can't pick a lock, he's not allowed to play with matches, and he can't shoot a bow and arrow," Annie said, beginning to be angry.

"If my mother knew some of the things I did when I was five, her hair would have turned gray overnight," Keene said.

"I'm getting really tired of this," said Annie. "There's a homicidal maniac out there stalking women, probably stalking me, and you keep trying to blame everything on my husband and my five-year-old son."

"We usually find, when these kinds of incidents occur, that a husband or boyfriend or family member . . ."

"Oh, stop it," said Annie. "Use something besides your textbook for a change. This killer doesn't play by your rules. And look at this."

She walked quickly to the closet of the smaller bedroom and put her hand on the door, but looked back at Keene before opening it because she wanted to see his face when he saw the quiver of arrows and the bow.

He was following her, but had stopped partway across the room. "You ought to keep that window closed, ma'am," he said, pointing to an open bedroom window.

Annie frowned. "It was closed," she said. "Anyway, look at this." She swung the closet door open. Keene's expression remained unchanged. Annie looked into the closet. It was empty.

"There was a bow and arrows in here," she said.

"Might have something to do with the open window," said Keene, in a dry tone that was the first indication Annie had noted that he might have a sense of humor. He looked outside, then climbed through. Annie started forward in alarm, expecting him to fall, but he didn't. He stood, apparently on air, pushing back the evergreen foliage that pressed against the house.

Annie put her head out the window. There was a small decorative balcony under it, hidden by the mass of leaves. Why had these shrubs been allowed to grow so tall?

"What window is that?" he asked, pointing to the house. "Which room?"

Annie leaned forward. From the balcony, the main house was in perfect view. "My bedroom," she said.

"You could get good aim from here," he said. "Just have to push these branches aside, then let them spring back after you fired. You're lucky he wasn't a better shot."

"Yes," said Annie, but she knew her luck didn't consist of the archer's lack of skill. She knew the branches, unable to stop him, had managed to deflect his aim. This time, she thought apprehensively, even while she put out her hand to touch the plants and thank them.

Chapter 19

Annie sat in a booth at Burger King and read a map while David finished his hamburger and fries. She'd had a headache by the time she got out of the bank, but it was abating now that she'd eaten. It didn't seem like a request for a receipt should have been that difficult for bank personnel to comprehend.

"Are we in a hurry, Mommy?" David asked.

"Not anymore. Take as long as you like."

"You said we were in a hurry."

"That was this morning. But we were so long at the bank, it made us late for Mrs. Avent, and when I called the retirement home to tell them, they said in that case it would be better to come after her nap, so that's what we're doing."

"I didn't like that lady at the bank."

"Which one?" Annie asked.

"All of them. I didn't like the lady who yelled at me."

"She did seem nervous around children. I don't know how she

could think you could possibly knock over that planter. It must weigh a hundred pounds," Annie said. She'd found two roads on the map that they could take, one a highway, the other marked "scenic."

David leaned forward and whispered to his mother, "I put an acorn in her machine."

"What? What machine?" Annie said, looking up from the map.

David sat back and smiled, pleased to have her full attention. "That TV that just has writing on it. I put an acorn into the hole in back."

"That's a computer, David. What hole?"

"There are these little holes, and it was broken there. I put the acorn in."

"Must be a break in the air grille," Annie said. She wondered if an acorn would do any harm, rattling around inside a computer. It didn't seem to be a well-maintained bank. "Don't do that again. Don't put acorns into machines again."

"She was mean."

"Well, the acorn wasn't. Now it'll never grow."

Frowning, David pushed a french fry through the pile of ketchup on the paper his hamburger had been wrapped in. "I thought we were in a hurry," he said.

"No, there's no need to rush."

"I'm full," he said, annoyed.

Annie laughed. "So stop eating. You don't have to finish everything just because we have time. Come on, let's go for a nice drive in the country."

The road led them through farm country, past hayfields and grazing land where big black-and-white cows rested in the shade of a maple.

"Look, Mommy! Cows," David said.

"Yes, but don't lean out the window, honey."

It was a sunny summer day of seventy-degree weather and low humidity. High above, pale wisps of cirrus clouds hung motionless against the intense blue beyond. Annie pointed out a red-winged blackbird.

"That's something you don't see in the city," she said.

They drove with the windows open, the smells of new-mown hay pouring through with the wind. Gradually the road climbed, and the fields on their right fell away to rocks and a broad stream below, while those on the left became steeper. The hillside above the fields was heavily wooded.

"Mommy. Bambi," David said, awe in his tone.

A group of five deer had appeared in the field, just at the edge of the woods. Two of them looked around, ears twitching, while the others ate. The car moving on the road below seemed not to concern them.

"Aren't they beautiful?" Annie said, and David nodded.

Suddenly a covey of quails rose from the meadow. The deer bolted into the woods. Annie could feel herself drawn into the quail, but resisted, knowing she had to drive. She caught one confused glimpse ahead, of the road disappearing into an oddly thick forest.

They drove up and up, winding toward the top of the mountain.

"My ears feel funny," said David.

"Swallow," Annie said. "It's the altitude."

Annie felt an uneasy prickling, as though her body were warning her there was danger ahead. But that was silly. They were in dappled shade now, woods on both sides of the road, ordinary beech and maple, sycamore and white pine. Soon they would reach the summit, perhaps stop for the view if there was an overlook.

Just when she expected the road to make its final climb, it suddenly veered right and dipped. Annie followed, and found herself in a hollow filled with enormous tropical trees. The air was hot and still, humid, the sky shut out by layer upon layer of greenery. The tree branches were decorated with pendulous orchids whose roots and blossoms hung down in the still air.

"Wow," David said.

Annie slowed and looked in the rearview mirror. They had been swallowed by the rain forest, but the road behind remained open. Should she turn around? That would mean she wouldn't get to talk to Mrs. Avent, not today, not traveling on this one road that went over the mountain.

A flock of parrots flew screeching toward them, circled the car. Annie looked for the reason for their flight.

"Roll up your window, David. Quickly."

"The birds won't hurt us."

"I'm not worried about the birds. I'm worried about that archer," she said, pointing ahead to the space between two trees through which the birds had come. A man in laced boots and shorts stood there. His head was masked, and he held a bow, arrow ready, in his hands. Waiting.

"What archer?" David said, but he obeyed quickly. With the windows closed, the air in the car was hot and still, the sound of shrieking birds muffled. Large raindrops fell, splattering the car.

"Somebody doesn't want us to talk to Mrs. Avent," Annie said. "Hang on, David. We're going through."

She pressed down on the gas pedal. They drew nearer the rain-blurred figure by the road. The rainfall increased to a torrent, and the wipers fought to clear a sheet of flowing water from the windshield. Lightning crackled, leaving behind thunder and a smell of ozone. The road became a small stream, awash with leaves and orchids. Annie held to the road, avoiding the tangled forest that whipped down on either side, and suddenly they were past him. They burst through the storm into calm weather and a dry road through pine and cedar.

David twisted around in his seat, looking behind them. "It's gone," he said.

Annie checked the mirror. "Yes. Didn't you see the man that time?"

"No," David said. "But something bad was back there."

The road they were now on was past the summit, and winding down. "I guess we had a detour," said Annie.

They found the retirement home a mile or so along the road, convenient to both the scenic route and the highway. When they got out of the car in the parking lot, another arriving visitor looked at them in surprise.

"Where did you find rain?" she asked. "Everything's dry as can be."

"We came over the mountain. Sudden squall," Annie said.

The woman nodded. "Mountains are like that. Must have been a torrent, to break all those plants loose."

Annie looked back at her car. It was wet, with bits of foliage clinging to the roof and hood. Stuck in the bumper, there was a tangle of orchids.

"What are those plants, Mommy? They're not the tree's flowers," David said.

"No," said Annie. "They just live in the trees. Rest on them, and get their water and food from the air."

"Can I take one to Mrs. Avent?"

"Yes," Annie said.

David plucked a sprig of white blossoms from the car.

They found Mrs. Avent sitting by a cast-iron table in the garden. She was a sweet-faced woman with a mass of wispy white hair more or less piled on top of her head, and she wore a fluffy rose-colored sweater. Annie was surprised to see she was smoking a cigarette in a long ebony holder. She greeted them warmly and invited them to sit.

"I've asked them to bring tea," she said, "and a pitcher of lemonade. I thought you'd probably want something cold to drink after your drive, but for me, now that I've got so old, I do seem to want a good, hot cup of tea in the afternoon on all but the hottest days."

"Oh, speaking of tea," Annie said, reaching into her bag, "Mariah sent you this."

"Herbal tea. How kind of her. That's one of the things I miss, Mariah's herbal tea."

David leaned forward and put the spray of orchids on top of the package of tea.

"What's this, dear?"

"We got it in the forest," David said.

"Orchids," said Mrs. Avent.

"We drove through a tropical rain forest on the way here," said Annie.

"Did you now?" Mrs. Avent said. She raised the cigarette holder to an elegant angle and inhaled thoughtfully.

"I've been saying things like that to people for weeks now," Annie said, "But you're the first one who's believed me."

"Of course I believe you, dear. I sold you the house."

Annie was very glad she had come. "So you can tell me what's going on? Please explain it all."

"Oh, I can't do that. Not entirely."

"Is it a secret?" David asked.

"Not one that I'm keeping, dear. I just don't know."

An efficient-looking woman in a sensible skirt and blouse brought them a tray of tea, lemonade, and thinly sliced pound cake.

She wrinkled her nose at the cigarette smoke before returning to the house.

"They're so easily shocked here," Mrs. Avent said, smiling. "They think they've seen everything, but they're really quite sheltered." She lifted the cigarette to her lips again. Annie could picture her as a young girl taking this same delight in shocking people with her smoking.

"I didn't know you smoked," Annie said, trying to conceal her disappointment at Mrs. Avent's confessed lack of knowledge.

"I haven't for years, until I came here. It's just boredom, and I happened to come across my old holder." She stubbed the cigarette out and poured tea. Annie gave David lemonade, but accepted a cup of tea for herself.

"I was hoping you'd be able to tell me something about . . ." Annie thought of the garden, and the birds, and the Indians and arrows and murders. "About a lot of things," she said.

"I can tell you what I know," said Mrs. Avent. "I can certainly do that."

Annie waited while Mrs. Avent sipped her tea. "Not as good as Mariah's," she said, setting the cup down. "Well now. It's an odd story."

"I'm getting very good lately at believing impossible things before breakfast," Annie said.

Mrs. Avent smiled. "I never had children," she said. "I was supposed to, you know, but . . . No, that's getting ahead of my story. I was pregnant once, but it ended in a miscarriage, and I was told I wouldn't be able to have any more. It was very sad for me and my husband. I took it harder than he did. Anyway, I felt worse and worse, just couldn't stop thinking about my baby, and the closer it got to when the baby was supposed to have been born, the more unhappy I became. Then, one day in June, I was in the garden. The garden was glorious that year, but it was all ashes to me, when I suddenly . . . was transformed. The garden was transformed. I knew my baby was born, and she was in the garden, and I had to wait for her there."

"Was she under the pine tree?" David asked.

"No, dear. It was her soul that was in the garden. It had become the garden."

"Oh," said David. "I play with her."

Annie wasn't sure how to take all this. It seemed unfair to accuse Mrs. Avent of eccentricity when she herself expected people to believe some pretty weird things and felt aggrieved that they didn't.

Mrs. Avent was smiling at her. "I remember the day vividly. It was June 16, 1965."

"That's my birthday," said Annie.

"Of course, dear," said Mrs. Avent.

"I don't understand," Annie said.

"Neither did I. People thought I was crazy, but since I had perked up and stopped moping, they didn't mind. I wanted an answer though, and I asked everybody: priests, doctors, scientists, anybody with a claim to knowledge, and a lot of frauds along the way. I finally found a really talented medium, though, and we held a séance."

"In the house?"

"Of course. The library. And we made contact with a spirit, at least I did, because no one else saw him or heard him. Just me."

"Was he an Indian?"

Mrs. Avent considered this. "Not exactly. Not an American Indian, not the kind you see in the cowboy pictures." She stroked the orchid. "He was from the rain forests. He had a big nose, and a sloping forehead."

"Was he wearing parrot feathers?"

"I don't remember. But he told me you had been born, my daughter had been born. You were supposed to be my daughter, but something went askew, he didn't explain what, and you had been born to someone else. He said I had to wait. He said your spirit was in the garden, and in this child, and I had to wait to make sure you and the garden got together. That's what I was supposed to do for you."

"But my soul can't be in me and in the garden at the same time," Annie said.

"Of course it can, dear. You're a Gemini."

"Can't everybody's?" said David.

"No dear, I've tried," Mrs. Avent said, looking tired suddenly. "I'm so pleased you came. I hope we can chat again. Anyway, I've told you what I know about what happened. I'm sorry I'm not able to tell you why it happened."

"Of course," Annie said, hugging her, but wondering how her mother would feel to be told she wasn't really her mother. "Thank you. Come on, David. We mustn't wear Mrs. Avent out." She took David's hand, but he broke free and ran to the old lady. He kissed her.

"Good-bye, Grandma," he said.

When Annie glanced back, Mrs. Avent was still smiling at them.

They drove home along the same road, but didn't pass through a rain forest. Instead, they paused at the summit to enjoy the view.

Chapter 20

 "So how will your mother feel, to learn that even though she gave birth to you and raised you, she's not really your mother?" Mariah asked.

Annie laughed. "I'm not going to tell her."

Both women were seated on the cushioned Adirondack chairs that made up Mariah's lawn furniture. David and Erica played in a wading pool nearby, but out of splashing distance. Annie took a sip of iced tea, then leaned back and looked up into the oak tree that shaded them.

"It's all so metaphysical," she said. "Mrs. Avent is a sweet lady. Once you believe all the other things that have been happening, then what she says makes sense." She turned to Mariah. "Only I have the feeling it's not the whole story."

"You seem happier for having heard it," Mariah said.

"Do I?"

"More relaxed."

"Ah. That's from driving by that archer and not getting any arrows shot at me. I have a feeling . . ."

There were happy shrieks from the pool.

"Keep the water inside the pool!" Mariah shouted.

"I have the feeling," Annie went on, "that nothing really bad is going to happen before the next full moon. We have until then to prepare."

"Prepare what?"

"I don't know, but we've got about three more weeks to do it. Anything in that coda of your grandmother's?"

Mariah snorted. "Sure. If you gather marigold flowers when the sun's in Leo, and wrap them in laurel leaves with a wolf's tooth, nobody will be able to speak ill of you."

"Might be useful if you're going to court. Sun in Leo, that's August, right? Good time to gather marigolds."

"Or," said Mariah, "if you take an herb called hound's-tongue, wrap a frog's heart in it, and put it under your big toe, all the dogs in town will gather together and will be unable to bark when you go by."

"That's disgusting," Annie said.

"There's a better one," Mariah said. "A love charm. You take the flowers of periwinkle and beat them to a powder with worms, and feed it to the people you want to be lovers."

"Worms? How do you get them to eat it?"

"Put it in their meat."

"That is a sick book," Annie said.

"It's all supersition. And petty," said Mariah. "They do have some nice recommendations for plant combinations for wreaths. I'm going to try some, so looking through the book wasn't a total waste of time."

"Nothing to help you see the truth? Or to protect the community from danger?"

"I didn't see anything like that, but you're welcome to look." The amusement in Mariah's expression gave way to seriousness. "They're not into big stuff much. Maybe there's a reason."

"What do you mean?" Annie asked.

"Maybe they knew something, that it's not wise to try. I think you should be careful, Annie."

"Was there some kind of warning?" Annie asked.

Mariah shook her head. "Nothing explicit. But there's a total absence of charms that are supposed to bring great wealth, or power, or change on any grand scale. This book wasn't put together by just one person, or at one time. Maybe what looks like preoccupation with petty concerns is really a kind of wisdom."

"And it could be they just never had the courage to try," Annie said.

"I think you should go slowly and carefully, that's all," said Mariah.

Erica came streaking by, the ruffles of her bathing suit flicking out drops of water. "Fun!" she said to her mother, then ran back into the pool.

"We ought to take them to the lake," Mariah said. "I haven't been even once this summer."

"Do you think they're ready for a lake?" said Annie, watching as David lost his footing and slid onto his butt in the water.

"Oh sure, there's a lifeguard, and the shallow part's roped off. The kids would love it. And we're probably safer in a public place these days than in our backyards."

"We're all right this afternoon," Annie said, but she listened to the rustle of the hedgerows just to check the garden's pulse.

A litter of twigs and leaves showered down on them. Annie put her hand over her tea.

"Squirrels," Mariah said. "Cleaning out their nest. I swear they like to wait till I'm sitting out here to do it."

There was shrill chatter high overhead.

"Worse than monkeys," said Mariah. "They throw acorns sometimes, too."

Annie was leaning forward, staring into her tea. "I wonder what the rain forest has to do with all this," she said. "Or Mayans. Or whatever part of it that's important. Maybe the parrots." She set the glass down. "I guess David and I need to make a trip to the library."

"Why don't you ask your father?" said Mariah.

"My father?" said Annie, surprised.

"I thought he was some kind of expert on Indians or rain forests or something."

"He's an anthropologist."

"He's still alive, isn't he?"

"Yes."

"Then it should be easy."

Annie laughed and shook her head. "Telephone lines run to the south of France, but that doesn't make it easy."

"Don't you two get along?"

"We get along fine. But asking my father questions, especially anything more complicated than what he would like for breakfast, is not easy. You never know what quirky perspective the answer's coming from."

"Surely he could contribute something," Mariah said.

"Oh sure. But you know how the ancient Greeks and Romans used to go consult an oracle when they had some big problem, and the oracle would give them an answer that made them think everything would be fine? Then all hell would break loose, and it would turn out that the oracle was right after all, but in a completely different way from what they had expected. That's the way my father answers questions. It's not helpful."

"I think you should call him anyway. I think your father is the key to this whole situation."

"My father? How can my father be the key to serial murders happening on the other side of the world from him?"

"I didn't mean to the murders," Mariah said. "Of course not. I meant to the other situations."

"What other situations?"

"This idea that you can communicate with plants, that you can make them do what you want, and that they protect you. Also the visions you've been having. Don't you see the connection with your father?"

Annie considered this for a moment. "No."

"That story you told, about him being in the rain forest when you were born. You keep seeing visions of a rain forest, because unconsciously you're looking for your father's affection. If he were a botanist, the plant things would make more sense, but it's close enough."

"I've got my father's affection," Annie said. "He's a little crazy, maybe, but he loves me. And if you think this is all in my head, how do you explain my hand healing so quickly?"

"The mind is a powerful tool," Mariah said. "I think it's capable of healing a lot of conditions."

"Damn," Annie said. "I thought you were starting to believe me."

"Unfortunately, I am," Mariah said. "But I don't want to. This is not rational. At least, it doesn't fit in with any rationality I know."

"What would your grandmother think?" Annie asked.

Mariah drew in her breath sharply, then smiled. "She'd believe it. But she might not like it. Her philosophy was one of cooperation with nature."

"I am cooperating with the garden. We get along just fine."

"But not in any way I've ever seen before. Not in a natural way."

"So maybe I'm supposed to start a new kind of cooperation."

Mariah looked worried, and Annie decided it was time to get off the subject. "So when should we take the water babies to the lake?"

Mariah brightened. "Why don't we try for the next sunny day?" she suggested, and Annie agreed.

After getting David into dry clothes, Annie had taken him to the library. They'd both come home with armloads of books. Annie had fed him and read to him and, once she'd put him to bed for the night, had settled down with her own stack of books, which comprised the library's entire collection on rain forests.

"Planning a trip to a rain forest?" the librarian had asked.

"No, not planning," Annie had said, "but you never know what's going to be around the corner."

The librarian had laughed politely, recognizing this as a joke without understanding it.

Now Annie sat at the oak table. A book with descriptions of trees and ecosystems rested in front of her in the lamplight. A breeze strong enough to billow the curtain but not aggressive enough to riffle the pages came through the open window. She was getting sleepy, but she didn't want to call her dad much before midnight. She wanted to be sure it was morning in France.

Annie went into the kitchen and brewed some strong coffee. She needed something to jolt her awake. When it was ready, she took it onto the kitchen porch and sat on the railing, sipping coffee and looking at the night.

The leaves were rustling slightly, but only with the wind; there was no warning in the sound. The night sky was clear and stars were plentiful, but the gibbons moon gave just enough light to differentiate the masses of shadows. As she looked at the garden, a pair of bright eyes looked back at her. A raccoon, probably; she was glad she'd planted extra rows of corn.

When she was sufficiently awake, she returned to her reading. At a quarter to twelve, she placed the call to her father. The photo album from Mrs. Avent was still on the library table, and while waiting for her call to go through, she slowly turned the pages until she came to the one taken in the year of her birth. She supposed she was attracted to that picture for just that reason: the year printed clearly under it. It seemed to her there was something else, something she was seeing and not seeing, but that was probably just her imagination. The coincidence of the date accounted for it.

At last the call went through. "Bonjour," said her father's voice at the other end.

"Hi, Dad. It's me, Annie."

"Annie! Nice to hear from you."

"I didn't wake you, did I?"

"No, I was up. I've just been for a swim. It's a beautiful morning. Your mother's sleeping, of course. She doesn't like mornings. It must be the witching hour where you are, though; is anything wrong?"

"No, everything's fine. What do you know about rain forests and Mayans?"

"Rain forests? Quite a lot. The most important thing to know about them right now is they're being cut down; but could you be a little more specific, pin down the area of knowledge you're interested in?"

"I know about their being cut down," Annie said, thinking of her flight with the parrots over the stubble-covered mud. "I guess I want to know what they have to do with me. Not in global terms," she added quickly. "I don't want a lecture, I've got about six books here full of that stuff."

"I told you about the incident with the witch doctor before you were born," he began.

"Yes, Dad, I remember," she cut in.

"I don't know how to answer," he said. "You always ask such impossible questions. I never seem to get the point of the inquiry. And you always seem so frustrated with my answers."

"Okay, Dad. What about Mayans?"

"Mayans? I've studied their civilization. It's one of the reasons I went to South America."

"Did you meet any Mayans?"

"No. Of course not. They're all gone."

"Gone?"

"In about, oh, our tenth century, which would be their Fourth Age, they all disappeared."

"Where did they go?"

"Nobody knows. If I knew where they went, I wouldn't say they disappeared, would I?"

"What are the theories?" Annie asked. "Disease, natural catastrophe, the Spanish invasion?"

"Not the Spaniards," he said, sounding shocked. "They didn't come till the end of the fifteenth century. Didn't you pay better attention to your lessons than that?"

"Sorry, Dad. So what do you think happened to them?"

"There's no evidence of natural catastrophe: the cities look like the people just walked away. Disease is possible, although there's no evidence of it. There is a theory I go along with. The Mayans were great astronomers, and they built their wonderful pyramids for astronomical observation. They also believed they were living in the Fourth Age and when that ended, man's time on earth would be over. Based on their astronomical observations, they knew precisely when the Fourth Age would end, and when that time came, they disappeared."

"But where did they go?"

"Into the jungles, into oblivion, nobody knows. It was by way of being a self-fulfilling prophecy. Why do you ask?"

"Nothing, Dad. I just keep seeing this Mayan lately."

"Do you now?"

"At least I think he's a Mayan. Sloping forehead, big nose. Wears a mask sometimes."

"That sounds like a Mayan, yes. They tied boards to their babies' heads to flatten them. Where do you see him?"

"In a rain forest."

"Ah. Is this a vision, or an actual rain forest?"

"Both. I can bring things back."

"It's starting, then."

"What's starting, Dad? What's going on?"

"Your mother and I don't know exactly, dear. We did our best to prepare you for whatever's coming, and we have every confidence in your ability to handle it. But if you like, I'll come back and take care of things."

"You call offering to take over an expression of confidence? Thanks a lot, Dad," Annie said sarcastically. If he came, he'd make her the subject of a study, and she didn't want that.

"Don't take that tone with me, young lady. It's not easy preparing a child for a world without knowing what that world is going to be like. We did our job, and then we did the next thing that's required: We let go. That's the hardest part of all. You just wait till David grows up, and you'll see what I mean."

"Dad, let's not fight. We're too far apart to waste time fighting."

"I agree. So. Do you think you'll see this Mayan again?"

"I don't know. Probably."

"If you get a chance, ask him where they all went." The intellectual hunger in his tone made Annie laugh.

"I will, Dad."

"Would you like me to prepare a reading list for you? It'd be no trouble."

"That's okay, Dad. I'll field 'em as they come."

"Ah. Baseball. Don't get in any ball games with these Mayans. The victors cut the heads off the losers."

"I thought you said they were civilized."

"They were. Within limits. At least they didn't go around dropping bombs on people."

"Just cut their hearts out, right?"

"Yes. Well. Religion."

"I'd better go now, Dad. Take care of yourself and Mom."

"You be careful," he said. "Your mother and I love you. Annie," he added, filling the sound of her name with a sense of urgency, "be careful. Assume nothing. Remember: An act can look the same in two cultures and still have two completely different meanings. That can be dangerous. If you feel it's getting to be too much for you, I can fly home."

"Thanks, Dad. I promise I won't get eaten."

She hung up, and sat thinking. Her father was right—she didn't know enough, and there was no one who did. It was too late to turn back now, though. In fact, she didn't think she'd ever had a choice.

Chapter 21

 Annie had expected a sandy beach in the swimming area. Instead, a lawn stretched to the water's edge, and under the shallow water, a layer of pebbles made the lake bottom reasonably comfortable to walk on. In the deeper water, the pebbles gave way to mud.

Annie and Mariah had taken the children in wading. Now all four sat on a blanket stretched over the lawn. They dried themselves in the sunshine and ate sandwiches. Several other groups were scattered on the lawn, mostly mothers with small children, but there was one group of teenagers sunning themselves. Annie recognized the baby-sitter and waved to her. Tiffany smiled and waved back.

David held a peanut butter and jelly sandwich in one hand, and was lining up a collection of lakebed pebbles with the other. "Now these won't grow," he said to Erica in a knowledgeable tone.

Erica reached for a pebble, but Mariah stopped her. "Don't let her have any, David," Mariah said. "She'll only put them in her mouth."

"Put them in your treasure box," Annie said, pulling out of her bag a cardboard box covered in shiny foil paper patterned with zebras.

"Fancy," said Mariah. "When I was a kid, I just had a cigar box."

"That's all this is," Annie said, "Only covered with glitzy paper, so they can sell it to kids instead of just letting them wait till Granddad's emptied his cigar box."

"Grandpa doesn't smoke cigars," said David.

"A lot of grandpas don't," said Mariah.

"Maybe that's why the cigar-box people are making these," Annie said. "To keep from going out of business."

A slight breeze lifted the edges of the sandwich wrappers and rustled the leaves of the trees that framed the bathing area on either side. Annie watched it ripple across the lake. The tethered raft put in for swimmers to rest on was within her line of sight when a large man pulled himself out of the water and stood dripping on the raft. He turned and Annie recognized Harley Baer. He looked fatter without his clothes, but had better muscle tone than she'd expected. He reminded her of a sumo wrestler, especially now, with his dark hair slicked back and wet. Annie shivered.

"Cold, Mommy?" David asked.

"No, honey. I'm all right."

Mariah, whose gaze had followed Annie's, said, "There's nothing he can do. Not with all these people around."

Erica yawned, her half-eaten sandwich forgotten in her hand. Mariah rolled up a towel for a pillow and settled Erica for a nap on the shady end of the blanket.

David looked at the raft, then moved closer to his mother. "I don't like him," David said.

"Neither do I," Annie said.

"Nobody does," said Mariah.

Harley dove into the water and swam for the pier.

"He swims good," said David.

"It's all that fat," said Mariah. "He can't sink."

"If I get fatter, can I swim out to the raft?" David asked.

"If you learn to swim, you can swim out to the raft," Annie said.

"Okay," David said, getting up.

Annie put her hand on his arm. "Not now. You just ate," she said, but she was watching Harley's progress along the pier.

"After he's gone, can I?" David said.

"If you go in swimming too soon after eating, you'll get a cramp," Annie said. "Would you like to go up to the pavilion and go on some of the rides?"

"Yeah," David said, but sighed when he saw Harley walk across the lawn and up the stairs to the pavilion.

"A little later," Annie said.

"Well, what can I do now?" David asked.

"I brought a book for you. Would you like to read?"

"I can do that at home," David said, pouting, but then his expression brightened. "Can I go watch the fish?"

"Yes, but stay out of the water until I go in with you," Annie said.

David ran to the pier. There were few people on it: just the lifeguard in his chair and two boys taking turns diving into the deep water. David sat at the edge, staring into the shallows. A moment later Tiffany came to stand beside him and chat.

"I wonder why Harley's here in the middle of the day in the middle of the week," Mariah said.

"Maybe he's on vacation, or maybe he doesn't have a job," Annie said.

Tiffany left David and walked to the lifeguard, and Annie

smiled, sure that the blond, tanned, muscular young man had been the reason for Tiffany's stroll on the pier all along.

"Harley's got a job," Mariah said.

David walked along the edge of the pier, gazing into the lake, and squatted down again near the diving board, where the water was deepest.

"What does he do? Oh, speak of the devil," Annie said, seeing Harley come back across the lawn. He was finishing an ice cream cone, and he crumpled a paper napkin and tossed it onto the grass just before he stepped onto the pier. Annie wondered if she should call David back.

"He works for a collection agency. Repossesses cars, hounds people for money. That sort of thing."

"I'll bet he's good at it," Annie said, standing up. She saw Harley say something to Tiffany, who frowned and shook her head, the cluster of brass bells at her ear catching the light as they moved. Then Harley turned to Annie, looked straight into her eyes, smiled, and jumped into the water, deliberately knocking David off the pier as he went.

"Oh my God," Annie said, already running. Before she could reach the end of the pier, Tiffany was in the water, and the lifeguard was close behind her.

David surfaced, gasping, and immediately went under again, but Tiffany had seen him and swam after him. She brought him up, clinging to her, and the lifeguard helped them both back to the ladder. They pushed David ahead of them and Annie held him while he gasped and coughed and got his breath back.

The lifeguard grinned and poked Tiffany's arm. "That's my job," he said.

"Thank you," Annie said, looking up at both of them.

Tiffany shrugged. "Well, I saw where he went. It can be hard to see under the lake."

"You did good," the lifeguard said.

Tiffany pushed her wet hair out of her face and frowned. "That stinker did that on purpose. Bully," she said, and looked out at the raft.

Annie looked too, expecting to see Harley gloating, but the raft was empty. The lifeguard looked quickly around, and that was when they realized Harley hadn't come up.

"Shit," the lifeguard said, and dove into the lake.

"Let him drown!" Tiffany yelled, but the teenager was swimming underwater, searching. He came up, got a breath, and swam down to look again.

David was breathing more normally now, but Annie could feel his heart beating against her chest. "It's all right, honey. You're safe."

David drew in a rasping breath, but seemed to be finding it hard to talk, more because of emotion than because of the water. "The weeds," he said.

"Weeds?"

"The weeds." He gulped and spoke again. "The weeds are holding him." He pointed to the water.

Annie looked at him carefully. "The weeds are holding him to keep him from hurting you?"

David nodded. Annie stood up and scanned the surface, then saw a clump of green beneath the water. "Tell them to let him go," she said.

"Okay," David said.

When the lifeguard surfaced again, Annie pointed and shouted to him to look in the weeds. He swam to the patch of green and dove under.

"Those old things are never any problem," Tiffany said. "They're not tangled enough or strong enough to hold anybody down."

The lifeguard brought Harley to the surface, and Annie didn't know whether she was pleased or sorry. Harley was evidently unconscious, and the teenager towed him toward the ladder but stopped, looked at the ladder, looked at Harley, then changed direction and swam for the shore. The people who had been crowding around ran to watch, and helped drag Harley onto the grass.

Annie put her arm around David. "Did you ask the weeds to hold him?"

David nodded, tears coming into his eyes. "I was scared."

"Of course you were, honey. It's all right. You did the right thing."

She walked with him back to the blanket, carefully skirting the scene at the shore. While she was drying David, she heard Harley cough and throw up. "I guess he's going to be all right," she said ruefully.

"Pity," said Mariah. "Maybe it'll teach him something."

"What?" David asked.

"Not to eat an ice cream cone just before he goes into the water," Mariah said.

Sirens sounded, coming closer, and stopped when they were at their loudest. A couple of paramedics came running onto the beach.

"Can we go home now?" David asked.

"Soon, David," Mariah said. "Let's wait till the ambulance is gone from the parking lot, okay?"

"Okay," David said. He looked at Erica. "She's still asleep," he said incredulously.

Mariah laughed. "That's how babies are."

The crowd at the water's edge began to break up and Harley, wrapped in a blanket and flanked by the paramedics, walked unsteadily up the beach. His color was grayish and his eyes red. One of the paramedics said something to him, but Harley pulled away and said, "I don't need no stretcher." He veered toward Annie and David and stopped at the edge of their blanket, dripping onto it.

"You think you're something, don't you?" he said to Annie. "I'll tell you something. I know who put the police on my tail. Don't think I won't do something about it."

Annie felt her stomach go cold. So much for Trooper Keene's discretion. "Stay away from my son," Annie said, "or I'll do more than just talk to the police. I'll have you put in jail."

"No you won't, bitch, because I'll cut your heart out first."

The paramedics led Harley away, and Annie looked at the wet spot he'd made on the blanket's edge, then turned and saw him leave the beach, a huge, hunched figure wrapped in a blanket.

"Colorful speaker, isn't he?" Mariah said.

"A collection agency," Annie said. "Does he do collecting for the bank?"

"I expect so," Mariah said. "There's only one agency like that in town. They do the collecting for pretty much everybody."

Chapter 22

Annie had never seen Mark so angry. She was glad he wasn't angry with her, and she was glad his first impulse when angry was to pick up a phone, because it certainly wouldn't help to have him engage in physical violence with the bank, the collection company, or the police. As it was, he was making everybody he spoke to almost as angry as he was himself, and Annie knew she'd have to deal with the consequences of it all, because Mark would be out of town again in a day or two.

David came to her in the kitchen, where she'd gone to escape Mark and the telephone. He looked unhappy. "Why is Daddy yelling at Trooper Keene, Mommy?"

"It's about that man who pushed you in the lake. Daddy thinks Trooper Keene told him something he shouldn't have."

"I like Trooper Keene."

"I do too, honey." *When he's not being infuriating,* she thought. "And I'm sure he'll still like you."

"I don't like Harley," David said. "He's mean."

Annie looked at the small, pouting face and a picture of David disappearing into the lake flashed into her mind. Her stomach tightened the way it had when she ran to the pier. "We'll have to watch out for him extra carefully," she said.

David leaned forward and patted her hand. "It's all right, Mommy. I took care of it. He won't bother us no more."

Annie opened her mouth to speak, but just then Mark burst into the room. "There is some justice in the world," he announced, and Annie saw that he was smiling. "Harley Baer was riding his motorcycle not two blocks from here, and a tree branch fell on him."

Mark went to the counter to pour himself a mug of coffee. Annie glanced quickly at David. "Is he all right?" she asked Mark.

"Unfortunately yes, but the motorcycle was demolished." He opened the refrigerator and looked in. "Where's the half 'n' half?"

"Second shelf." She turned to David and spoke softly. "What did you do?"

"I asked the trees to keep him away. He wants to hurt us."

"But two blocks away? I didn't know you could do that."

David looked puzzled.

"I didn't know you could talk to plants outside the garden."

"Oh," David said, enlightened. "The garden taught me."

Annie thought about the acorns in the mall; he had said he'd told the roots to grow down deep. When she flew with the birds, she'd never been confined to the garden—it had just been a starting point. Did that mean she could influence the properties of plants outside the garden? Was this a fixed ability they had, or were they both learning and growing? Like the plants?

But Mark had sat down opposite her. "Hey there, Tiger," he said, punching David lightly on the arm.

"Are you happy again, Daddy?"

"I think I've got things pretty well under control. The police are going to double their patrols around this house, and they're going to be watching Mr. Harley Baer. Plus I'm going to see about having a security alarm system put in. The line of defense around this house is going to be so tight, nothing can get through."

"I don't want a line around the house," David said. "I want to go out and play."

"You can do that," Mark said.

"Daddy doesn't mean he's going to draw a line around the house and that we can't cross over it. He means he's going to fix it so if somebody tries to break in, an alarm will go off."

"Oh," said David. "We don't need that."

"I say we do need it, young man," Mark said. "And what I say still goes. Now, I'm going to finish my coffee, and then you and I can go put up the net and I'll teach you to play a little badminton. How about that?"

"All right!" David said enthusiastically.

"Don't expect too much of his coordination. He's only five," Annie said to Mark.

Annie left David and Mark to their badminton, and went into the garden. The afternoon was sunny, and a slight, pleasant breeze stirred the ripening seed pods of gas plant and lunaria. Pink asters sprawled across their bed and into the path, and a single black butterfly sat on them and slowly fanned its wings. Under the apple tree, yellow jackets were feeding on dropped and broken fruit.

Annie decided this would be a good time to do a little work in the quarry garden. With David occupied elsewhere, she wouldn't have to worry about him on the steep hillside or near the water. She got her pruning shears from the potting shed, stuck them in her jeans pocket, remembered she wanted to oil the gate back there, and picked up a can of household oil. Then she set out across the meadow.

The tall stems of grass had ripened their seed and dried to a mellow, golden color. Tiny grasshoppers fled Annie's coming, whirring clumsily on inadequate wings. When she reached the gate, she saw that bindweed had overgrown the stone wall and twisted itself around the iron gate. Its white morning-glory flowers were open in the shade, but closed and shriveled where the sun hit them. She oiled the hinges, then unwound the plant stems from the lock and opened the gate.

The garden was in good shape, considering how little attention it got. Some tufts of grass grew where they shouldn't, and there were broken twigs from the apple tree littering the path. She tidied up, discarding the unwanted plant material in an out-of-the-way corner to decompose.

The rocky hillside was hot, and the sun beat down in a way that made her wish she'd brought a hat. A trickle of sweat ran down from her hairline, and she brushed it aside. The air was heavy with sage, and she felt she was floating on the scent. Getting out of the sun would probably be a good idea.

She went lower in the garden, to the pool at the bottom, already shaded by the sheer rockface that separated it from the street. There was a welcome temperature difference when she stepped into the shade, and coolness seemed to flow from the water. She sat on the flat stone bank and looked at the pool.

The surface was still, a black mirror reflecting the sky. She could hear water spilling out the runoff, and noticed the water was at exactly the same level as it had been in the late spring. That seemed odd—in August, after a fairly dry summer. She wondered how deep it was, and was tempted to go in for a swim, but her inability to see beneath the surface made her uneasy.

A leaf fell onto the water. It floated, drifting toward the runoff.

Annie put her hand in. The water was shockingly cold, considering the sun must have been beating on it right through midday. She felt nothing under the water but more water, bottomless, as cold as melted snow, as though ice formed so deep in winter that it never all melted. She withdrew her arm, then cupped her hands and splashed water on her face and neck.

The caw of a crow behind her made her turn. There were two of them, not five feet from her, as large as chickens and shiny black. They were fighting over the remains of something furry. When had they come?

Annie got up and they backed off, still playing tug-of-war with what seemed to be the remains of a squirrel or possibly a groundhog. There was blood on the rocky outcrop behind them, as though it had run down from the tablelike surface. Not all the blood was fresh.

Annie moved closer and the crows flew off. She was back in the sun, and her shadow fell on the granite altar. It could only be an altar. Four feet high, with a shallow bowl carved out of the top. The bowl held a heart and entrails drying in the sun. She would have thought the birds would have gone for that first.

Who had done this? And how had they gotten in without tearing the vines from the gate? She opened herself to the plants, asking them if there was danger, but they were somnolent and ... different. Different from the rest of the garden, as though they had some purpose beside which everything else seemed trivial to them. They calmed her, but like a parent telling a child: It was only a bad dream, go back to sleep and let us sleep. They didn't share her fear the way the other plants did.

Annie's head vibrated with a humming that was almost painful. Perhaps it was from the sun. She turned and looked at the top of the rockface, where the sun now hovered. It was a dazzle of rays at the edge of the rock, and its disk should have been partly hidden, but a break in the edge made a niche in which it seemed to rest. She was directly between the sun and the altar, in its concentrated beam as the rest of the quarry darkened rapidly.

Annie stepped out of the way, and the humming ceased. The shaft of sunlight fell directly on the altar as though planned. Curious, she stepped back into the light and was slammed by an intense pain that made her gasp and draw back. No warning this time, just get out of the way. Then the sun slid behind the rock and the quarry was in twilight. She looked at the altar. The bloody offering was gone.

Thoroughly frightened, Annie wanted only to leave. She climbed the steep, rocky steps, forcing herself to go carefully. At the top, she found sunlight, and the gate still open.

When she got back to the house, Mark and David were still playing badminton. She watched the plastic birdie fly into the air when Mark hit it, only to fall in the dust by David's feet. David put the birdie on his racquet and flipped it toward the net. It hit the net, fell to the ground, and David tried again, intense concentration on his face. This time it barely cleared the net, and Mark had to run forward to catch it. Annie thought he looked winded, probably from having to run forward all the time to get the birdie, then back to serve it. He was moving back now. When he saw her, he smiled and waved.

"David's going to be a great player in a few years," he said, definitely out of breath. "In the meantime, let's buy a beach ball. Last serve, Tiger." He hit the birdie and it flew over the net, a piece of white plastic in the dusk.

An innocent game, but it sickened her. This birdie was made of plastic, and before that they were feathers, and before that, what? The body of a small bird, smashed back and forth like that? Probably not. Probably just a birdie because it had been made of feathers and the players sent it flying, but Annie couldn't shake the image of a small bloodied bird, lifeless in the air.

She closed her eyes. An echo of the humming was in her head, just a memory. Or perhaps a reminder.

Chapter 23

Annie watched Mariah make wreaths. The kitchen table was heaped with artemesia, baby's breath, stalks of dried delphinium, and a sampling of every flower Mariah grew that could possibly be dried. The colors were faded from their summer freshness, but just now the setting sun was mellowing the faded prettiness to something softer and nostalgically elegant.

"I wish I could package the lighting," Mariah said, holding up a wreath of gray artemesia wired with daisies and strawflowers. It seemed made of silver and gold leaf, so old and wafer-thin the light shone through it.

"What do you do with them all?" Annie asked.

"There's a crafts place downtown that takes them on consignment. Abby's Attic. Lots of starched lace and fancy boxes and Caswell-Massey soap, and enough potpourri in the air to knock you out for the day if you're susceptible to migraines."

David came in and leaned glumly against the table. "Erica's asleep," he said.

"It is past her bedtime. And she's just a baby," Mariah said. "You can play with her toys, if you want."

But David was watching Mariah twist a length of wire around a bunch of lavender, then attach it to a circular form.

"Do they do anything? The wreaths," Annie asked.

Mariah smiled. "Purely decorative. You can look in the book, if you want. They might symbolize different things."

But Annie shook her head. She fingered a sprig of apricot-colored celosia. It was flamelike, but just a dried husk: a token of summer rather than a source of power.

"They're empty," David said.

"Yes," said Annie. "Maybe we could fill them up."

"Can I make a wreath?" David asked.

"Sure. Help yourself," said Mariah. She sneezed. "Lavender's dusty. I always sneeze if I breathe too much of it. I'm going to take a break. Do you want a glass of wine?" she asked, going over to the refrigerator.

"Sure," said Annie.

"How long's Mark gone for this time?" Mariah said, filling two glasses and bringing them to Annie's side of the table.

"A week and a half. They keep sending him farther and farther away."

The light was fading quickly. Mariah turned on the lamp that hung over the table, making a cozy island of light against the twilight. David blinked but kept twisting stems of baby's breath into a progressively thicker circle.

"We have a guest room. I've offered it before, and it's still there," said Mariah.

"I'm fine," Annie said. "I'll be more fine when the police catch this guy. And if by some chance the mad archer turns out to be Harley Baer, that would solve two of my problems at the same time."

"That would be something, wouldn't it?" said Mariah. "Fat Harley. I remember him from sixth grade."

"I'd have thought he was older," Annie said. "Was he a bully then?"

"Yes," said Mariah. "Liked twisting girls' arms behind their backs, especially the ones who were developing something in front." She glanced at David, and seemed to decide not to continue that part of the story. "Sixth grade was where the social promotions stopped in our school. You had to actually do some work to get out and into junior high. Harley arrived in sixth grade a year before I did, and he was still there when I left. Getting bigger and bigger and learning how to use his size."

"I wish there was something I could do," Annie said.

"Harley can't hurt us," David said.

"I meant for everybody," said Annie.

"Oh," said David.

"Don't we all," Mariah said.

"We could ask the plants to make him stop," David said.

"I wish we could," said Mariah. "But that tree branch falling on his motorcycle was just an accident, David." She waved toward the plants hanging from the beams, the jars of herbs lining the walls. "Plants can't really do things like that."

"Yours can't," said David. "But my mommy's can. Ta da!" He held up his finished wreath, a mass of tiny white flowers with dried blue cornflowers set in at random.

"Very nice," said Mariah.

David set the wreath on Annie's head. "My mommy's queen!"

"She certainly looks like one," said Mariah.

Annie smiled. The wreath was light and mildly fragrant, but she was thinking less of it than of David's underlying suggestion.

Could they set sentinel plants around town to watch for violence and stop it? Or, if not stop it, warn her, so she could call the police? The moon was waxing again.

"What if I told you Harley's accident with the tree branch wasn't quite so much of an accident as it looked?" Annie said.

"What do you mean?" said Mariah.

"The tree did it on purpose."

Mariah laughed. "Clever tree."

"Yes." Annie winked at David. "We'll have to show Mariah sometime."

"We can do it now," said David.

"No. Another time. Now, I'm going to take you home and put you to bed." She reached up to take off the wreath, but the hurt look in David's eyes stopped her.

"Better wear your crown home," Mariah said, and added, too low for David to hear, "Aren't you lucky you don't have to go home along the street?" She walked them to the kitchen door, but stopped Annie at the threshold. "He's really caught up in this game."

"It's not a game," Annie said, "any more than healing with herbs."

"No," said Mariah. "There's a big difference between believing in the medicinal powers of plants and believing they can drop branches at will on people you don't like."

David tugged at Annie's arm. "Mommy. Let me show her."

"David, the plants are asleep. It's not nice to wake them up just to make them show off."

"That one's not," he said, pointing to the moonflower vine growing on a trellis outside Mariah's door. Its leaves were a layered mass in the darkness, but the white flowers stood out.

"You're right, it's awake," Annie said. "All right, go ahead."

David smiled. "Watch, Mariah."

The flowers, which had twirled open at dusk, all suddenly closed, then blinked open and shut, open and shut, in a random pattern, on and on, like a carnival of moths all fluttering their wings.

"I'm not seeing this," Mariah said.

"But you are," said Annie.

The light from Mariah's open kitchen door made a path for them across her patio and onto the lawn. After that, Annie and David had just the risen moon and the stars, but they were enough. At the hedgerow gate, Annie turned and waved to Mariah, saw the figure in the doorway wave back and the fan of light shut and disappear.

"Will she believe us now, Mommy?" David asked.

"I don't know, but we gave her a lot to think about."

Crickets sang around them, and something rustled in the fallen leaves under the hedge. David unlatched the gate and climbed onto it, riding it as it opened.

"David, I want you to help me talk to the plants. I want them to help stop the bad things that are happening."

"Okay. You mean you don't want Harley to bother anybody, not just us?"

"That's part of it."

"Okay. You want me to tell them to kill him."

"No, no. I don't want anybody killed. I want them to stop all the killing."

David jumped off the gate. "Okay. But the foxes and cat and owls will be hungry if they can't kill anything."

"That's not what I mean. I mean I want people to stop killing people."

"Even when we're not there?"

Annie took David's hand and walked with him into the meadow. "Especially when we're not there. I want them to help protect all the people."

"How?" said David.

"What do you mean, how? They protect us. They stopped Harley from coming here."

"That's different," David said, breaking free and running ahead.

Annie was finding this more difficult going than she'd expected. "How is it different?"

"They protect us because they protect us. They stopped Harley because I told them to. How will they know who to stop if we're not there to say?"

"They should just protect anybody who's in trouble."

David groaned and threw himself down into the grass. Annie wondered what the problem was. She reached out to the trees, trying to sense their mood. How did they see the situation, what made them act? She was puzzled and upset, and could feel a calming effect in the rustling leaves, the protective spread of branches. "Surely they know what an attack is," she said.

David groaned again and popped up out of the grass. "They know feelings. And they know what they're told."

She could sense his frustration, in fact she shared it, because she couldn't understand what he was trying to tell her. She stood in the center of the meadow and raised her arms to the stars. "I wish somebody would explain this to me."

She sensed a rift in the trees' sensibility, as though they'd been momentarily distracted.

"Your crown has stars in it, Mommy," David said, looking up at her.

"You must be seeing the sky through the baby's breath,"

Annie said. She touched his cheek, soft and cool in the night air. "It's time you were in bed. We'd better get back to the house."

But David was twisting to look behind her. "Who's that, Mommy?"

Annie turned. Someone was sitting cross-legged on the quarry garden wall. He raised a sloping profile to the moonlight.

Annie gasped. "The Mayan," she whispered.

Startled, the man hurriedly grabbed his bow from where it lay beside him. Annie pushed David behind her, but the Mayan set the bow down again.

"Oh, it's you," he said.

"You tried to shoot me," Annie said.

He shook his head. "Me? No."

"On the mountaintop."

"No. I'm not one to shoot a woman's spirit in a bird's body. That kind of thing can only cause trouble."

"On the other mountaintop. In the rain."

"Must have been somebody else."

"Oh sure. There are so many Mayans wandering around. How did you get all the way from the rain forest to here?" Annie asked.

"It's not far."

"It's a hemisphere away. It's thousands of miles."

"I took a shortcut. Same as you." He looked at David. "Hi there," he said encouragingly, but David kept hidden behind his mother. "Shy boy."

"He's got reason to be. We've had a lot of problems around here lately."

"Ah," said the Mayan. "Those things happen."

"They shouldn't."

The Mayan shrugged. "This used to be a nice neighborhood."

"I thought all the Mayans were gone," Annie said. "And if you're supposed to be Mayan, how come you speak such good English?"

"I was just going to ask how come you speak such good Mayan."

Even in the moonlight she could see his smile. It was a nice smile, and almost made up for the big nose and sloping forehead.

"You wanted something?" he asked.

"Me? I want the killings to stop. I want to know why people are being killed. I want to know who shot me, and who's making sacrifices around here, and why my son can talk to plants and I can fly with birds."

"That's a lot to want to know," the Mayan said. "I can't help you."

"Then why are you sitting on my garden wall? Going bird-hunting by moonlight?"

"Why do you want to know all that stuff?"

"I want to know what to do."

"That's different. You already know that. The kid's been telling you, the plants have been telling you, the sun's been telling you. If you won't listen to them, why would you listen to me?"

"Well, since you look like an adult human being it might be that I thought you could tell me in words. It might be something like that. I could use some clear answers instead of more of this mystical shit."

The Mayan stood up on the wall and slung his bow over his shoulder. "You need to listen," he said, walking away.

"I need to hear something that makes sense," Annie shouted.

The Mayan looked back at her over his shoulder. "If you see a guy in jaguar boots, stay away from him. He's no good."

"I suppose he looks just like you."

"No. He's ugly. Not handsome like me. He wears a mask a lot."

That jolted Annie's memory back to the other times she'd seen the Indian. He'd worn boots when she and David hid, fur boots. She wasn't sure what jaguar skins looked like, but those boots were of spotted, silky fur. And the one in the rain, the masked one, had worn the same boots. So how did Harley fit into this, and who was the other man with the Indian in the meadow?

"He's gone, Mommy," David said.

Annie looked up. The wall was empty. She thought of her father then, and called out, "Where did the Mayans go?"

But there was no answer.

David leaned against her.

"You saw him that time, didn't you?" Annie asked.

"Yes," David said. "I saw that one."

Chapter 24

The next morning, Annie bundled David into the car. "We're going to talk to the trees around town," she said. "We're going to ask them for help."

David slumped in his seat and twirled the loose knob on the door handle. The plastic spun with an annoying whir, and as soon as it stopped, he started it up again.

"You don't seem to have much enthusiasm for this," she said.

Still whirring the knob, he began rhythmically kicking the underside of the dashboard.

Annie wondered if she'd be able to do much without his cooperation. Since he usually liked the park, she drove there first and parked as near the lake as she could. "I brought bread for the ducks," she said, reaching into the backseat for the bag of stale bread.

"Can I feed them?" said David, scrambling out of his seat belt.

"Sure thing," Annie said, happy for the distractibility of small children.

David took the bag and ran to the lake. Alarmed by his approach, all the ducks onshore waddled hurriedly into the water and swam out of reach.

"You're frightening them, David!" Annie called.

David reached into the bag, then threw out a handful of bread. The ducks quacked excitedly and swam toward the floating bread.

Annie sat on a bench and considered the willows growing around the lake. She tried to communicate with them, but got very little response, as though they could hear her but only in a muddled way. This wasn't like being in her own garden, and she suddenly felt exposed, unprotected outdoors when she had grown used to feeling safest there.

"All right, Mom," David said, dropping the empty bag into a trashcan. "What do you want them to do?"

Annie resented being patronized by a five-year-old, but he was the only one who might be able to help. "I want the trees to stop anybody who tries to hurt anybody else."

"How?"

Annie looked at the trailing branches, and said, "Could they just tangle up and hold the person?"

David took a few steps forward and gave all his attention to the trees. Annie was able to listen in on the conversation, but only on a poor connection, or from far away. David was speaking from somewhere deeper in himself than she could reach in herself, that was the main difference. The trees seemed . . . amused. Responsive, but amused.

"Okay," David said, turning to his mother.

"What did they say?"

"Didn't you hear them? They think it's silly, but they'll do it."

"Did you tell them it was important?"

"No," David said, "it's not important. It's silly. Can we go home now?"

"First we're going downtown. Maybe some of those oak seedlings you have growing are tall enough and flexible enough to trip people. And lots of trees have acorns and seed pods now: they could throw them. Come on."

She led him to the car, David shaking his head in disapproval.

"Then I'll buy you lunch," Annie said.

"Pizza?" David asked.

"Sure. I have to go to the bank, too, and pay the mortgage again."

Annie felt the trees downtown were looking at her as though she were a little odd. "Will they do it?" she asked David.

"They want to know if you're sure."

"Of course I am."

David raised his hands in a gesture that denied responsibility. "She's sure," he said.

They walked to the bank then, passing through a ragged group of picketers protesting some of the bank's investments.

"What do those people want, Mommy?"

"They don't like where the bank spends its money. Not doing much for their cause: Three people don't make much of a line."

Annie took David's hand firmly and led him through the revolving door. At least this month she knew where to go to make her payment, and marched past several partitions and straight to the desk of Mrs. Pratt, the sour-faced woman who seemed to handle all the difficult cases.

"Yes, I remember you, Mrs. Carter. This is all so unnecessary," she said, shaking her head. She went to a cabinet for the receipt forms.

David was staring at the computer terminal on Mrs. Pratt's desk. Annie saw, this time, the break in the plastic ventilation grate that had allowed him to drop an acorn inside. You'd think a bank would maintain its equipment better than that. Looking around, she saw that this whole section of the bank was poorly maintained, dusty, the carpet worn. She supposed they didn't care about impressing the customers who had to deal with Mrs. Pratt.

"Please don't let the child touch anything," Mrs. Pratt said before turning her back.

"Mommy," David whispered, "orchids can live on air."

Mrs. Pratt elaborately examined the check Annie had written, then just as elaborately wrote a receipt, taking great pains to let it show that all this was an unreasonable imposition. David fidgeted in his chair, and Mrs. Pratt glanced at him sharply, then at the seat of the chair he sat in. "He is toilet-trained, I hope?" she said to Annie.

"Yes, of course," Annie said.

David blushed crimson.

Mrs. Pratt gave Annie her receipt. "If you're going to keep doing this, you're probably going to keep getting late notices. This just goes completely against our system."

"Change the system," Annie said sweetly, accepting the paper and scrutinizing it as closely as Mrs. Pratt had done to her check. She put it carefully away. "Ready to go, David?"

David looked at her pleadingly. Annie frowned in puzzlement, and David looked briefly at the computer, then back to her. Annie understood. She smiled and nodded. The kid deserved some fun, and Mrs. Pratt certainly deserved whatever happened.

As soon as they were outside the bank, David burst into uncontrollable laughter.

"Quiet, David," Annie tried to say, but found she was laughing as hard as he was. The protesters stopped marching to stare at the two of them, and Annie tried to explain the laughter wasn't directed at them, but couldn't stop long enough to talk. She hurried David away, across the street and into the pizza restaurant. They chose a table by the window, and he sprawled happily in his chair while she ordered a medium pepperoni pizza and two Cokes.

"So just what did you tell that acorn to do?" Annie asked after the waitress had left with their order.

"I told it to grow. I said it should grow little teeny roots into all the spaces in the machine."

"Did it show you what the inside of the machine looked like?"

The waitress served the sodas. David picked up a paper-covered straw and carefully peeled the end open. "Roots don't see. Roots feel their way."

"So what kind of spaces are in there?" Annie asked, looking across at the demonstrators: a ponytailed boy in jeans and T-shirt, a middle-aged housewife, and an older woman whose gray hair hung loose in a sixties style that must have been young for her when she first started wearing it in that fashion.

David blew the straw paper at her and she looked back at him. "In between the wires and plastic. In these little tracks. Lots of places."

"I guess it's good I pay in person, because it sounds like next month our bill could be even more messed up, if that's the computer they bill us on."

"Pizza!" David said as the waitress set it down on the table. Annie put a slice on his plate.

"It's hot," she warned.

"Having a day on the town?" said a man's voice behind her, and Annie looked up to see Charlie Legere standing there. Her first thought was that the bank had found out about David's acorn, but Charlie was smiling, so that couldn't be it.

"Something like that," Annie said.

"And how are you, young man?"

David, his mouth full of pizza, scowled. Clearly he remembered this man who wanted to take their garden away.

"So Charlie, have you started looking at other sites?" Annie asked.

Charlie smiled. "We keep an open mind. We're still hoping for your property, but if it's not to be . . ." He shrugged.

"I'm glad you realize that," Annie said.

Charlie's smile faded. "I'm sorry you seem so resentful of our offer," he said. "It was a generous offer, considering what you paid for the property and how short a time you've owned it."

"The offer was fine. It's your means of persuasion I object to."

Charlie seemed at a loss for words and at a loss for a smile. He paused for longer than she'd ever seen him flustered before. "Do you mind if I sit down for a moment?" he asked, sitting before she could answer. "Have I done something to offend you?" he asked.

"You personally?" Annie said. "No. Not really. Not that I know of. It's the way you do business."

"Annie," Charlie said, "you seem to think I know what you're talking about, but I don't."

"I'm talking about the bank threatening to foreclose because Mark was out of town and the mortgage payment was late. I'm talking about this guy you've got working for you in the collection department, the one who keeps threatening me."

Charlie frowned at the tablecloth. "Are you behind in your mortgage payments?"

"No. And I've got receipts to prove it."

He nodded sagely. "It's probably the computer. These things go out automatically on certain dates. But I don't know why the collection people would be involved, not this soon, not even if you'd never made a payment. I'll look into it. Do you remember the name of the person giving you a hard time?"

Annie hesitated. Oh why not, how much more trouble could there be between her and Harley? "Harley Baer," she said.

"Don't know him. But don't you worry about a thing: I'll take care of it. We don't do business by intimidation," he said, standing up. "Enjoy your lunch," he told David, mussing the boy's hair. He left carrying his order.

David frowned and pushed his hair back. "I still don't like him," he said, watching Charlie go into the bank across the street.

A screech of brakes followed by the crunch of metal striking metal riveted their attention to the corner. One car had crashed into the side of another, both drivers evidently having thought they had the right-of-way. Annie looked at the traffic light. This was one of those bright, sunny days when all lights look green.

The driver of the first car got out unhurt. The driver of the second car was slower, and held a blood-soaked handkerchief to his head. They walked toward each other, each obviously not pleased with the other, and suddenly a hail of chestnuts pelted down on them. They raised their arms to protect their heads, and the already bloodied man slumped to the ground. People ran to the men, and chestnuts rained down.

Annie's hand flew to her mouth.

"I told you, Mom," David said. "They don't know."

The bystanders pulled the two men into the protection of a nearby shop.

"The trees don't know how to interpret human aggression," Annie said. David just stared at her. "Maybe we have to explain better," she told him.

David shook his head.

"I wasn't trying to make things worse," Annie said.

"I think you should talk to that guy," David said.

"What guy? Mr. Legere?"

"The one last night, with the big nose."

"The Mayan?"

David nodded.

"He was no help," Annie said. "He talked in riddles and then he walked away."

"Mom. You yelled at him."

"He was such a smartass," Annie said.

David looked pointedly out the window. People were beginning to peep cautiously out of the shop doorway, looking up to see if chestnuts were still falling. A chestnut falling from high up could make a painful bruise. Or worse. Annie sighed.

"All right," she said. "I could try again. I guess I could apologize."

David sat back and ate his pizza.

Annie wondered how she'd get in touch with the Mayan. It wasn't as if she had his phone number.

Chapter 25

 Of the two places she'd seen the Mayan, the rain forest and her back meadow, the meadow was the easier to get to, so Annie decided to start looking for him there.

"Come on, David," she called. He'd run back to the house for something, and she heard the kitchen door slam, then slam again as he emerged. He ran toward her carrying the wreath she'd been wearing last night when they'd seen the Mayan.

"You might need this," David said.

"I might at that," said Annie. "But I think it's becoming un-raveled."

David looked at the wreath, which had lost large pieces of it-self in his run from the house. "Oh," he said.

"It's okay," Annie said. "I think he came because we called him. Remember, I wished somebody would explain things, and there he was?"

David nodded. He dropped what remained of the wreath and

accompanied her to the back part of the meadow, near the quarry garden wall.

"I wish somebody would explain things to me," Annie said.

They waited. A flock of sparrows landed in the grass, where they hopped around eating seeds and chattering to each other. A squirrel ran along the stone wall, saw them, and ran back. The bindweed flowers wilted in the sun.

"It didn't work," David said.

"Maybe it's the wrong time of day," Annie said.

"Maybe you need your crown."

"We can come back later, after dark, and try again. I wish there were some way to leave a message for him," Annie said. She looked at the sun, tangling itself in the tops of the trees. It would be a couple of hours yet before dark. Then she thought of the quarry. "Maybe we can," she said. "Come on."

"Can what?" David asked, following her through the gate.

"Leave a message. Careful on these stairs, honey: They're steep."

They went to the bottom of the quarry and stood beside the pool. The altar was empty of sacrifices today, but the sun was getting into position. Annie searched her pockets. "I hope I have a pencil and paper," she said, and found an old shopping list. She could write on the back, but she had nothing to write with. "Do you have a pencil?" she asked David.

His pockets contained an assortment of rocks, some tangled string, a dead beetle, and a crayon.

"Great!" Annie said, grabbing the crayon. It had a blunt point, and the paper was small. What was the shortest message that could work? *Please come,* she wrote, then set the paper in the bowllike depression on the altar.

"Now what?" David said.

Annie glanced at the sun, which was still above the wall, but not far. "Now we wait," she said, taking David's hand and stepping back from the altar.

The quarry stones radiated heat, and a scent of crushed thyme hung in the air. The sun slipped into the niche in the wall. Its rays focused on the altar and dropped the rest of the quarry into shadow. As Annie watched, the substance of the paper thinned, and the altar stones hummed with a high-pitched whine like distant locusts. David clung to her.

No longer solid, the paper rode the end of the light ray and brightened with increasing energy. Annie expected it to build up enough energy to fly along the light at any second, but suddenly the humming decreased and the light ray halted before it reached the altar. The end of the sunbeam thickened, growing in length and breadth as the white light split into colors. At last the figure of a Mayan in a parrot-feather cape stood beside the altar, his feathers a burnished green in the sunlight.

"Not a good idea," he said in a voice filled with disapproval. He picked up Annie's message, which had reverted to an ordinary scrap of paper. "You shouldn't do this. You don't know who'll come."

"I was just trying to get in touch with you."

Frowning, he waved his hand toward the altar, then toward the sun. "It's a party line," he said. He sat on one of the steps cut in the rock and took a pipe out of a pouch he wore on his belt. "What do you want?" he asked, filling the pipe.

"First, I want to apologize if I offended you last night."

He grunted, struck a spark from a flint, and set fire to her note. Then he used it to light his pipe. "I suppose you didn't mean to," he said.

Annie thought this over. "Actually, I did mean to, but I'm sorry anyway."

He smiled at this and motioned her to sit down.

"I need some help," she said. "I mean, I'm trying to do something about the problems we're having here, but I'm not sure it's working."

He blew a stream of smoke into the air. "Parlor tricks," he said. "Little games."

David had come over and stood gazing thoughtfully at the Mayan. "Are you dead?" he asked.

The Mayan seemed amused. "No," he said.

"David thinks," said Annie, trying to phrase this carefully so as not to give offense, "that you're one of the Mayans who all kind of disappeared in the tenth century."

"He's right."

"Why did you go?" asked David.

"It was time to leave," said the Mayan.

"You're still here," said David.

"Earth's my old neighborhood. I like to visit." He offered the pipe to Annie.

"No thank you," she said. "I don't smoke."

"Smoke," he said, still holding it in front of her.

"Tobacco's bad for you. That's one of the things we've learned in this century," she said.

"It's not tobacco," the Mayan said, still holding it toward her.

It didn't smell like tobacco, Annie thought, but it didn't smell like pot, either. To be polite, she accepted the pipe. Determined not to inhale, she drew smoke into her mouth. It tasted like fire and ice and burning wood. She coughed and gasped for fresh air.

"It takes some getting used to," the Mayan said, accepting the pipe she pushed toward him. He slowly inhaled through the long stem.

"One of the things I don't understand," Annie said, her voice sounding ragged in her own ears, "is why, if you're an ancient Mayan, you speak such contemporary English."

"I don't," he said teasingly, then relented. He pointed to the beaded headband he wore. "It's the translator."

Annie saw a crystal woven behind the beads, cradled just above his ear.

"I speak Mayan," he said. "You hear English. You speak English, I hear Mayan. Works for writing, too. It's very good at hitting the idiom, provided there's an equivalent in the two cultures. If there isn't, it has to approximate."

"Mayans invented that?" David asked.

"Oh no," the Mayan said. "I bought it. Let's see, I think it was on Rigel IV. Or maybe that little place the other side of the Crab Nebula."

"You space-travel?" David asked, his voice squeaking.

"Oh no," the Mayan said. "I take shortcuts."

"Shortcuts," said Annie.

"Things aren't as far away as they seem. It depends on how you're looking at it."

Annie pressed her hands to her eyes. She'd like to begin at the beginning, if she could figure out where that was. Plus, the smoke from the pipe was making the world seem tenuous, as though all the molecules were getting farther apart. She had to get a firmer grasp on reality.

"What has all this got to do with the murders that are happening here?" Annie asked.

"How should I know?" said the Mayan.

"All these sacrifices of birds and hearts and entrails. I keep finding them practically on my doorstep."

"Do you now? That's interesting," said the Mayan.

"And you have nothing to do with it."

He inhaled deeply and blew the smoke into the air. It settled around them in a light cloud.

"Didn't the Mayans sacrifice hearts?" Annie asked.

The Mayan smiled, pipe clenched in his teeth, then removed the pipe to speak. "Human hearts," he said.

David moved closer to his mother.

Annie felt an increase in tension, but also felt that her responses were rubbery from the smoke. "Did you sacrifice the women who've been killed?" she asked.

"No," he said. "They weren't my enemies. We only make sacrifices of our enemies."

"I guess I'd better stay on your good side," she thought, but when he chuckled she realized with alarm that she'd spoken. "Do you know who did kill them, then?" she asked.

He gazed into the cloud of bluish smoke he'd made around them. "What do you mean by that?" he asked.

"You sound like a psychiatrist," Annie said.

"It's a complicated question," he said, his voice prickly with dignity.

"It seems simple to me. Either you know who killed them, or you don't."

He shook his head. "It's a . . ." The last word was unintelligible.

"What?" said Annie.

He tried again, but with no clearer results. He tapped the crystal in his headband. "It's the translator," he said. "You have no equivalent concept." He looked at her earnestly, obviously trying to be helpful. "It's like with the plants," he said.

That might explain everything to him, but it explained nothing to her. And the moon was close to full. "Is there anything you can tell me that would help me fight this?"

He stood up impatiently. "You've been told all that. You've been shown it all." He went to the altar and emptied his pipe into the bowl. The herbs, whatever they were, continued to smoke. Annie lifted her hand to shield her eyes from the sun, which was streaming through the niche at the top of the wall.

"What about your friend with the jaguar boots? Could he have done it?"

"He's not my friend."

"He's a Mayan, isn't he? From your time?"

The Mayan's face drew down in an expression of disgust which seemed even more deeply carved because of the harsh angle of the sun. "His mother must have slept with a Toltec," he said, and spat on the ground beside the altar.

"Who is he?" Annie asked, thinking if she could get a name her father might be able to help.

The Mayan said something unintelligible.

Annie sighed. "What's the closest equivalent in our culture?" she asked.

The Mayan turned to the sun for a moment, and his sloping profile became hard-edged with light. Then he faced her again. "He is Death."

He stepped back, out of the light. The sun was in her eyes for a moment, then it was gone behind the wall. The altar was empty. The Mayan was gone.

David leaned against her. He felt cold. "Can we go home, Mommy?" he asked.

Annie looked at the shadowed pool, smooth and dark, waiting. Premature twilight had come, and she felt frightened, as she had the last time she'd been in the quarry when the sun left it.

"Yes, honey," she said, putting her arm around him. "I don't think this is a good place to be after dark."

Chapter 26

Annie and David walked across their familiar meadow, where the sun still warmed the ripening grass and the apple tree was happy to see them. Eager, in fact. It wanted to know how things went. All the plants did.

"What is this?" Annie said. "Nothing happened."

David walked backward, looking at the pine tree, trusting the meadow grass to cushion his fall if he tripped. "I think they like him," he said.

"The Mayan?" said Annie, listening to the trees. David was right. They were acting like a favorite uncle had come to visit. "You weren't this excited last night when he came."

A bit of a sulk crept into the garden's mood.

"I know I didn't tell you he was coming last night. I didn't know. I didn't tell you this afternoon, either."

The plants protested. She thought about having stood there calling the Mayan, waiting. "All right, maybe I did. But nothing happened. He was no help. There's no point in getting so worked up."

The plants were clamorous for information. As Annie and David made their way through the perennial garden, the sunflowers turned toward them, the asters brushed against their hands, the rosebushes caught at their clothing.

"Why are they so excited?" she asked David.

"They think something's going to happen."

"What?"

David shrugged.

"They think it's going to be something good. They remind me of you on Christmas Eve." She stopped on her back porch steps and looked out on the garden. "Settle down," she said. "I don't know what you expect, but nothing's going on."

The plants ignored her words, apparently happy for reasons of their own and convinced she'd understand eventually. She went inside to fix supper.

When she called David to come eat his chicken, he brought in the stack of mail from the front hall. "You forgot this," he said, plumping it down on the kitchen table.

"So I did," she said, going through it quickly and dropping the junk mail in the trash.

"Is there anything for me?" David asked.

"Not today. Daddy will probably call tonight, though."

"I like the pictures of where he is. And the stamps," he said. He looked at the drumstick on his plate. "Can I pick this up?"

"Okay, just don't do it in a restaurant, or when we have company."

After supper, Annie sat on the library window seat and looked out into the garden. Dusk mellowed all the colors, and the air coming through the screens was mild and smelled of roses. The bush reached up and tapped its thorns on the window frame, inviting Annie to come outside.

"Sorry, guys, I can't. I'm waiting for a phone call."

The branch arched itself in curiosity.

"From Mark," Annie said.

The bush rustled its leaves in disgust.

"Why don't you like him?" Annie asked.

The rose sent a series of associations into her mind: the stink of printed money, the stink of Charlie Legere's aftershave, the ugliness of parking lots all merged into feelings of ill will toward the bank. As far as Annie could put it together, the plants thought Mark was on the bank's side. She had to concede they had a point.

The phone rang. Annie answered it.

"Hi, how're things going?" said Mark's voice.

"Pretty good," Annie said. "I paid the mortgage. And I ran into Charlie Legere, and he claims all this mess is a mistake and he says he's going to take care of it." David came around the doorway.

"Well, that's one good thing," Mark said.

"I don't like the sound of that," Annie said. "Are you having problems?"

"You might say that. Absolutely everything leaks. Have to go over the whole system tomorrow. I don't know when I'm going to get out of here."

"So you'll be gone longer than you expected again?" David leaned against her, trying to hear.

"Maybe not. But don't count on me till I'm there. How's the Tiger?"

"He wants a postcard. And he wants to talk to you," she said, as David pulled on the phone cord pleadingly.

"Okay, put him on. And I'll call again in a couple of days when I know better what's going on. I miss the two of you."

"Take care," Annie said, relinquishing the phone to David.

She looked at the clock. Eight-thirty. David should be in bed, but, tired as he was, he'd never have settled down before his father called. She was tired, too, and although she wanted to talk to her own father, she didn't think she'd make it till midnight. She could call him in the morning and catch him in the early-evening hours over there. He and her mom didn't usually go out to dinner.

"How are things going over there?" her father said when she reached him.

"Pretty good. How are you and Mom?"

"Great. Just sitting here enjoying the sunset."

"Tell her we want her to come for a visit," said her mother's voice in the background.

"Did you hear that?" said her dad.

"I can't now, Dad. Mark can't take time off now."

"So come without him. Just you and David."

"We'll pay your airfare," said her mother.

"Did you hear that?" her dad said.

"Dad, I can't now."

"We're worried about you. The newspapers from home finally caught up with us. We had no idea all these murders were going on so near to you."

"Dad, I've seen the Mayan again."

"I wouldn't doubt it. This business of removing the victim's heart is a very ancient South American Indian thing to do. He's part of why I think you should get out of there. A spirit who can murder living people is nothing to fool around with."

"He didn't murder anybody, Dad."

"Oh?"

"He told me so."

"And you have complete faith in him, of course."

"No, I don't. But . . . it's a long story. He says there's another Mayan hanging around, though. Some guy in jaguar boots. The closest he could come to the guy's name was to say he's Death. Do you have any idea who he might be, or what he might be like in their mythology? So I'd know what to watch out for."

Some French bird sang in the pause during which her father thought this over. "Beyond the obvious, no," he finally said. "There's a lot we don't know about their mythology. The jaguar boots would indicate a warrior, also a member of the upper classes."

"He might be part Toltec," Annie said, not sure whether that had been the truth or some kind of insult.

"Toltec?" Alarm crackled across the transatlantic cable. "He's a Toltec?"

"Is that a problem?"

"The Toltecs were particularly harsh, bloody people. The Mayans had human sacrifices, yes, but the Toltecs not only ripped their victims' hearts out, they flayed them and wore the skins in future rituals."

Annie could hear her mother's voice in the background, the sound quick and excited, but unintelligible because both parents were speaking at once. "Dad," Annie said, "Dad—I'm not talking to the Toltec. I don't even know what the Toltec has to do with all this. Probably nothing. What are those clicking noises?"

"Nothing. I'm just moving, the sun's in my eyes, and I hit the phone on the railing. I don't like these spirits hanging around; maybe you should get some help. If you were in South America, I'd say contact a medicine man."

"Oh, Dad, I asked the Mayan for you where they all went. He said it was time to go, so they just went."

"Did he say where to?"

"He didn't say exactly how he did it, but apparently he's been to various places around the galaxy. He says they travel by taking shortcuts."

"Did you say the Mayans had spaceships?"

"No. I said they took shortcuts."

"I'm having trouble hearing you. There's interference on the line, plus this damn sun is so strong."

"Dad, do you have a headache?"

"What?"

"Does your head hurt?" she shouted into the receiver.

"Yes. It's just the sun."

"I know. Get out of the sun, Dad. Good-bye." She hung up.

She hoped she'd broken the connection soon enough. She'd have to call him back, make sure he was all right. And she'd have to be careful not to call at sunset again.

Chapter 27

 When Annie called an hour later, her mother answered the phone and said her dad was fine, but resting. They chatted for a while, and her mother promised to call if there were any problems, but when Annie hung up she still felt anxious about her father. Could what was happening here put him in danger so far away? The idea made her feel lonely and depressed.

She went outdoors. The garden welcomed her. The plants were spreading their leaves to a cloudless sky, soaking up energy in optimum amounts, and their feeling of well-being was correspondingly high.

Annie found David under the apple tree. He was collecting seeds from broken apples and spreading them on a rock to dry in the sun. He looked up and smiled when she came. "Hi, Mommy."

"Hi. Going to plant those?" she asked.

"Yes. The tree likes me to. What's the matter, Mommy? You look sad."

She sat on a rock near the one he was using. "I guess I'm just feeling a little down. I could use a hug."

He put his arms around her as far as they would reach and squeezed. "Is that better?"

"Much better, thank you."

"Good. Because I have work to do," he said, picking up another apple.

The mood in the garden suddenly changed to fear. She and David looked at each other in shock; Annie had never felt such terror from the plants. She stood up to see better.

A man wearing a suit was coming toward them through the perennial garden. The trees shivered, the flowers drew back as he passed.

"It's just Charlie Legere," she told the garden. "Just the banker." But for once the plants were afraid for themselves, not for her. "I won't let him buy the land," she said, but it did no good.

Charlie was smiling, coming toward her with his hand held out. He said something in greeting, but it was hard for her to concentrate with all this emotional upset going on around them.

"I have some news for you," Charlie was saying. "Nice piece of property," he added, looking around. "I can see why you're fond of it. We'd leave as much of it as we could, you know. Pave over the meadow . . ."

She lost the rest of what he was saying, because she had to restrain the apple tree from dropping an extremely heavy limb smack on top of him. The tree knew the branch was rotten and likely to go at the first snowstorm. She had to convince it this wasn't a better time to let it go.

"I think we should talk inside, Charlie," she said, interrupting something he was saying.

"I really do appreciate the outdoors," he said.

How could she convince him that if he wanted to live, he'd better come inside? "I think I've had enough sun," she said.

His expression changed to concern. "By all means let's go in," he said, "if that's the case."

She led him to the house by the most direct route, through the herb garden. David stayed behind, which was just as well because he obviously thought this was funny and was being no help at all. All the way in, Annie had to make plants behave: They were all eager to trip the banker. She'd never seen such animosity in them toward anybody. You'd think he was Hitler, she thought.

Charlie cried out in pain. Annie turned abruptly to look at him.

"I guess I wasn't watching where I was going," he said, disentangling himself from the rosa rugosa that grew at the edge of the herb garden. From his position and the plant's, she knew he hadn't walked into it: The branch had snapped forward. She told the plant to quit it and it slunk back.

"Pretty plant," Charlie said. "Sharp thorns, though."

"And not very well behaved," Annie said, wondering how he could be deaf to the savage wildness that wanted to shred him. "You'll need to clean that," she said, as he wiped his forehead and looked with dismay at the blood that came away on his handkerchief. Annie waited while he went safely into the kitchen. "Calm down," she said to them all before she too went indoors.

Charlie had found the kitchen mirror. "It's just a scratch," he said, and seemed to be mostly concerned with keeping the blood away from his suit.

Annie wet a kitchen towel, wrung it out, and gave it to him. "If you just sit down and hold that to the cut for a few minutes, the bleeding should stop."

"I don't think your garden likes me," he said jokingly, sitting on a kitchen chair.

"No, it doesn't," Annie said. "What was it you wanted?"

"I just wanted to reassure you. I checked your account, and everything's in order. All paid to date."

"Yes, I know that," Annie said.

"It must have been a computer error. Don't worry about it."

"Okay. Well, thanks for looking into it," Annie said, although she intended still to pay in person and get a receipt.

"We do have these glitches from time to time. Today, a third of the computers at our main branch are down, and nobody knows why."

"Oh?" said Annie, thinking of David's acorn.

"It's just the terminals, nothing to do with the mainframe, but these things are inconvenient. And I wanted you to know that other matter is taken care of, too." He checked the cloth, saw he wasn't bleeding, and set it neatly in front of him.

"Other matter?"

"Harley Baer. He's been fired."

Great, now he'll really want to kill me, Annie thought, and when I'm gone Mark will sell the house to you. It was a flippant thought, but she immediately realized it could be true.

"I didn't want you to fire him because of me," she said.

"It's not just because of you. He's stepped over the line before, and been warned before. In fact, I was careful not to mention your name, but if he makes any trouble, you just let me know."

And what'll you do, fire him again? she thought, but she said, "Thanks, Charlie."

"My pleasure. We like to keep our customers happy, even the ones who won't cooperate," he said flirtatiously. "So. I'd better be getting back to the bank." But he did not move from his chair. "Mark away?" he asked.

Oh no, Annie thought. I should have fed him to the garden. "Due back any minute," she said. "I'll tell him you were here." She got up and opened the door to the hall. "You'd better go out the front," she said, taking him to the front door.

He stopped in the doorway and smiled. "Here's my card," he said. "Wait." He wrote on the back, and handed it to her. "I put my home phone on the back," he said, putting his hand on her shoulder. "Call me if you need anything. Anything at all."

"Will do, Charlie," she said, pulling away from the hand that was massaging her shoulder. He walked to his car and she watched him to make sure he got past her bushes safely.

"Aw shit!" he said. "Tree sap all over the Porsche. I thought they only dropped that at night. And so much of it!" Still muttering, he got into the car and drove away.

Annie laughed. The garden, happy to see him go, shook off its fear and anger.

"Annie?" It was Mariah's voice, coming from the back of the house.

"Be right with you," Annie called out, then closed the front door and went to the kitchen. Mariah was standing by the table.

"David said you were in here, but there was no answer when I knocked."

"I must not have heard you. I was showing Charlie Legere out the front door."

"I didn't know you knew him."

"He's our banker. Do bankers often make house calls in this town?"

"Did he make a pass?"

"Well, not exactly. It was more like he was hoping he'd get lucky."

"That's Charlie. Anytime you see his car pull up, give me a call and I'll be happy to come over and get in the way."

"Have you had problems with him?"

"Sort of, while John was interning, but I semi-accidentally

dropped a jar of bay leaves on his head while he was 'helping' me get it down from a high shelf, and he hasn't bothered me since."

"Well, my trees sapped his car, so maybe it's taken care of. Isn't a Porsche a little expensive for a mid-management banker?"

Mariah thought this over. "You would think so. But he's divorced, no child support, and flashy cars are important to him. It doesn't necessarily mean he makes a lot, just that he spends what he makes on his car."

"Could be," Annie said.

"And, I don't know, do bankers get bonuses and commissions and things?"

"I have no idea," Annie said, "but if that bank is doing that well they ought to spend some of it on new furniture and a bigger cleaning staff for their office. The back is a mess. So. Was there anything special you wanted? Could I make you a cup of tea?"

"Don't bother about tea," Mariah said. "But I was wondering if you have Mrs. Avent's cookbooks? She had a recipe for pear jelly that was just delicious, and I thought she might have left it with you."

"Come look in the library," Annie said, leading the way. "She left quite a few books behind. The books on that side are all things we brought, but these were Mrs. Avent's." She stopped at the bookcase beside the window seat and ran her hand along the spines. "Cookbook," she said, pulling one out. "Cookbook. And another."

"It was called something about home preserving. Oh, here's the old album," Mariah said, pleased, taking the velvet-covered book from the shelf and bringing it over to the round oak table. "I loved to look through this when I was a kid."

"Home preserving! Found it," Annie said. She put the other books back and brought that one to Mariah.

Mariah was paging through the photo album. "She always said she was going to pass this on to her daughter when she came

214

to live in the house. Sad, isn't it, the way people's dreams don't come to pass?" She paused. "But I suppose, in a way she thinks she did. My favorite," she said, skipping to the back, "was always this one. I always wondered who this was, behind the lace curtains in the library."

"I hadn't noticed anyone," Annie said, looking at the window in the photograph. There was an outline there.

"All the family's on the porch," Mariah said.

"Maybe it's just the way the lace falls. It just looks like someone," Annie said, but the hairs at the back of her neck were standing up. There was something familiar about the shape.

"I always pretended it was an Indian," Mariah said. "I don't know why."

"Probably because of Mrs. Avent's story about the séance," Annie said. "It would have happened around the time of this photograph. Maybe it's a ghost."

"What séance?" said Mariah.

"Didn't she tell you that story?"

"No."

"Then how do you know she saw an Indian?"

"I didn't. That's just what it looks like to me."

They looked at the picture again. Annie noticed she was still holding the cookbook, and set it down. "You know, the moon's approaching full," she said. "We ought to do something."

"You mean have a séance?" said Mariah. "What good would that do?"

"I don't know. We might learn something, get a handle on more power. Or protection. It helped Mrs. Avent."

"Who would hold it?" said Mariah. "Do you know a medium?"

"No, but I know the relative of a witch."

"Me? I don't know anything about séances."

"But you know the ghost." She pointed at the album. "You've seen him for years. And basically, don't they always sit in a circle, hold hands, and call some ghost?"

"Two of us won't make much of a circle."

"We'll be enough."

"Well, okay," Mariah said. "It might be fun. I always wanted to meet the face behind the curtain. We don't have to do this at midnight or anything, do we? I'm not much of a night person."

"No. It should be after dark, though. And tonight, while the moon is still waxing."

"Tonight's good," said Mariah. "John will be home watching his baseball game. I'll come over after I get Erica to sleep. This is bizarre, but maybe it'll distract you from worrying about those murders." She giggled. "I haven't done anything like this since I was a teenager and we used to have séances at slumber parties. I'd forgotten about those. Nothing ever happened, though, Annie."

"This one will be different," Annie said. "Don't forget the cookbook."

She waved good-bye to Mariah from the kitchen door. Should she have told Mariah it wasn't ghosts they were after? No. Too hard to explain. And maybe they were some kind of ghost, anyway. How could they still be alive after all these years? Anyway, she felt better just to be doing something. Between asking the trees for help, even though that wasn't a perfect solution, and now the séance, she felt she was getting a handle on the situation.

Chapter 28

 Mariah arrived with her grandmother's coda under her arm and an assortment of candles and pens in one hand, a flashlight in the other.

"What's all that for?" Annie asked.

"I did some research," Mariah said, setting the things on the kitchen table with a clatter. A pen rolled off the edge and she caught it. "I thought we ought to know a little something about what we're doing."

"Can't we just sit at the dining room table, hold hands, and call this guy?" Annie said.

"Nope. Bad idea," Mariah said. She turned pages in her grandmother's book. "We could get a demon by mistake. We're supposed to draw a circle with a triangle around it for protection. Like this." She showed Annie the illustration.

"I've already put some vases of alder and fennel in the library. They both repel demons."

"I think we should draw the circle and triangle, too," Mariah said. "The pens are to write the spirit's name." She reached into her pocket and pulled out a bottle of ink. "I figured you'd have paper. The candles are to burn the paper, but also for light. Probably the medium didn't want too much light, so the people at the séance couldn't see the medium's assistant pretending to be a ghost."

"They talk about mediums in that book?"

"The chapters written in the nineteen-twenties do. It sort of comes at the end of a section on white magic; I think somebody was improvising."

"Like us," Annie said. "What's the flashlight for—in case the spirit blows out the candles?"

"Actually it was so I could see to go home, but that's not a bad idea."

The kettle shrieked. Annie turned the gas off and poured boiling water into a teapot. "I was just making some tea. Do you want some? It's not quite dark out, and besides, I just put David to bed and I'd like him to settle down before we start conjuring spirits."

"Sure," said Mariah, pushing the pens aside to make room for the teacups Annie was getting from the cupboard. "It's almost dark: The sun was just above the horizon when I came over."

"You weren't thinking about this on the way over, were you?" Annie asked.

"I don't remember. I think I was thinking about the news on Channel six. Why?"

"Nothing. Sunset's a funny time of day, that's all." She poured the tea. "So did John mind baby-sitting while we held a séance?"

"I didn't tell him about the séance, I just said I couldn't sit through any more baseball. But he got a call and had to go out, so he's taping the game and I got Tiffany to come over."

"I didn't mean for you to have to hire a sitter," Annie said. "I could probably have managed by myself."

"You don't even know about the circles and triangles. You'd get eaten by a demon," said Mariah. "Besides, I get really tired of having to change my plans. Obviously John has to go when he gets a call, but I've learned to set up avenues of escape, like a list of baby-sitters who don't mind coming over at the last minute." Mariah sipped her tea, then chuckled. "Did you watch the news tonight?"

"No," Annie said.

"So you haven't heard about what's happening at your bank?"

Annie put her hand to her head. "You mean about the trees pelting everybody with chestnuts?" She supposed if she were a tree looking at human behavior, she wouldn't be able to figure it out, either.

"No. Got a headache?" Mariah asked her.

"No. What was it, then?" Annie smiled what she hoped was a bright smile and poured more tea.

"It was about the demonstrators outside, and they showed Charlie going up the stairs and saying, 'No comment.'"

"I saw them there yesterday," Annie said. "They want the bank to stop investing in South Africa or something."

"Rain forests," Mariah said. "They want the bank to stop investing in South American development, because of the rain forests."

"Charlie Legere's bank is responsible for cutting down rain forests?"

"Didn't you know? They're one of the worst offenders. That's why John and I won't do business with them anymore," Mariah said.

"No, I didn't know," said Annie. That sure explained why the garden hated him. Only, how did the plants know? "But we only owe them money," Annie said. "So I suppose our mortgage is money they can't invest in South America." She took her empty cup over to the sink and looked out the window. "It's dark out. Should we get started?"

Mariah gathered up her paraphernalia and they moved into the library. "How are we going to draw the circle and triangle?" she said.

"The table's a circle," Annie said. "Can't we just use that?"

"I don't think it's exactly what the book had in mind."

"This is a good carpet. I don't want to draw on it," Annie said. "Suppose we use the table for the circle, and set up a triangle of candles around it. We can put alder and fennel at the points. That should be an improvement over the book."

"Okay," Mariah said. "But we'll need more candles."

Annie rummaged through the kitchen and dining room drawers and came up with an assortment of tapers, votive candles, and half-burned Christmas novelties. She and Mariah attached them to saucers and set up a triangle of light around the library table.

"We should get inside before you light the last one," Mariah said, and stepped over the last unlit candle.

Annie held a match to the wick of a half-burned snowman. "I can't believe we paid to have this moved," she said.

"It's coming in handy," said Mariah. She sat down by the pad Annie had supplied, and dipped a pen in ink. "I'm supposed to write the name of the spirit we want to summon. I'm pretty good at calligraphy, so we can give him an elegant invitation. What's his name?" She looked at Annie.

"I have no idea," Annie said. "I hadn't thought of that. How do you summon a spirit when you don't know what his name is?"

Mariah put the pen down. "Could we just call him the Indian in the picture?"

Annie looked at the photograph by the light of the one candle they had reserved for the table. She saw Ada Avent and her family on the porch, and an uncertain shape behind the lace. "Are you sure it's an Indian you see?" she asked, thinking of the Mayan's warning to be careful who she called.

"That's what it's always looked like to me," Mariah said.

"I just don't want to say Indian and get some Toltec in jaguar boots," Annie said. "What if we call it the spirit who was at the séance? So we'll get the same spirit."

"Sounds good. I don't see why we'd get a Toltec, I know I wouldn't want one," said Mariah, writing. It did look elegant when she'd finished. She put the cap back on the ink bottle. "Now what?"

"I thought you knew," Annie said.

Mariah pulled the book over. "They've got different incantations you can use, but they all use the names of powerful spirits, and I don't know if I want to get into that. What if this turns out to be real? We could be in big trouble."

"All we're doing is sending an invitation," Annie said. "I don't see why we have to do it in anybody's name but our own."

"Okay. Let's make a circle and try it," Mariah said.

Annie quickly discovered that two people cannot hold hands and form a circle around a table the size of the one in her library. "None of this is going according to plan," she said.

"Maybe the circle isn't that important," Mariah said. "Let's sit opposite each other and try." They faced each other over the candle. "Spirit of the séance, come to us!" Mariah said, and giggled.

"You have to take this seriously," Annie said, feeling a little foolish herself.

"I know. Let's try again." She called out again, but nothing happened. They looked into the darkness around them. The candles that surrounded them cast multiple shadows on the walls, but the shadows were all their own.

"It's not working," Annie said.

"I know!" Mariah said. "I forgot. You're supposed to burn the paper."

"I'll get an ashtray."

"No, no, you can't leave the triangle of protection. You'll spoil everything," Mariah said. "Just sit down and concentrate." She held the paper to the candle flame and called the spirit. The paper blazed up, sending dark smoke away from the light, and she dropped it into the candle when it got too small to hold. It burned there for a moment, and sent a river of melted wax into the saucer. They listened, but heard only the creakings of an old house at night. A breeze came through and fluttered the candle flames, but it was only a breeze.

"Maybe it feels we're ordering it around," Annie said. "Maybe if we just sit here and think about it, invite it to come, it'll feel more comfortable about showing up."

They sat in silence, Annie feeling discouraged. She could use a friend about now, somebody who could give her a little guidance and some help in figuring out what to do. A lot of help, actually.

"I hear something," Mariah whispered.

Annie could hear it, too. They turned toward a shuffling noise in the hall.

David appeared at the edge of the candlelight.

"Oh, honey, you're supposed to be asleep," Annie said.

"You scared me," said Mariah. She shook her head ruefully. "I guess this is a bust."

David looked across the table at a point midway between his mother and Mariah. He smiled. "Hi, Grandma," he said.

Annie and Mariah turned to follow his gaze. Ada Avent was standing just outside the triangle of candles. She was a dim figure, like someone seen in an old mirror whose silver backing is worn thin. She smiled.

"Ada!" said Mariah.

"Hello, dear," Ada said to David. Then, to all of them, "It's so nice to see you all again."

"But . . . but you're not a spirit," Annie said.

"We're all spirits, dear," Ada said.

"All right," Annie said. "What I meant was, you're not a ghost. How can you be at a séance when you're still alive?"

"Oh no, Annie," Ada said. "I passed over . . ." She waved a hand vaguely, as though trying to concentrate. "Recently. It's so nice of you to visit me so soon."

"I'm sorry you're gone," Annie said.

"I'm not gone. I'm just on the other side. You've done nice things with the house, and the garden looks lovely."

"Thank you," Annie said. "We were hoping to get some help, Mariah and I, with some of the problems we're having here."

"Why don't you ask that nice Mayan gentleman you've been talking to? It seems to me I saw him around somewhere when I was coming."

"Is he the same Indian who came to your séance? I wasn't sure," Annie said. "Is he the one Mariah sees in this photograph?" She held the album up for Ada to see.

Ada stepped through the candles. Mariah gasped, then she and Annie looked at each other, realizing Ada was unhurt, and the candles didn't even flicker. Annie quickly said to David, "Don't you try that."

"Yes," said Ada. "It's the same gentleman. I never noticed before that he was in the photo."

"We wanted to ask him some questions," Mariah said. "We held this séance to get in touch with him. Although it's very nice to see you instead."

"We did just ask for a spirit who was at the séance," Annie said. "And Ada was there, she just wasn't a ghost yet. Do you know his name?" she asked Ada. "We could try again."

"It wouldn't do any good," Ada said. "You can only call people from the other side with a séance. He's still on your side."

"But he came to your séance," Annie said.

"Oh. So he did. How odd. But I didn't know then that he wasn't of the spirit world. I couldn't tell. Now I can—the difference is obvious. Maybe his coming just had nothing to do with the séance at all."

"Maybe you just called him," Annie said.

"Perhaps I did. I have to go now. I'm new at this. It was charming seeing you." She passed through the table to lean down and kiss David. "Good-bye, David."

"Will you come see me again?" David asked as Mrs. Avent faded.

"Yes, dear. I will. Look for me in your dreams."

And she was gone.

"Well," said Mariah. "That was a surprise."

"Yes," Annie said. "David, would you get the light switch, please?" David put the lights on, then helped Annie and Mariah blow out the candles. "I always thought people would know everything once they died, but that doesn't seem to be true," Annie said. "It was a silly assumption, come to think about it. Why should you know more just because you're dead?"

"It's hard to think of her as dead," said Mariah.

"Yes, it is," Annie said. She went to the telephone table, looked up a number in her address book, and dialed. In a few moments, the nursing home answered.

"I'd like to speak to Mrs. Avent, please," Annie said.

There was a brief pause. "I'm afraid that won't be possible," the person at the other end said.

"Is she all right? This is Annie Carter, I visited her not long ago."

"Yes, I remember. With your son. She enjoyed your visit very much."

"I just had the feeling, tonight, that something was wrong. Is she all right?" Annie asked again.

"Mrs. Avent passed away this evening. A few moments ago. It was very peaceful. She just drifted away, I don't think she was really with us for the last couple of hours. Then, at the last moment, she smiled and said, 'Good-bye, David.' That's your son's name, isn't it?"

"Yes."

"Well, she was thinking of him at the end."

"Thank you for telling me," Annie said. She put the receiver down gently. Mariah and David were looking at her. "She died this evening," Annie told them. "I wish I'd visited more often."

Tears spilled out of Mariah's eyes. "I don't know why I'm crying," she said. "She seems perfectly happy."

David patted her hand. "It's okay, Mariah. She'll still play with us."

Chapter 29

 The moon had risen and David was yawning over the cocoa his mother had made him by the time Annie and Mariah had finished discussing the séance.

"I think it's time you went back to bed," Annie said. "Go on up. I'll come tuck you in soon."

"I ought to be going back myself," Mariah said as David shuffled off to bed, "and let Tiffany go home."

"I'll walk with you," Annie said.

Mariah laughed. "And do what, see that the plants protect me?"

That was Annie's intention, but she said, "It's a pleasant night. I'd like some air."

"You ought to stay inside. Nobody's after me particularly, but you've already been shot once," said Mariah, going out the kitchen door.

Annie followed her. "All the more reason for me to come with you. You wouldn't want to be mistaken for me if somebody's after me."

"I didn't mean after you especially. Just that you should be careful, which as far as I can tell, you're not." Mariah switched on her flashlight, but said, "I don't even think I need this, the moon is so bright."

"It's better not to walk around with a light if you're at all worried about being a target," Annie said.

Mariah turned the light off and they walked through the herb garden and into the meadow. Fuzzy gray clouds moved across a darker sky, and the moon hung low, its rocky face leaning toward Earth. Craters and stress lines spoke of past violence. The top of the pine tree showed black against it.

Annie sensed from the woody plants a feeling somewhere between expectation and apprehension. The grasses were sleepy, but they lived a more hurried life and had less emotional stamina. She thought that meant some event was probable, but not imminent, or the meadow grass would be sounding its alarm. Looking around the borders of her land, she could feel no intruder.

"It's a beautiful night," Mariah said. "We should be able to relax and enjoy it. It's a shame, all this going on."

"Yes," said Annie. A quiver of activity at the farthest edge of the hedgerow rippled through the plant's consciousness to her mind, then subsided. Something settling to wait, perhaps a dog or raccoon. The intention behind the vigil wasn't clear.

"Mrs. Avent always loved the garden. I feel her spirit's at peace here somehow, don't you?" Mariah said.

"I don't think so," said Annie. "Not from anything I can tell."

"No? I can sense she visits here, and my grandmother visits, too. It's not something I make a habit of telling people, but it's there. I always thought it was just a romantic fantasy, but now I'm not so sure."

"Do you talk to the plants?" Annie asked.

"I've never tried."

"Until tonight.

"That's true," Mariah said. "I get no feeling from the plants at all."

"And I don't sense ghosts," Annie said. They were at the gate. This section of the hedgerow slept lightly, prepared to respond if need be to an intruder at the far end.

"You're listening to your plants again, aren't you?" Mariah said. "Plants don't know everything."

"So you do believe in them?" Annie said, interested.

Mariah shrugged. "You're talking to somebody who just saw a ghost. I'm open-minded on just about anything right now. But unsettled. By tomorrow morning, I'm not sure I'll even believe in the ghost." She swung the gate open and stepped into her own garden. "It's been a remarkable evening. I wouldn't want a lifetime of supernatural occurrences, though."

"How can you avoid them?" Annie asked.

"By living in reality," said Mariah, stepping firmly across her own mown lawn. "Look, give me a call when you get home. I mean it."

"All right. But Mrs. Avent is a part of reality," Annie said.

Instead of returning directly home, she watched Mariah's silhouette approach the house and enter. Only when she was sure Mariah was safely inside did she step away from the hedgerow and into the full moonlight.

Every plant on the perimeter was watchful. They were faithful sentinels. The only soft spot in the garden's defense was the quarry garden. The stone wall had no plants, the plants below were . . . fey. They just couldn't believe in the importance of what concerned the rest of the garden. They thought they were eternal. But they shouldn't matter. The drop from the wall was too steep for anybody to come in that way. Any human she knew anyway, except maybe the Mayans, and what could they do without the sun?

Were the murders always completed before sunrise?

She walked briskly across the meadow. Lights burned in her kitchen and in the upstairs hallway. The house was her shelter from the dark, the garden her shelter from outside evils. She just had to make sure she extended that shelter over the entire neighborhood.

"We'll catch him tonight," she said to the plants. "We'll put a stop to him."

The plants were agreeable.

She went inside and locked her door, then went straight to David's room.

She could tell from his breathing that David was sleeping soundly. His arm hung over the edge of the bed, and moonlight highlighted his hand and arm and the soft curves of his profile. She withdrew and checked the rest of the house before going into the darkened library.

The room smelled of candlewax. Annie sat on the window seat and put a cushion between her back and the wall. She could see the perennial garden, its borders silvered by the moonlight, and the shadowy mass of the hedgerow beyond. How long would her vigil be?

An owl cried. It was a good night for hunting, with the ground brightly lit. Annie quickly submerged herself in the owl, and they were flying before the moon. She could see her owl-shadow below her, wings beating across the meadow. The owl was hungry. She stooped and caught a field mouse and then, strengthened by the meal, rose into the sky and wheeled around the neighborhood.

Annie saw her own house and gardens, and Mariah's, all peaceful. On the street, there were three teenagers waiting at the bus stop, giggling and horsing around. A police car drove by, then turned left and headed downtown. A girl walked along the sidewalk toward the corner, eating ice cream. A couple dawdled by the street side of her quarry garden wall, and the boy threw a pebble over the wall. It splashed in the pool below.

Annie made a larger circle, and could see the edge of the park, the busier streets downtown. A column of heat from the pizza restaurant's chimney caught her off guard, but she quickly corrected for it. She flew toward the little shopping area near her house, crowded with people coming out of the movie theater. All was well.

She flew upward then, delighting in the flight, and tore through the edges of a cloud. Wisps of it trailed after her, and the moon seemed near enough to grasp in her talons. She rode the currents, gliding lower and lower, in smaller circles, back to her garden.

An archer stood on the quarry wall above the pool. His face was masked, but his bare chest and arms gleamed in the moonlight. He was scanning the sky, but she wasn't frightened, not even when he fitted an arrow into his bow and aimed at her. Surely no one could hit a bird in the dark.

He loosed the arrow and it came straight toward her. She could see the relentless stone arrowhead, broader than the shaft, rising to intercept her flight.

Annie folded her wings and plummeted. The arrow passed harmlessly. Annie opened her wings again and, shrieking, reached into the sky for speed. The roar of her own feathers sounding in her ears, she swooped toward the archer and ripped the mask from his face.

She screamed again and circled for a fresh attack. He fitted another arrow to his bow, and as she came for him she saw an unfamiliar face, but with a flattened profile similar to her Mayan's. Black blood welled from a cut in his cheek.

Before he could loose the second arrow, she struck again. This time the bow went flying, and he fell backward, his quiver of arrows scattering like pick-up sticks. He shouted something in a language she could not understand, then rose to his feet and stood, arms outstretched, challenging her.

She circled higher, picking up speed, positioning herself so the empty darkness and the fall to the pool would be behind him. She fell on him then, gathering momentum, the sound of her passage through the air harsh in her ears. He reached for her and caught one of her legs as she struck him; they fell together toward the water.

The black pool glittered below, filled with stars. Annie clawed the Indian with her free talon, and bit his hand, and freed herself just before he plunged into the water. Aching, she rose to the sky and circled once.

The quarry was still, the water without a ripple.

Tired, she flew to the top of the pine and concealed herself among the branches that were home. A comforting, resinous smell surrounded her.

Her Mayan had been right: the Toltec was uglier.

She stretched the injured leg tentatively. It felt strained, but not broken. She tried it on her perch, and could hold well enough, could even put weight on it.

The owl rested. She looked at the moon and blinked.

After a time, she could hear a distant wail of emergency sirens and, from the quarry, there came a faint sound. Annie recognized it as laughter.

Chapter 30

 A yellow light was flashing outside. Curious, Annie leaned forward on the window seat as she reached to push the curtain farther back. She still couldn't see the street, but from the overlapping patterns of flashing lights, there seemed to be several emergency vehicles in front of her house.

She got up to investigate, and found her left leg sore and stiff. She limped into the entrance hall and looked out the front window. There were an ambulance and two police cars out front. The activity centered around an area on her lawn, which the police were cordoning off. A small crowd had gathered, and faces peered over and around the obscuring policemen. She could hear the crackle of a two-way radio, and a siren approached, then was cut off as a third police car drove onto her lawn and parked.

She was about to open the front door when a noise from the back of the house stopped her. It sounded like somebody was trying to get in the kitchen door. She moved quietly down the dark hallway and into the kitchen.

In the moonlight outside, she could see a dark figure through the glass. The door handle rattled, then metallic scraping noises told her the person was trying to pick the lock. With three police cars out front?

But maybe it was a good time. The whole neighborhood's attention was drawn to the front of the house. No one would notice a stranger at her door. A burglar might have trouble carting off loot with all those police around, but the motive could be something other than burglary.

She could still run down the hall and out the front door, bring the police back with her, but that would leave David alone in the house. She couldn't risk it.

The lock clicked home and the door opened, only to be stopped short by the chain. A hand reached in to undo the chain.

Annie threw herself against the door, slamming it against the hand. The chain rattled free, but the intruder cried out in pain.

Annie needed a weapon, tried to think where the nearest heavy or sharp thing might be. The knife rack! It was on the wall, just out of reach. She let go of the door to get to it, and as she did the door swung open. She grabbed a carving knife and swung around just as the intruder turned a flashlight beam on her. She could see the round light, and the long, shiny blade that she held in front of her with both hands.

"Mrs. Carter? You can put that down. It's me."

The voice was familiar, but she didn't quite place it, and all she could see of him was his flashlight. She held the blade pointing firmly toward him. "Who are you?" she said.

"Trooper Keene. I mean, police," he said. "Look." He pointed the flashlight beam toward his own face.

"What do you think you're doing?" she said. "You scared me half to death." She lowered the knife and switched on the kitchen light. They stood blinking in the sudden glare. "Aren't you supposed to yell police or something when you break into somebody's house?"

"I was too busy screaming in pain. I think you broke my hand. Could I have some ice?"

Annie set the knife down and piled ice onto a dishtowel. "Why didn't you just ring the doorbell?"

"I did. Nobody answered."

She shouldn't have gone completely into the owl. That must be why she hadn't heard the bell. "I guess I dozed off," she said. She tied the towel around the ice and gave it to him. "That looks nasty."

"It hurts like hell." He looked at her, smiled, and said with apparent sincerity and relief, "I'm real glad to see you."

"Me? Why me?"

"Well, your neighbor called. Mrs. Fenton? She saw the police cars on your lawn and was worried about you. Apparently you were supposed to call her when you got back inside, and you didn't. Considering what's been going on around here, I figured I ought to check it out. And when you didn't answer the doorbell . . ."

"I forgot I was supposed to call. What did happen?"

"Another woman got murdered."

"Oh no."

"And I thought . . . Well, the body's on your lawn and all, and with you missing . . ."

"So why were you trying to get into my house?"

"The boy. He's upstairs, isn't he? I just didn't want him to wake up and see the police cars and all, and be scared. I thought, well, we seemed to hit it off all right, and I'm not a stranger to him. I didn't think he should be alone."

"That was kind of you," she said.

The melting ice was dripping through the towel. He dropped it into the sink and flexed his fingers, checking them out.

"I'm sorry I hurt your hand."

234

"It's my own fault. I should have followed procedure."

"Who was she? The woman who was murdered."

"I don't know. I thought it was you. I don't suppose you saw anything?"

Annie slowly shook her head. "It happened right in my front yard?" she said, the closeness of it sinking in at last.

"I'm afraid so."

"I walked Mariah home," Annie said, thinking aloud. "Through the gardens. Who might be going along the sidewalk after that?" She stopped then, jolted by a possibility she didn't like: Tiffany. She had seen Mariah home safely, but she hadn't thought about Tiffany leaving Mariah's and going along the sidewalk.

"What?" said Trooper Keene.

Annie ran out the kitchen door and toward the front of the house. Keene followed quickly behind her.

"Mrs. Carter! You don't want to go out there."

She ran toward the emergency vehicles, to the ring of light focused on the still figure draped in a sheet. The cordon was to keep away people approaching from the street, and she was able to get quite close before Keene caught hold of her.

"It's real bad," he said. "You don't want to see."

But Annie could already see. Trampled into the grass, but still glittering in the spotlights, a glint of gold. She bent down and, reaching forward, picked up a tangle of crushed bells and wire that had been an earring.

"It's Tiffany's," she said, having trouble getting the words out because she was trying not to cry. "She baby-sat for Mariah tonight."

She handed the metal to Keene, who took it with a puzzled expression.

"An earring," Annie said.

He nodded. "We'll look for the other one."

"She only wore one," Annie said, turning away from him, because now she couldn't stop the tears from coming. Keene patted her shoulder. Annie pulled away, then faced him. "Did he cut out her heart?"

"Yes," Keene said. Technicians from the ambulance wheeled a stretcher over to the body. "I think you should go inside now."

Chapter 31

Because the front door was locked, Annie walked back to her kitchen door. When she got inside, the phone was ringing. She went into the hall and picked up the receiver.

"Hello?"

"Annie!" Mariah said. "I'm so glad you're all right. I mean, you are all right, aren't you?"

"Yes. But a woman was killed in front of my house."

"I know, it's on the news. Do they know who it was? Was it somebody from the neighborhood?"

"It's Tiffany."

There was a pause at the other end of the line. "But she was just here a few hours ago," Mariah said.

"Is that Daddy?" David asked sleepily from the landing.

"No, honey. It's Mariah."

"She woke me up," he complained, walking slowly downstairs. "What's going on? Why are there police cars in front of our house?"

"Another person was killed," Annie said.

"Tiffany?"

"Yes."

David stood on the bottom step and leaned on the banister. "Will she still baby-sit for me?"

"Sounds like you've got your hands full," Mariah said. "Is there anything I can do? Do you want me to come over?"

"No. Thanks, but stay home. They haven't caught him yet."

"Good luck with David. I'll stop by tomorrow," Mariah said.

"Thanks," Annie said again, and hung up. She sat on the stairs beside David and sat him on her lap. "Tiffany's on the other side with Mrs. Avent."

"So she can still come to visit me?"

"Yes, but probably just in your dreams. She won't be able to baby-sit."

David put his arms around Annie's neck and hugged tight. "She won't bring me movie tapes," he said.

"No, David. She won't." Annie stood up and carried him upstairs. "Let's get you back to bed."

"Why did Tiffany go to the other side? She wasn't old."

"No, she wasn't." Annie settled him in his bed, and sat beside him. "Somebody sent her there, and it was wrong. The police are looking for him."

"Will they find him?" David asked, and yawned.

"He's a bad man, and his badness will catch up to him. Don't you worry about anything."

David closed his eyes. Annie hummed a lullaby, waiting for him to fall asleep. She looked out the window at the rosebush that protected David. Its clawlike thorns shone in the moonlight, and the scent of its flowers flowed into the room, soporific and soothing. When the sound of David's breathing told her he was sleeping, she went downstairs and out onto the back porch.

Annie felt a deep sadness, but wasn't sure whether it came from the garden or herself. She understood now about the predator in the hedgerow. How had she overlooked it before? Not a dog or raccoon, but a murderer hiding, waiting. To the garden, they were all much the same. The garden had given her information she had misinterpreted.

But that wasn't the worst of it. She sat on the back steps and looked up at the moon. It was much higher now, small and cold. All her snares, all her plans had come to nothing. He had not only murdered again, he'd murdered on her front lawn. There was a special kind of malice in that, and she took it personally.

The small leaves fluttered silver, the herb garden released carefully modulated chords of scent, the effect much like the lullaby she'd hummed to David. The plants tried to comfort her, but they were themselves disappointed. Under the affection and the comradeship of the garden, there was fear. She appreciated their courage, and knew she had let them down.

How had he done it? How had he gotten through all their defenses as though they didn't exist? Had it been entirely her incompetence?

She thought back. The murder must have been happening while she flew. She'd made a big mistake, becoming so completely part of the owl that she was unaware of what was happening around her human body, had kept no contact with the garden through it. If she hadn't gotten so involved fighting the Indian . . .

That was it. While she was fighting the Indian—one to distract, while another murdered. No wonder he'd been so easy to defeat, and no wonder he'd ended by laughing at her. Not only had she been stupid, she'd been suckered.

A wave of anger swept through her. She rushed into the kitchen, grabbed the carving knife, and went back outdoors, through the herb garden, into the meadow.

Annie stood in the open meadow and strained to catch a hint of the intruder the garden had warned her of earlier. The meadow grass presented a sealike surface to the moonlight, the arching curves of the stems mimicking waves. Dew had fallen, and the general wetness added to the feeling that she was walking through water. Her jeans flapped wet and cold around her ankles.

Overhead, the sky was clear and cold. The brighter stars patterned the darkness with their familiar outline, one that shone even on hazy nights, but in between, bursting from the surrounding glow of the bright stars and spilling out of the darker patches in clusters and crowds, were all the dim and distant stars of the Milky Way. Annie could see thousands upon thousands of stars whose names she would never know. How many had her Mayan visited?

A twig snapped, returning her attention to Earth. She raised the knife and held it before her with both hands, looking into the darkness under the apple tree. Leaves rustled as something jerked a branch down, let it snap back up. Something large was under there. A deer stepped forward, into the meadow.

A deer in this neighborhood? Then she thought of the wooded area nearby, and how it connected with the larger woods on the outskirts of town. Why not? The night belonged to the wild things who were wise enough to avoid people.

The deer had been eating apples, and was chewing while it considered her. Its eyes gave no hint of its thoughts. It lost interest in her, and moved leisurely toward the hedgerow.

If the murderer is human, Annie thought, he'd have moved off when the police came, or before. He'd be long gone. And if he weren't quite human, but was whatever the Mayans had become . . . ? But the garden said no Indian, no human, was here.

If she were looking for one of the Indians, the place to look was the quarry garden. Annie was uncomfortable with the idea of going there, especially at night, both because of the steep stairs, which would be treacherous in the dark, and because of the raw power in the place, power she had no idea how to use. She had to go anyway, because that was where she was most likely to force a confrontation.

She found the quarry gate open. Her already strained nerves wound tighter at that, because she never left it open. She was careful about it, because she didn't want David to wander in. Going as silently as she could, she slipped through the gateway.

The garden put her in mind of a crater on the moon, all rock and harsh shadows. The pool at the bottom was black and still. She felt drawn to it. Carefully, she made her way down the stairs, feeling the ground before trusting her weight to it. The shadows were deceptive, some lying simply on rock, others concealing a sharper drop or a patch slippery with pebbles.

At the bottom, she stood beside the water. It was dead water, colder than ice, a black lens reflecting the stars. She shivered from the cold. She held out the carving knife, trying to keep it steady, and touched its tip to the surface. A single ring spread out from it, disturbed the surface, and was gone. Not knowing why she did it, but trusting her instinct, she thrust the blade into the water as far as the knife handle.

It disappeared at the surface. Even in the moonlight, even underwater, she expected to see that blade taper away, not end abruptly. And it was cold. Her hand ached with holding it, as though the metal were conducting the absolute cold of space back up her hand and arm and to her heart.

She pulled the knife out and fell back onto the ground. She dropped the knife, and it clattered, the metallic sound reverberating against the rock walls. The water rippled briefly, then was still as before, untouched, open to the sky. Annie sat on the quarry floor and shivered. When she moved the hand she'd used to steady herself in her fall, she found it was sticky.

She looked behind her. She'd fallen before the altar, and something black and shiny stained its side and flowed across the floor. She sniffed. The smell of fresh blood was in the air.

Annie scrambled to her feet and moved away from the altar. She didn't want to see this sacrifice, not even by moonlight, not the offering made on the night of Tiffany's murder. Tiffany's blood was on her hand and she found that unbearable. She knelt by the pool and plunged her hand into the searing cold, washing the blood away. The pain made her gasp, but then her hand became numb, and the cold drew her toward sleep. She could sleep forever in the pool, and let others worry.

The garden was pulling her back, urging her to come back to the meadow grass and the pine needles, to come back to David. The thought of David gave her the strength to break free. She ran from the pool, stumbling up the quarry steps to the warmer air above, and achieved the meadow.

It had been another defeat, she knew, not finding the Indian. Images of the cold, still pool, of the sun blazing in its niche, conflicted in her mind. A place of fire and water. A place of elements. If you count air and earth, which are always around, a place of all four elements.

Why had that come to mind? A random thought?

She thought of her father by the seashore at sunset. Fire, water, air and earth. Symbols of power in most ancient cultures.

The garden welcomed her back. She was tired, drained. It didn't matter. Elements didn't matter. Her mind was just running on empty. She dragged herself toward the house and went into the kitchen.

The Mayan was sitting at the table, smoking. He had on his parrot cape. When he saw her, he took the pipe stem out of his mouth and shook his head.

"You've got to stop doing this," he said.

Chapter 32

Annie stared at the Mayan in disbelief. "I've got to stop doing this?" She slammed the kitchen door. "What do you mean, I've got to stop doing this? Your friend just murdered a young girl. Why don't you tell him to stop?"

The Mayan sucked on his pipe and blew a cloud of smoke into the air. "Don't get excited," he said. "You're wasting time."

The sugar bowl was on the table. Annie resisted the impulse to throw it at him. Instead, she opened the kitchen door to let the smoke out. "You've got a real problem with that pipe," she said. "You should get help."

He looked puzzled. "The pipe? It's a good pipe."

Annie pulled a chair out from the table and slumped onto it. "Denial. The first sign."

"Does it bother you?"

"Yes."

He tamped it out. "It's good for strength. But if you have a weak head . . ." He shrugged. "It's going to be a long night."

"It's already been too long," Annie said. "I'm beat."

"You can rest later," the Mayan said. "We have to go on the attack, catch him when he doesn't expect it."

"We?" said Annie. "Are you finally going to help?"

"I've always helped." Annie gave him a look that she hoped conveyed complete disbelief. He sat up straighter and pulled the parrot cloak tighter around him. "You don't look so good. You need energy. How do you make a fire in this place?" He looked around. "I want to heat a pot of water."

"Well, don't start piling up sticks on my kitchen table," Annie said. "We use a stove." She put a saucepan of water on for him and turned on the burner. "Don't even need your flint."

"You get sarcastic when you're tired," he said. "It's not an attractive quality."

"That's it. I'm going to bed. Let yourself out and lock the door when you're done."

"He'll be back."

She sat down and, pillowing her head on her arms, rested on the table. "Wake me when he gets here."

The Mayan went over to the stove. Annie could hear him rattling things around on the stove and in the cupboards. She was drifting off to sleep when he put two mugs down on the table, banging them so the vibration brought her awake.

"Drink this," he said.

Annie looked at the mug, which held a steaming brown liquid with flakes of something floating in it. "That smells like coffee," Annie said.

"It is coffee."

"Why didn't you tell me you wanted coffee? There's a coffee machine right over there." She pointed to the counter between the stove and sink. It was littered with coffee grounds, spilled coffee, the dirty saucepan. "Instead of making that mess. At least you turned the stove off."

"Those machines are no good. They take all the grounds out."

"Is that what's floating in here?"

"It's the best part."

"I can't drink this."

"Drink it. You'll need it."

It wasn't a suggestion, Annie could tell from the changed tone. She sipped the hot liquid, and the cobwebs cleared from her brain. "I wish you'd keep your murderers in your own time," she said.

"He's not a murderer. He's a priest." He nodded toward the coffee. "Good, isn't it? It's my own special blend."

Annie took another sip. The grounds were settling to the bottom, so she kept the surface as still as possible when she drank. She could feel the fatigue sloughing off, strength returning to her muscles. "So this is all some sort of religious thing? I thought you said you only killed your enemies."

"We do."

"But he's different because he's a Toltec, is that it?"

"No. You're his enemies."

Annie set the mug down. "Why? What did we ever do to him?"

"You're blasphemers. And you're ready for another cup."

It was making her feel better. "Easy on the grounds," she said, as he poured more from the saucepan. "How are we blasphemers?"

The Mayan sat down and frowned, evidently trying to think how to explain this. His fingers toyed with the bowl of his pipe. "You're not religious people; it's hard to make you understand," he said.

"Go ahead and smoke if you want to," Annie said.

He relit his pipe immediately, not giving her any time to reconsider the offer.

"Are you a priest too?" she asked.

"Yes. But I'm more tolerant than he. He's . . ." The Mayan waved the pipe in the air. "He's orthodox. Conservative."

"Seems more like a fanatic," Annie said.

"No. You really shouldn't be here."

"Why not? Just because you left?"

"It was the end of the Fourth Age," the Mayan said. "It was time for man to leave. It was time for a new age. We did the decent thing; we left. You people didn't, and you're an affront to morality. You're delaying the rightful next age. You're a blasphemy on the face of the Earth. That's the way he thinks of it."

"But you don't agree with him?"

The Mayan sent a stream of smoke up to settle down around them. "I think he presumes too much. He acts like he's a god, to sit in judgment. I say the gods choose how to go about their own plans, and who is he to say you aren't a part of the plan? I say wait and see what becomes of you."

Annie thought back to what her father had said, about their leaving in the tenth century. "And you've been waiting about a thousand years already, and nothing much has become of us? And he's tired of waiting?"

"What's a thousand years in the eyes of the gods? Nothing."

"He's not going to get very far, killing one of us a month. It's not like he could kill us all. He's just making a political statement, right?"

The Mayan looked at her as though she'd said something very odd. "Of course he means to kill you all." He inhaled and blew out smoke. "It's not up to him to decide he's tired of waiting. It's not up to him to interfere past his time. He's the blasphemer."

246

"Can't you just lock him up somewhere? Keep him away from this planet?"

The Mayan laughed so hard, she was afraid he'd choke on his pipe smoke. When he got control of himself, he took a handful of sugar cubes out of the bowl and lined them up end to end on the table.

"I could line these up on the floor all around you," he said, "make a complete square, with no openings. Could you get out?"

"One cube high like that?"

"Yes. But with absolutely no openings. You'd be boxed in."

"I could step over it."

"That's what he'd do to your locked room."

Annie considered the sugar cubes. "This has to do with how you travel, doesn't it? How do you travel?"

"I told you: we take shortcuts." He pushed his cup aside and leaned toward her across the table. "There's a long way and a short way to get anywhere. You only see the long way. You only see the surfaces. You reason, and you feel, but you ignore all the input you get from your other means of communication."

"I haven't been lately. And neither has David. But I still don't understand how you travel."

"Space is bent. If you look at the world the way it's really shaped, you can see the shortcuts and step through them. If you only look at the surface, you only see the long ways. You don't know how to think." He sat back, sucked on his pipe, and blew smoke into the air. Annie was glad she was sitting near the open door.

"And that's how you travel to other planets?"

"An enhanced form of that, yes. You've neglected your astrology, too. Conjunctions, alignments, various configurations of the planets and stars can give a power boost if you use them. We use them."

"And can you be in more than one place at a time?"

He squinted at her through the smoke haze. "No. Don't be ridiculous."

"Then how could he be killing Tiffany at the same time he was fighting with me?"

"One of his creatures killed Tiffany, but he's still responsible. It was done at his direction."

"I suppose he's immortal, too."

"No. Space travel slows down aging, that's all. You catch a ride on light, and use astrological forces to speed up from there, and biological time slows down, goes backward, even."

"So you're not the only two Mayans left. Can't you all get together and stop him? He's a murderer."

"He's a priest. He's allowed to kill people."

"Oh, that's a nice philosophy. Such a nice, civilized, superior people you are. Too bad your thinking never left the tenth century."

"You're getting excited again. Besides, this planet is a forbidden place. Only priests can come here."

"And how many priests are there?" Annie asked.

"Two. Him and me." The Mayan knocked the remaining ash out of his pipe and into his mug of cold coffee.

"That smells disgusting," Annie said, and dumped the whole mess down the sink drain. "I don't suppose you're going to do anything about him? Since all he does is murder people, and he has every right to do that."

"I'm going to kill him," the Mayan said. "He's a blasphemer."

"Well, good. I'm glad to hear it. I wish you'd done it a few months ago."

"I was waiting for you to get stronger. You're almost strong enough now."

"Me?"

"I need your help. You don't want me to go up against him alone, do you? If he kills me, then who can help you?"

Annie leaned against the sink and studied him. "What do you want me to do?"

"You're going to be bait."

"Oh, that's nice. I'm almost strong enough—not quite but almost—so you want me to be bait in a battle between two guys who think it's perfectly within their rights to kill somebody like me because they're priests and I'm . . . what? A sacrificial victim?"

"To him. But you're his enemy. You're my friend."

Annie wondered about that. As far as she could tell, all she and this guy ever did was argue. Was that friendship? "Why can't we wait until I am strong enough? I'd like to live through this," she said.

"The conjunction we rode in on is breaking up. We'll be leaving soon."

"So let him leave. Solves my problem."

"For one thing, he'll be back. For another, what he's started will continue unless we stop him."

Annie sat down. The air from the doorway was colder, and she shivered. "I wouldn't want David to have anything to do with this."

"No," the Mayan said. "He's too young, too innocent to see evil clearly. His part comes later, after this is settled. If it's settled in our favor. Otherwise . . ."

Annie looked at him sharply.

"The boy would be an obstacle to his plans."

"All right," Annie said. She grabbed a sweater from the hook by the door and put it on. "What do we do?"

Chapter 33

The Mayan stood up and adjusted his parrot-feather cloak. Annie saw the quiver of arrows that had been leaning against the chair and the bow on the floor behind him. "We have to get the murderer to come here," he said. "I want you to communicate with him."

"Me? What do you think I was out there doing before you came? I can't get him to come."

"I want you to telephone him."

"This Toltec has a telephone?" Annie said.

"No, no, not the Toltec. Phone his creature. The murderer. Tell him you saw him tonight, and you're going to tell the police in the morning."

"I don't know who he is."

"Of course you know him. He's the one who shot you in the hand."

Annie looked at the Mayan's impatient face and saw the

world in front of her become misty and gray. She could feel the blood draining from her face as she held on to the table edge.

"It's that big guy with the motorcycle, the one who keeps coming around," the Mayan said.

Harley Baer. Annie's heart resumed beating. "Okay," she said. "I don't suppose you have his number?"

The Mayan looked puzzled at that, so she got out the phone book. How many Harley Baers could there be? She ran her finger down the column. Only one.

Annie punched the number into the kitchen wall phone and waited. It rang five times before a groggy voice mumbled something at the other end. The son of a bitch had been sleeping. *Sleeping.*

"I saw you tonight," Annie said.

The breathing at the other end halted momentarily, then resumed.

"I saw you kill that girl," Annie said.

"Who's this?" The speech was slurred, but he was definitely waking up.

"You know who this is. I'm going to tell the police what I saw."

"It's just your word against mine," he said in a self-satisfied tone.

"Tell him he left his footprints in the quarry," the Mayan said softly.

"You left your footprints in the quarry. In blood," Annie said.

"Listen, bitch," Harley said, but Annie hung up.

"He was becoming abusive," she said to the Mayan. "Now what?"

"Now we go out there and wait for him to come and try to kill you."

"What about the other one? How do we get him to come?"

"Oh, he'll come. He wants to kill you himself."

"Why wouldn't he just let Harley do it for him?"

"You're the main thing that might get in the way of his plans. He wants to sacrifice you. It would strengthen his cause."

"I'm so glad I asked," Annie said.

The Mayan shouldered his arrows and picked up the bow. "Come on."

"I want to check on David first."

The Mayan nodded. "Don't be long."

Annie went upstairs to David's room. She warned the rosebush and it crept farther into the room, setting a protective thicket of thorns around the bed. She checked the locks then, wishing Mark had carried through on his plan to put in an alarm, and lit a nightlight in the guest room as a decoy. Before joining the Mayan outside, she picked up a flashlight and locked the kitchen door.

"He'll be all right," the Mayan said. "As long as we're all right." He looked solid and tall there in the moonlight, more in his element than he had in the kitchen. "What's that for?" he asked, pointing to the flashlight.

Annie switched it on, then off, in demonstration. "Flashlight," she said. "To make it easier for him to find us."

"Good idea," the Mayan said. They set off across the meadow. The insects were still, the night without sound except for the slight rustling she and the Mayan made passing through the grass. But the plants tingled with expectation. Annie could feel them stretching for information, preparing for what might come.

"Do you think Harley will be dumb enough to fall for this?" Annie asked.

"You've met the man. How do you estimate his intelligence?"

"He thinks he's so great, no dumb broad could outwit him.

He'll show up," Annie said. "What do we do if they both get here at the same time?"

The Mayan ignored this. He stationed himself on top of the quarry wall and looked around. The parrot feathers had an odd sheen in the moonlight, and his profile against the stars took on a mythic look.

"What should I do?" Annie said.

"Just wait. You can go down by the pool if you want."

"I'd rather not. I don't like it down there."

"No? Why not?"

"For one thing, there's a sacrifice on the altar, and for another, that pool gives me the creeps."

"It's just a power station. A gateway."

"That water's freezing. It's colder than ... It's colder than that." She pointed to the night sky.

"Ah," he said. "You've come that far? Stay away from it, then. You have a little knowledge, enough to put yourself in danger, but not enough to be able to use what you know."

"Does having fire and water come together have anything to do with how you travel?"

"Yes. Opposing forces."

"And earth and air?"

"No. They support each other."

"I suppose you have a lot of places like this scattered around."

"Yes."

"It must get confusing."

"No more than an airline terminal. Look, are you going to keep asking me questions so he'll know before he gets here that there are two of us?"

"Well, he can see you standing out there plain against the sky. What difference does it make if I talk?"

"I'm going to hide as soon as I hear him coming. If I can hear him over your chatter."

But Annie turned then, alarmed by the garden. An intruder had come and was making his way toward them. When she turned back to warn the Mayan, the wall was empty.

"Oh, great," Annie muttered, hoping he was at least hiding nearby. She looked across the meadow. A bulky figure, backlit by the street lights, made its way into the perennial garden and halted. He seemed to be hesitating between the house and the quarry garden. Annie switched on the flashlight and he moved toward the light.

Annie thought she could use a decent-sized branch, and the apple tree obligingly dropped one in front of her. "Thanks," Annie said. She picked it up, stepped through the gate, went halfway down the stairs, and set the light so that it shone upward toward the gate. Then she went back up and crouched behind the wall, hiding just inside the gate. She held the branch ready. It wouldn't be long: She could hear him trampling toward her.

Harley strode through the gate. Annie poked the branch between his feet and he tripped on it. He hurtled headfirst down the stairs, shouting as he fell. The flashlight, dislodged by his passage, fell with him and bounced to the quarry floor. It rolled to a stop, its beam sliding back and forth along the ground until finally, its momentum spent, it shone across the stone toward the altar.

There was silence in the quarry except for the murmur of the runoff. The altar cast a huge shadow up the wall, and before it, resting in the flashlight's beam, Annie could see the carving knife she'd left behind.

Harley was down there somewhere in the dark, indistinguishable from the mounds of shrubby plants. But what condition was he in? He'd taken a bad fall. He could be dead. He could be unconscious. He could be gathering himself together to attack. And she'd better get to her knife before he did.

She made her way to the bottom of the quarry, avoiding the larger clumps that might conceal an attacker. This path brought her to the edge of the altar, and as she stepped forward to get the knife, Harley suddenly emerged from the darkness behind the flashlight, picked it up—picked the knife up—and stood shining the beam on her.

"Thanks for the light," he said.

Annie thought this would be a really good time for the Mayan to come back. When he didn't, she moved so the altar was between her and Harley.

Harley tracked her with the flashlight, letting the beam linger just a bit on the altar. He held the carving knife forward then, so the flashlight illuminated it, and said, "You're about to join your friend." She could hear the smile in his voice.

So. He had the knife. He had the light. No Mayan. She reached out to the quarry garden plants, but without much hope of a response considering how indifferent they'd always been, and was surprised to find they were listening. Sniffing. Best of all, they didn't like Harley. They still didn't care about her one way or the other, but they didn't like Harley.

They were small plants, though. Able to fight with scents and resin, thorns and leaves, but without much physical power behind them. She called to them, and moved slowly closer to the water.

Harley kept the light beam and the knife trained on her, and also his attention. He didn't notice the carpet of leaves edging in front of him, or the sap oozing onto the leaves and making them slippery. He stepped forward, then lunged with the knife.

Annie jumped aside. The leaves pulled back suddenly, and Harley, carried by his own forward thrust and assisted by the plants, plunged into the water.

As he fell, he dropped the flashlight and Annie caught it before it hit the ground. Exultant, she turned the beam onto the water.

He was done for; he'd never escape that cold, not falling in completely the way he had. One down, one to go.

Harley bobbed to the surface and tossed water out of his hair. He swam toward her, and she could see he'd kept hold of the knife. So all that blubber was protection enough? How?

He pulled himself out of the water and stood dripping, the intent to murder clearly written on his face.

So he had the knife. At least she had the flashlight.

Right—and she was using it to show him where she was. She flicked it off and dodged behind the altar just as he lunged. He missed. As she was getting ready to try braining him with the flashlight, a harsh voice called out a command. The language was one she didn't know, but the intent of the tone was unmistakable.

Harley stood and turned toward the voice. His stance seemed relaxed, docile, and Annie was tempted to shine the light on him again to get a better idea of what she might expect, but was afraid to reveal herself to the speaker. Instead, she lifted her gaze to where Harley was looking.

The Toltec stood on top of the quarry wall, high above the pool. He was without the mask she had stripped him of when she was the owl. She recognized the moonlit face, the scratched cheek, the boots. She hoped he couldn't see her, but he chuckled and seemed to look directly at her. Slowly, and with deliberation, he took an arrow from his quiver, fitted it to his bow, and took direct aim at Annie.

Chapter 34

Before the Toltec could loose his arrow, Annie heard the sound of another arrow and saw it strike the Toltec's shoulder a glancing blow. The Toltec grunted and his own arrow went wide. He looked across the quarry, then fitted a second arrow to his bow. Annie hid in the darkest shadow she could find.

The Mayan stood on the quarry wall opposite the Toltec. Between them was empty space; below them, the pool and Harley's immobile figure. The stars faded in the purple sky behind him. The Mayan shouted something that sounded like a challenge, but Annie couldn't understand the words. Apparently he wasn't using his translator, which made him seem inaccessible and different. He looked different, too: His hair was tied back tightly, and his skin seemed shiny, as though he had oiled it.

The Toltec spoke then, in an equally challenging voice but at far greater length. He kept his weapon ready, arrow fitted into place, but stopped short of aiming it. When he finished his harangue, the Mayan's answer was flat, forceful, and brief. The Toltec began again, but the Mayan interrupted with one short, barking word, dropped his own bow, and pulled a knife from the scabbard on his belt. He held it up to the sky and shouted a somewhat longer sentence. Annie guessed he was claiming some right.

The Toltec spat out one word that sounded like something the Mayan had just said, then threw down his own bow and quiver of arrows. He too drew a knife, and they advanced toward each other along the top of the wall.

Annie remembered Harley, and looked to see what he was doing. He still stood in the same position, a bemused, docile expression on his face, the carving knife dangling from his hand. He seemed harmless enough, but since she didn't know how long this state would last, she decided this would be a good time to get the knife away from him.

Annie moved as quietly as she could, keeping to the shadows, trying not to draw attention to herself, ready to run if Harley snapped out of it when she reached for the knife. Harley let it slip from his fingers as though he didn't know it was there. His behavior made Annie wonder if the Mayan priests had hypnotic powers that made it easier to subdue their victims. She shuddered and drew back into the shadows.

When she looked up, the two Indians were standing on the wall above the pool, knives ready, knees bent in a fighting posture: dark figures against the predawn sky. The Toltec lunged and a stone came loose from the top of the wall. It fell the distance to the pool, then splashed and disappeared. The Indians struggled, and she could no longer tell them apart. Pebbles fell, and larger stones; then, with a sudden rumble, the section of wall they stood on gave way and slid into the pond, carrying them with it.

Afterward, the water was quiet. Annie waited. She wondered if this particular drama would play itself out on some other world.

Surely they couldn't have drowned each other. She looked at Harley, but he was still standing by placidly.

The water in the pool bubbled up as though something were churning its way upward from a great depth. Annie moved back, but it exploded all over the quarry, drenching everything, but especially Harley. The water returned to the pool, running down the quarry steps and joining rivulets that ran down the uneven stones to the basin.

The Mayan was back, and the Toltec. Both were bleeding from various minor cuts. Both were wet and sleek, and each was absorbed in the total concentration required to kill the other.

Annie considered whether this wouldn't be a good time to leave, or at least seek safer ground. The Toltec made a successful feint, and managed to carve out another small piece of the Mayan. Annie gasped at the sudden welling of blood, but her friend made no sound. Should she try to help? It was a fair fight now, one on one. . . . She thought of Tiffany. Who the hell cared whether this guy died in a fair fight or not, so long as he died?

She walked toward them, trying to position herself so she could help. The way they kept moving back and forth and circling made helping difficult.

The Mayan said something, probably to her, but without the translator she had no idea what he meant.

The Toltec noticed and barked out an order. Harley came out of his daze at that, and looked confused, then alarmed. The Toltec repeated what he had said, and Harley, apparently unwillingly, moved toward the fight.

"Hey, Harley. I'm over here!" Annie shouted, waving the knife at him.

Harley looked at the fighting Indians, then at Annie. He smiled. "And what are you going to do with that knife?" he said, circling the fight to get to her.

The Toltec spoke again. The Mayan was backing him toward the altar, washed clean by the flood, and there was an edge of panic in his tone. Harley, however, was apparently not so foolish as not to know his own best interests. He followed Annie as she led him up the quarry steps.

"Better give me that before you hurt yourself," he smirked.

Annie, trying to divide her attention between Harley and the fight below, wondered just what her chances were. Harley outweighed her two to one. With luck she'd have one shot at him, but as soon as she got close enough for him to grab her, the knife would be his.

"Maybe I'll be nice to you," Harley said. "If you ask me real nice, that is."

They were by the wall. To get away, she'd have to edge to the gate and slip through. Which way was it? She didn't like to look away from Harley. That would give him his chance.

A scream from the quarry made all the hair on the back of her neck stand up. She looked toward it, and Harley took the moment to seize her arm. They struggled for the knife, Harley winning, while the scream rose in intensity. Then Harley struck her, and she flew back against the wall. When she looked up, Harley was standing over her. He was holding the knife.

The scream abruptly ended.

Harley leaned toward her, but his expression changed to surprise and she saw him jerk backward. The bindweed from the top of the wall had hold of him, his ankles, his legs. He cut at it, but the blows did no good. The weed encircled him, pressed around him until he was held, helpless, on the top of the wall. A sacrificial position.

Annie drew in a deep breath. Then she saw David, in his pajamas, standing in the gateway. He ran to her and she hugged him tight.

"Are you all right, Mommy?"

260

"Yes. Thank you. That was a good idea."

But David was straining to see around her, down into the quarry. Annie looked too, at the altar with the Toltec stretched across it, just in time to see the Mayan reach into the Toltec's bloody chest and lift out his heart. The Mayan held up the heart and chanted. Blood ran down his arm. The heart was still beating.

The sun rose behind Annie and David to the accompaniment of welcoming birdsong. Light flowed into the quarry. When it reached the altar, all sight of the lower quarry disappeared in a dazzle of rays. They grew bright, like a small, separate sun, then diminished and were gone.

The Mayan stood alone. The sacrifice was gone.

Annie made her way slowly toward him. "Are you all right?" she asked, not sure how much of the blood on him was his own.

He gave her a funny look, then touched the translator in his headband before speaking. "It's over," he said.

"Are you all right?" Annie asked again.

"I think so."

David peered round the altar, but there was no sign of the body. "Is he gone for good?"

"Yes," the Mayan said. He smiled, then touched a bloody thumb to David's forehead, leaving a smudge behind. He did the same to Annie before kneeling by the water to wash the blood off his head and chest and arms.

"No more murders?" Annie said. "That's done?"

The Mayan rested, sitting cross-legged on the stone floor. He laid his knife in front of him, and let the sun dry him and it. Imitating him, David sat cross-legged too.

"His creatures are still here, but I've cut out . . ."

"You've cut out their heart, I know."

"It's up to you to make what you can of your age. I've ended the blasphemer's interference."

"So everything should be all right now?" Annie said.

"You still don't understand, do you?" He shook his head. "See that light?"

David looked where the Mayan pointed.

"Venus," Annie said.

"Bright in the morning sky, the last to fade," said the Mayan.

"It's pretty," David said.

"It's a hellhole," said the Mayan. "And so will this be."

"The greenhouse effect?" said Annie. "That's what you're talking about, isn't it?"

He nodded. "The blasphemer wanted you all dead. That's how he was doing it. Waste of a good planet. And one that was home."

Annie put her hand on his arm, because she could hear the pain in his tone, but she still didn't know what he wanted her to do. "Surely now that he's gone, he can't hurt us anymore," she said.

"I like greenhouses," David said.

"Honey, if there's too much carbon dioxide, the air heats up and can't cool down and nothing can live. The plants take the carbon dioxide out for us, but too many of them are being cut down, like in the rain forests and all," Annie said.

"So we'll just make more grow back," said David.

The Mayan smiled and patted the boy's head. "Listen to the kid," he said. He stood up. "I've got to be going. But I'll take care of that one for you first." He picked up his knife and nodded toward Harley.

"Wait," Annie said. "You can't go."

"I have to. This isn't my place anymore. You have to work this out. I could only stop the blasphemer; I won't become one myself."

"How did Harley get involved in this in the first place?" Annie asked.

"He was bent according to his nature. The same as the others. What you and David can do with the plants, the Toltec could do with Harley."

"And you can do with us," Annie said.

The Mayan smiled. "You're my friend," he said, and she supposed that was one part of friendship. A friend could get her to do things an enemy never could.

The Mayan was walking up the slope.

"I don't want you to kill Harley," she said.

The Mayan stopped and looked at her. "He killed Tiffany and the others."

"But because of the Toltec. He'll stop now."

"No. He won't. He's grown this way now, he can't go back."

"It still wasn't all his fault. Let him be. You said we have to take care of things now; it's our turn."

The Mayan shrugged. "What'll you do, lock him in prison for the rest of his life? My way is better."

"Let's ask him," Annie said. "Hey, Harley, what would you rather have? Do you want to go to jail for life, or would you like him to cut your heart out right now?"

"Keep that crazy Indian away from me," Harley shouted.

The Mayan shook his head. "I think it's cruel, but if that's what you want . . ." He put his knife in its sheath and walked toward the pond.

"Will you come back?" David asked.

"From time to time. I like to keep in touch." He smiled, then said to Annie, "Say hello to your dad for me."

"My dad?"

The Mayan stood in the sunlight at the edge of the water, his feet firmly on the stone floor. "Your dad's a good guy. I haven't seen him for years now. We met before you were born." He smiled. "In the rain forest." And then he stepped backward and was gone.

Chapter 35

Annie took David's hand. "We have to get the plants to hold Harley while we go back and call the police," she said.

"They're already here," David said, pointing with his free hand.

Annie looked up at the quarry wall. Trooper Keene was in the gateway, standing half crouched, his gun out and ready to fire.

"Hi," Annie said, and waved to him. When he trained the gun on her, she put up her hands. David put his up too.

Keene lowered his gun and stood in a more relaxed position. "It's all right," he said, and two more troopers appeared from behind the wall.

"It is not all right," Harley said. "She tried to kill me."

"He killed Tiffany," Annie said, walking with David to the top of the quarry. "And he tried to kill me, too, last night." She pointed to the knife wrapped up with Harley inside the bindweed.

"It's not my knife," Harley said.

"You've got a pretty good hold on it," Keene said. "How'd you get yourself all tangled up like that?"

"The plants attacked me," Harley said.

"Didn't you hear me?" Annie said. "He killed Tiffany."

"You saw him do it?" said Keene.

"No. But I know he did. And I called him last night, and told him I knew and would tell you, so he came here and tried to kill me."

"I didn't kill nobody," Harley said. "You come get me when you've got proof."

"You called him?" said Keene angrily. "What did you think you were going to accomplish by that?"

"Get a confession from him."

"And after he killed you, what good would the confession do? A dead woman can't testify in court."

"She wasn't after no confession," Harley said. "She was setting me up. She had this Indian guy waiting to kill me, only he got in a fight with the other Indian and killed him instead."

"What Indian?" said Keene.

"Probably the same one killed all those women, cut their hearts out. He cut the other Indian's heart out. Jesus, didn't you hear the scream? Probably heard it all over town."

"That's why we're here. Your neighbor called us," Keene said to Annie. "Where're these Indians?"

"What Indians?" Annie said. "He screamed when he fell and tangled himself in the plants."

"The Indians!" said Harley. "Old Indians, like Aztecs or something. The one guy cut the other one's heart out right down there, on that altar."

Annie shrugged. "There's nothing there. See for yourself."

Keene went down into the quarry and inspected the area.

"I'm going to get you for this, bitch," Harley said in a voice low enough so the police couldn't hear.

"I'd lie quiet, if I were you," said Annie. "There's no poison oak in those leaves, but there could be."

"No body," said Keene. "No blood."

"In the water! They went into the water!" Harley shouted.

Keene stood at the edge of the pool gazing in. "Pretty clear for water that just had a man's blood supply dumped into it. It's so clear, I can see right to the bottom. Shallow too, but I don't see any bodies."

Annie and David exchanged a glance at that.

"Are the Indians a secret, Mommy?" David whispered.

Annie nodded. "And I think that pool is magic," she said. "Can you see the bottom?"

"No," said David. "It's deep forever."

"They're there!" Harley screamed. "They're there! They sacrificed those women, shot them full of arrows and cut their hearts out."

Keene shook his head. "What do you say, David? Did you see anybody here with a knife?"

David looked at the trooper solemnly and nodded, then pointed to Harley.

Keene walked briskly up the steps. "Get him out of those plants and take him in," he said to the other policemen. "Read him his rights." He turned to Annie. "I'd like to speak with you for a moment," he said, and went into the meadow. Annie and David followed.

"Do you have enough proof to convict him?" she asked.

"No," he said. "But this is enough to hold him, and enough to get a warrant to search his place. We'll find something to connect him to the murders: traces of the victims' blood, hair, maybe just on his clothing, but I bet we'll find the murder weapon. He's used the same knife every time."

"We're going to have to get pruning shears or something," one of the officers shouted.

"Let him go now," Annie whispered to David. David nodded. The vines went suddenly slack. Harley jumped up and the policemen pounced on him. Handcuffs flashed in the sunlight.

"Probably end up in a hospital for the criminally insane," Keene said.

Mariah appeared at the gate in the hedgerow just as they were leading Harley across the meadow.

"There's Mariah!" said David.

"Go on," said Keene, "You go to her."

David ran off, and Annie started to follow, but Keene said, "Just a moment." She turned to face him. His eyes were cold. "How did you know about him cutting their hearts out?" he said. "That's something we kept out of the papers. How did you know to ask me about that last night?"

"I didn't. It's something he threatened to do to me."

"Christ," he said. "You should have told me."

"I thought it was just a threat, just something he was saying. But when Tiffany died, I thought about it again and asked. And you said he had cut out her heart, and then I knew."

"And you still didn't tell me? You're lucky you're alive, you know that?"

"I guess I am," she said. "And you're right: I should have told you."

"Any witnesses?"

"Mariah one time, at the lake. I don't know if she'll remember."

Keene strode across the meadow toward Mariah. Annie

hoped she wouldn't have to tell too many more lies and half-truths to the police, because she was sure she'd mess up if she did. Only, they wouldn't believe about the Mayans anyway, so why worry?

The sun was already warming the morning air, and the dew that had made her cold and wet the night before now brightened every twig and leaf with reflected light. Annie listened to the garden. She sensed happiness, but also expectation. It wanted something more of her. She felt lightheaded, she supposed from lack of sleep, and could feel herself shifting toward some altered state.

A sprig of cornflowers was in front of her, weighted down with dew. It had two flowers the exact shade of the cloud-free sky overhead. Annie thought about the succession of buds along the stem, each waiting its turn, and pictured them all open at once. As she thought of it, so it happened, each bud opening to make the stem a small, blue-flowered arch.

She hadn't asked it to do that. This was something much closer to the plant acting from her thought rather than at her request. It wasn't something the plant did entirely on its own. It was more like symbiosis. Yes, that's what it was, symbiosis.

She wanted the blackberry to pull in its thorns while she passed, and it did. She wanted the burdock to keep a tight hold on its burrs, and it did. She wanted to smell the honeysuckle, and it released fragrance in her path. And it was all as natural and unplanned as walking across the meadow. She didn't have to think about it any more than she had to think about how to put one foot in front of the other. It came as second nature.

And there was David, part of this as he had always been, but only now sensing her through the plants. He left Mariah and Keene and ran to her.

"I told you you could do it, Mommy," he said.

Keene was wearing his official face, talking to Mariah, but

when he turned away he looked at Annie, smiled, and made a thumbs-up sign. So he must have gotten confirmation, she thought. He walked toward the road and Mariah joined Annie and David.

"I'm so glad it's over," Mariah said excitedly. The three of them trailed slowly behind Keene. "Harley Baer. It shouldn't surprise me, but I guess it does. It's hard to think of someone you know doing murder."

"Yes. They still have to get proof," Annie said.

"They'll get it," said Mariah. "This whole town is going to breathe so much easier."

"I know I am," Annie said.

"Are you all right?" Mariah asked. "You look done in."

"I didn't sleep last night."

"There's some kind of smudge on your forehead."

"Probably dirt," Annie said, rubbing at the Mayan's bloody thumbprint. It came away on her hand, and she rubbed David's off, too. The sign was gone then, but it didn't matter. They were permanently marked inside. They were part of something new.

They walked through the perennial garden. Annie could tell the plants liked Mariah. Many of them had started as cuttings from her garden, and they greeted her, but she passed by, oblivious. Yet the liking was mutual. Annie suspected Mariah had been one of the Mayan's failed experiments. He'd almost said as much.

"Did you ever see that Indian, outside the picture in Mrs. Avent's album?" Annie asked.

"I used to think I did," Mariah said. "When I was little." She shrugged. "Then I thought: You have to grow up, be practical. There are reasonable explanations for everything. Now I'm not so sure. You know what I did last night after I got home?"

"Besides worry about me? I'm sorry I forgot to call."

"It turned into a bad night," Mariah said, and Annie knew she was thinking of Tiffany. "Anyway, I couldn't sleep, and I went around the house, trying to find out if I could really see ghosts. It's an old house. I thought there'd be some."

Annie noticed a patch of chrysanthemums leaning over into the path. They were bronze, but the color was off, too greenish. "And you couldn't find any?" she said to Mariah while making an adjustment in the flowers. The bronze mellowed, grew warmer.

"Not at first," Mariah said. "What are you doing? You did that, didn't you?" She pointed at the flowers.

"Yes," Annie said. Mariah looked troubled and unsure of how she felt. Annie found it amusing that someone who had been looking for ghosts all night thought communicating with plants was odd. "So, how did it go with the ghosts?"

"At first I couldn't see anything, but then I stopped trying and it was easy. They're not around all the time. Just traces of them, afterimages and cold spots, like fossils of emotion caught in time. That's what people see when they think their houses are haunted. It's not the actual spirits."

"Did you try to call any spirits?" Annie asked, continuing to walk toward the front lawn.

Mariah shook her head. "Mrs. Avent was enough for one night. And I think I'll do some serious study before I try again. There aren't just dead people out there, you know—there are other things. But you know who I did see?"

Annie was puzzled. "The Indians?"

"Tiffany. She hasn't moved on, and she's very confused. And she can't hear me. I don't know what to do about it. There she is. See?" She pointed to the expanse of lawn and the beech tree at the corner.

"No," Annie said.

"She's very faint in the daylight," said Mariah.

There were two squad cars in front of the house, and one drove away as they rounded the corner onto the lawn. Harley sat in the backseat of the other one, waiting. Keene and another officer stood beside the driver-side door, trying to get, or give, instructions through the phone.

"Take David inside for me, would you, Mariah?" Annie asked.

Mariah glanced at Harley. "Sure," she said, leading David up the steps.

Annie went to the police car. Harley made a movement toward her, but the chains he wore restrained him. He snarled.

"Don't forget about me, bitch, because I'm going to get out. I'm going to beat this thing, get out on bail, or parole." A privet branch came in the car window, and he moved so it wouldn't be in his face. "And I'm not going to forget you." The stem wrapped itself around Harley's throat. "I'm going to get to you and make you beg me to put you out of your misery. . . ." The stem tightened and Harley let out a choked squawk.

Annie smiled. "Are you sure of that, Harley? Are you sure you want to do that?"

The stem tightened more and he gasped for air.

"Because wherever I am, I'm going to have plants around."

He was turning blue, so she loosened the grip.

"Do you understand that, Harley?"

He gulped air and nodded.

"Good, I'm glad you understand. Because I have a real way with plants."

The privet sprouted thorns where the stem entered the car and Harley could see them. His eyes bugged as he watched the line of thorns come closer to his neck.

"Plants like me, Harley. They like me a lot. They like my son, too. If I were you, I'd want to stay away from plants as much as I could. Do you understand that?"

She tightened the grip on his neck.

"Yes," he choked out.

"Good." The privet let go of him and slithered back out the window.

Keene had finished with the radio. He frowned. "We'll be going now. Everything okay over there?" he said to Annie.

"Fine. I was just pointing out to Harley that there aren't any plants in prison."

Annie stepped back, and the troopers got into the car. Keene was in the driver's seat, the other one beside Harley.

"Bitch tried to strangle me," Harley said.

The trooper beside him was looking incredulously at Harley as they drove off.

Annie waved.

Chapter 36

When Annie went inside, she found Mariah had made a pot of coffee and David had poured himself a bowl of cereal.

"Your coffeemaker's all right," Mariah said in a puzzled tone. She waved toward the mess of coffee grounds around the sink. "I thought maybe something was wrong with it."

"No, it's fine," said Annie. She poured herself a mug and sat at the table with Mariah and David. David noisily chewed Captain Crunch.

"Why was Harley after you, in particular?" Mariah asked. "Do you know?"

Annie sipped from her mug. Mariah made better-tasting coffee than the Mayan did, but his gave a much bigger energy burst. "He used to live in the apartment over the carriage house. His father worked for Mrs. Avent, but there were problems, and she made them move out. I guess he resented it."

"That's right, he did. I remember now. Sounds like Harley. Of course, he also has to be crazy," Mariah said.

"I made the plants grab him," David said, and put another spoonful of cereal into his mouth.

Mariah smiled at him. "Good move. Just don't do that to people too often, all right, David?"

David frowned. "He was hurting my mommy."

Mariah gave Annie a worried look and shrugged. "Well, I'd better get back to Erica so John can get off to the hospital. Do you want to go to the mall with me this afternoon?" Mariah asked.

"No thanks, not today. I've got stuff I have to do. Another time," Annie said.

After Mariah had gone, David put his spoon down beside the bowl, which now contained only sugary milk. "She doesn't think I should stop bad men," he said.

Annie wiped the milk off his chin with a paper napkin. "Not exactly," she said. "She just wants you to be sure they are bad."

"Oh," said David. "Can I watch TV?"

"All right. If you can find anything on this early."

David went into the living room. Annie sat staring at the tiny puddle of milk that had collected in the bowl of his spoon.

She missed Mark. She'd wake him if she called now, but maybe she'd try after she showered. She should be able to catch him at his hotel before he went out today.

"Mommy's going to shower now," she told David. "Then I'll help you dress and we're going downtown."

He nodded, but didn't take his attention away from the cartoons on TV.

Annie stood under the shower and let the hot water and steam absorb and wash away the images of blood and violence from the last

274

twenty-four hours. Traces of blood and dirt and crushed leaves swirled down the drain.

She put on a terrycloth robe and went to her bedroom to dry her hair. The bed was still made up from the day before, and sunlight was warm on the spread and pillows. She lay down to rest, just for a moment. The room spun around and she fell into sleep.

"Mommy! Mommy!"

David was shaking her. Annie came out of a deep sleep to find the sunlight gone and David standing beside her bed.

"I'm hungry," he said.

"All right," Annie said. "What time is it?" She looked around for the clock.

"I don't know," David said. "I can't tell time."

"One-thirty. Lunchtime."

"Granddad called."

"What?" said Annie. "When?"

"When you were sleeping."

"Why didn't you wake me up?"

"I tried. You talked to me, but you wouldn't get up."

"All right, all right. What did he say?"

David spoke carefully, as though trying to get the message just right. "He said he's feeling great, don't worry about the sun, he's flying over and he'll call you from the airport."

"Here? Granddad's coming over here?"

David nodded.

"I'm amazed. I had no idea he was even thinking about coming. David, what did you say to him? Just before he said he was coming here. Did you say something to worry him?"

"No. I told him everything was fine," David said defensively. "I told him the Mayan killed the Toltec, and we caught the murderer, and that's why you were tired."

Annie groaned and flopped back down on the bed. "Did anybody else call?"

"The phone ringed when I was in the garden, but they didn't wait for me. Mommy, I'm hungry."

"All right, I'll get dressed and be right with you."

"That's what you said before," David said. "I dressed myself."

"So you did," she said, wondering whether she should rebutton his shirt so the buttons went into the right holes. She didn't want to hurt his pride. "You look very handsome."

She made tuna fish sandwiches and, since her hands were shaking with what she assumed were coffee jitters, a pot of tea. As she ate, she felt better.

"We're going to go to the bank this afternoon," she told David, refilling his milk glass. "I want you to help me with something."

"Do we have to see that lady again?"

"Yes. And we have to talk to the plant in her computer."

"Okay," he said, brightening.

"Do you think it would do some things for me?"

"I guess so."

"Good."

"You want a breakdown of your mortgage payments?" Eugenia Pratt said. "Surely you have that information at home."

"I have my own records," Annie said, sitting down without invitation on one of the all-purpose chairs the bank seemed to favor. She hitched it forward so she could see Mrs. Pratt's computer screen. "I want to know whether they agree with the bank's. I've been paying extra toward the principal, and I want to make sure it's being credited properly."

"You can tell that from your statement."

"I don't get a statement. I have a coupon book, and I have no idea what you do with the money I pay you."

"You'll get a statement at the end of the year. Please keep the child away from my desk."

David was staring solemnly at Mrs. Pratt's blank computer terminal, making contact with the plant inside.

"He won't touch anything," Annie said. "And I'd like a statement now."

"I'm afraid I can't help you. My computer's down," she said smugly.

"Surely there's a functioning computer that you can use somewhere in this bank."

Mrs. Pratt sniffed.

"I am within my rights," Annie said.

"I'll have to speak to Mr. Legere about this," she said threateningly.

"Please do," Annie said.

Mrs. Pratt walked off huffily.

"Quick, David," Annie said. She opened her mind to the plant, and David reassured it, letting it know his mother was safe.

Annie felt her way through the root system, learning with satisfaction that it had grown through to the mainframe. She fed the plant images of what she needed, and the screen came to life with lists of transactions the bank had made regarding rain forest investments. Names rolled by, and investments, until she was sure the bank had sunk all available funds into this, to the point of reckless irresponsibility. The investments must have quickened to a frenzy the speed with which the forests were being destroyed for development. The Toltec had known how to use greed to his advantage.

"Annie, nice to see you. Mrs. Pratt tells me you have a problem," Charlie said.

"My computer!" Mrs. Pratt said, glaring accusingly at Annie. "It's been down all week."

"I didn't touch it," Annie said. "It just came on."

"Mrs. Pratt, please get Mrs. Carter the information she wants."

Mrs. Pratt sat down and tried to access the computer, but the lists of investments kept rolling by. Charlie looked at what was on the screen and turned a deep red.

"You really should get out of those," Annie said.

"That's confidential information," Charlie said, looking as though he wanted her to cover her eyes.

"Don't you feel at all guilty about what you're doing to the planet?" Annie asked.

"Nonsense. That's a lot of hype." He shifted his weight nervously from one foot to the other.

"I can't get in," Mrs. Pratt said as information scrolled past her.

Annie shook her head. "You really should pull out. For your bank's survival."

"That's absurd. These are excellent investments, and we're fully committed. We can't pull out. Mrs. Pratt, turn that off."

"I can't," she said.

Charlie pushed her aside and punched buttons on the computer.

Annie told the plant to access the mainframe, all the branch offices, and any other computer setup, to speak to this one. She told it to rescind all loans made to developers, and tell the bank's brokers' computers to sell all investments having to do with the rain forests. Any property it couldn't sell, she told the computer to erase. There was surely hard evidence of ownership, deeds and things, but the computers wouldn't know about it, and no computer in contact with this one would have any record of it.

"What is happening?" Charlie said in horror, looking at the screen.

"What is it, Mr. Legere?" Mrs. Pratt asked.

Annie told the plant not to let anyone get access to the system, and to keep growing until its roots were in every wire and microchip in the computer network.

Charlie stood up abruptly. "I've got to call our broker," he muttered, and hurried back to his office.

Annie smiled at Mrs. Pratt. "I'll come back another day," she said. Before she left, she followed the plant-computer through its telephone communications network, and had it pinch out all telephone lines but the ones it was using. That should frustrate Charlie for a few minutes, long enough for her plant ally to accomplish everything she'd asked and remove all traces of the bank's ever having had these particular assets. She was briefly tempted to get rid of her own mortgage while she was at it, but decided that would be unethical.

Outside, the protesters were marching glumly up and down, hanging on till closing time even though it was one of the bank's days to stay open late. They'd soon be happier people.

The early morning and busy afternoon had tired out David, and he was quiet in the car. Annie found that a pleasant change. She was tired herself, but felt satisfied with the job they'd done.

"You worked hard," she said to David. "We'll stop for a take-out pizza on the way home."

"Pepperoni?"

"Pepperoni it is. We've just about got time: I want to be back for the evening news."

They pulled into the driveway, and as soon as they got out of the car, the plants cheered. Everything that could flower had burst into a second season of bloom: the privet hedges, the wisteria, all the roses around the house. The trees, unable to do anything showy in the flower line, had instead rushed forward into their autumn colors. Their red and gold combined with the flowers' pink and purple and crimson for an effect notable more for its exuberance than its good taste.

"It's a party, Mommy," David said.

As they walked up the path, the privet dropped white flowers like confetti. On the porch steps, the climbing rose showered them with petals.

"More like a ticker-tape parade," Annie said, blowing petals off the pizza box. She waved to the garden. "Thanks, guys!"

Inside, they continued to feel themselves surrounded by riotous celebration. Annie set the pizza box down and opened it while David turned on the TV. The smell of tomatoes and cheese rose from the box, and Annie felt sharply hungry. The local news was starting. She hurried into the kitchen to get them each a soda.

"Mommy, it's on!"

Annie hurried back just on time to see a shot of the newscaster standing on the bank steps. ". . . tremendous excitement, as computer connections went haywire this afternoon. What do the police have to say about the situation?"

"Look, Mommy! There's Trooper Keene," David said.

"You're right," Annie said, as the reporter thrust a microphone in Keene's face.

"I'm not in charge of the investigation," Keene said, blushing in a way that made Annie's set look as though it needed adjusting.

The camera suddenly zoomed in on the three demonstrators being assisted into a squad car, and the reporter hurriedly told viewers that the apparent suspects were being taken in by the police.

"Oops," Annie said. But surely they couldn't prove anything against those people. She picked up a slice of pizza and ate, waiting for the financial news to come on.

"In financial markets," the announcer said, his voice becoming suitably deep and formal, "the Dow Jones plummeted due to a sudden drop in the prices of South American investments, especially land, beef futures, and lumber companies. The stock of First Savings Bank also plunged due to the bank's heavy involvement in the South American market. Other trading was light, and the market in general rose, the steep drop in the average being accounted for by the bottom falling out of the South American stocks."

"Yes!" Annie said, raising her fist.

"Is that good, Mommy?"

"Yes, David, it certainly is."

David stiffened, his attention caught by something outside the window. "Daddy's home!" he said, dropping his half-eaten pizza onto his plate.

"No, David, Daddy won't be home till the weekend," Annie said, but David was already running toward the front door. Annie looked out the window and saw a yellow cab drive away. She heard the front door open, David's footsteps thudding on the porch. She followed him.

David was on the front lawn. Mark was there too, kneeling, hugging David tight. Beside them the trampled grass was stained with Tiffany's blood.

"Mark," Annie said.

Mark raised his head from David's shoulder. There were tears on his cheeks and his face was crumpled with sorrow, but as Annie walked toward him the grief changed to relief, and then to pure happiness. He stood and folded her in his arms as though he thought she might break.

"Mark, what's the matter?"

"I thought ..." He waved a hand toward the bloodstained grass, then drew her and David away from the spot. "It was on the morning news that the serial murderer killed an unidentified woman. They showed our house and said she was found on the front lawn. I called, but nobody answered. I was frantic. I came right home."

"You didn't ring long enough, Daddy," David said. "Granddad rang longer."

They had walked into the rose garden. Soft flowers nuzzled Annie's hand, brushed David's cheek.

"Granddad's coming," David said.

"What?" said Mark.

"Mark, where's the car? Where's your luggage?" Annie asked.

"Atlanta. I just grabbed the first plane and left. I didn't even check out of the hotel." He folded her in his arms again. "I'm so happy you're all right, I don't even mind that your father is coming."

As he reached for her, a rose bent toward his arm. Mindful of the thorns, Annie was about to tell it to use velvet paws, but it just caught a thorn on his sleeve and nestled there. Annie realized it liked Mark. The feeling coming in from the roses and trees—the whole garden—was that they were glad he was home. They finally liked Mark.

Annie smiled. "Thank you," she said.